PAINTED EYES

A Novel By
Rubén Colón

PublishAmerica
Baltimore

First printing

This is a work of fiction. Names, characters, places, and incidents are the product of the author's imagination or are used fictitiously. Any resemblance to actual persons, living or dead, events, or locales is entirely coincidental.

PublishAmerica has allowed this work to remain exactly as the author intended, verbatim, without editorial input.

ISBN: 1-4241-9983-2
PUBLISHED BY PUBLISHAMERICA, LLLP
www.publishamerica.com
Baltimore

Printed in the United States of America

For Tom, Ashley, and Jaime…
May they enjoy reading my story as much as I enjoyed writing these pages.

PROLOGUE

L ate in the fifteenth century, the king of Portugal, Manuel I, decreed a stiffening of its hold on the Spice Route. This imaginary ocean road stretched from India, snaked along Java, Thailand and Indonesia, ending in the Imperial China of the Ming Dynasty. Along this watery artery, Portuguese ships laden with enormously lucrative nutmeg, cinnamon, cloves and pepper, funneled the spices to Europe.

Under a policy of Prince Henry the Navigator, Queen Isabel's great-uncle, King Manuel I sent a fleet—complete with two Arabic speakers and one knowledgeable in several Bantu dialects—to open trading ports on the Western and Eastern coasts of Africa and beyond.

While some seaports agreed to allow Portuguese ships to enter and trade, those ruled by sultans refused entry to Christians. Rebuffed by their requests for open harbors, the Portuguese resorted to force. Fighting erupted in Mombassa, Mozambique, Quilmana and other seaports.

During one battle off the western coast of Africa, on the pebbled beach of Mozambique, a young Spaniard named Sebastián Alejandro de Avíles, a former captain in Queen Isabel's army, stood in front of a ragged line of sailors and soldiers from three Portuguese caravels lying offshore.

Though wounded in shoulder and arms, Captain de Avíles rallied his men, raised his sword, and, with the Spanish battle cry of "St James," charged the Muslim defenders whose sultan had refused entry.

European swords clanged against Arab scimitars, daggers slashed, pistols cracked and smoke clouded the beach. Soon, the defenders lay dead or dying, and the officer and his men entered the city. The sultanate was now a port-of-call for the ever-expanding Portuguese Empire. Soon after, the captain returned to the caravel, *São Gabriel* to mend his wounds and see to the care of those wounded in battle.

On board the *São Gabriel*, the commander of the three-ship naval group, Vasco da Gama, congratulated Sebastián for his valor and the ships sailed farther south.

Before leaving port, Da Gama had received rumors about the presence of the much-sought Prester John, the Christian king, but the exact whereabouts of the fabled Nestorian kingdom, however, remained unclear. Disappointed at the nebulous information on Prestor John, da Gama ordered his ships to set sail for rounding the Cape of Good Hope and on to his final destination: India.

In Calicut, India, sword in hand, wounds barely healed, Captain de Avíles fought another battle when relations soured between the Portuguese and the Zamorin, the Hindu king and ruler of Calicut. Muslim merchants, jealous of the new traders, inflamed tensions higher by inciting the Indians to attack da Gama's men.

Crushing the Indian rebellion, the Portuguese turned their anger against the Muslim instigators. Again, Sebastián de Avíles led a charge against the enemies of Portugal. While the Portuguese suffered minimal losses, hundreds of Mohammedans died.

After fighting their way of the city and harbor, Vasco da Gama departed Calicut and set sail for Lisbon.

Disaster followed.

ONE

In the Year of Our Lord, Fourteen-hundred and Ninety-Nine, off the Western coast of Africa, the caravel *São Gabriel*, bearing several small cannon and flying the swallow-tailed royal pennant of His Catholic Majesty, King Manuel I of Portugal, shuddered to a stop.

Its weary timbers creaked and groaned in protest as a fluke of the iron-plated wooden anchor buried itself into the sandy bottom of the blue-green water in the secluded bay.

"Haul canvas!" deck officers shouted.

Tired and sick sailors roused themselves, shuffled barefoot to the masts and hauled lines. Yellowed canvas, the red moline cross of the Order of Christ painted on the center, furled into layers on the yardarms.

Outside the narrow channel, a second caravel, the *Berrio*, bobbed with the ocean swells and tacked back and forth on an oblong course like a wooden sentry.

Captain Sebastián Alejandro De Avíles, formerly of the Spanish Royal Army and late of the court of King Fernando and Queen Isabel, stood at rigid attention. The dimness in the *São Gabriel's* cabin failed to hide the keenness in his bright green eyes. His shock of black hair touching the ceiling's crossbeams, he stood poised as though on dress parade. His right hand grasped the pommel of his sword; the other cradled a burnished, metal helmet. At the rear of the helmet hung a panache of plumes—limp in the damp air—one red, one white—the colors of St James, the martyr and patron saint of Spain. White represented the saint's purity of heart and red for his blood—spilled by his beheading at the hands of King Herod Agrippa I. The saint's name soon turned into a rallying cry during Christian battles against the Moors.

A polished breastplate of tempered steel, embossed with his family's coat of arms of a rampant red lion on a blue shield, covered Sebastián's chest. He shifted his weight again, hoped da Gama would not notice his nervousness—any show of weakness or cowardice was unacceptable from a Spanish field officer.

Warm rivulets of sweat ran down the open collar of his blouse—his neck long bare of pleated ruff, the stiff lace cloth removed earlier in the voyage and used for cleaning and polishing sword and dagger. Perspiration had soaked through the linen blouse, drenched his leather jerkin and back. His heart pounded so hard he could feel the throb in his ears.

This moment, this particular moment, had filled him with dread since the ships had left India for the return trip to Portugal. Now, a cloud of melancholy hung over him, his mouth dry, hands clammy, he anxiously waited for his superior to speak. He lowered his gaze to Vasco da Gama, who, head bowed, sat behind a desk.

Patience strained, Sebastián waited.

Da Gama raised tired eyes. They glanced blearily at the young officer who stood at attention in front of him. Air inside the cabin, stale with dried sweat and hot with sickness, stifled breath. A clutter of books, maps and weapons added to the oppressiveness.

Several candles guttered, struggled to cut through the gloom while their small flames threw flickering shadows on the bulkheads and faces of both men.

Vasco da Gama masked his deep distress and bitter disappointment over his voyage home with seeming casualness. Disastrous, the only word he used for the outward sail to Portugal.

What previously had taken several weeks on the inward voyage to reach India had stretched into grueling months on the outward voyage. Out of the original four ships, only the *São Gabriel* and *Berrio* remained. The other two vessels either broken up or burned due to lack of sufficient crewmen.

The weather vacillated from merciless sun to blustering headwinds—his crews wasted by a multitude of foul diseases. The most odious illness of all: one that caused the limbs to swell, and black blood to ooze from the gums; those men too weak to move had been attacked by rats. With no physician and only infusions of herbs, boiling oil and the hot iron as cures, most of the crewmen—many of them convicts—died with hideous groans or cries. Except for the Canarians.

Columbus and all navigators thereafter—when gloomy accounts about life in the New World and the high death rate at sea, spread throughout Europe, and desperate for seamen other than convicts—eagerly sought these men from the Canary Islands as crews for their ships.

Men inured to heat or cold, toughened by hardship, Canarians faced death with equanimity and silence.

The thirty-four-year-old da Gama closed his eyes and silently issued a small prayer of thanks for being mercifully spared the sickness. Out of the original one hundred and seventy crewmen, only fifty-five had survived the rigors of the voyage and now headed back to Lisbon.

Among those less fortunate: his dear brother, Paulo, a ship's captain, who at this moment lay dying in the next cabin. Vasco da Gama opened his eyes and wiped his wet brow with a threadbare sleeve.

In addition to endless calamity on his ships, he now faced a disagreeable duty to perform against this finest of officers. His gaze turned toward the young captain, peered into the questioning green eyes under the furrowed brow. The time was now at hand to pronounce sentence on Captain de Avíles. Da Gama felt a hollow emptiness in the pit of his stomach. Such a great loss to Spain and Portugal! He felt his left cheek twitch as though in pain.

A deep sigh escaped his lips. "Captain Sebastián Alejandro De Avíles. His Majesty, my Lord King, has graciously granted me the discretion of deciding what to do about this warrant for your arrest from your sovereign, Queen Isabel. Let me amend that statement. It is a *request* for your arrest."

Da Gama picked up a worn gray vellum bearing the Spanish Royal Seal and ribbons, glanced at the contents a moment, then let it fall from his fingers onto the cluttered desk. Months before, a Portuguese ship had left the document at Mombasa and handed to da Gama on his return trip to Lisbon. His attention traveled again to the exemplary officer.

Sand in an hourglass trickled, formed a miniature pyramid.

The Captain's coolness this morning caught da Gama's admiration as it had done in the recent past, the time off East Africa, dealing with the sultans of the coast or again in negotiations with the Zamorin of Calicut, India. With

9

the sultans, da Gama had twice requested open trading ports for Portuguese ships. Both times the sultans refused. Da Gama replied with fire and sword.

Cannon shot rained on walls of cities, followed by bloody conflict.

In the ensuing violent confrontations, Sebastián not only offered sound military advice, but also showed presence of mind and unquestioned bravery.

Scratching his thick, dark beard, da Gama reached behind him, extracted one of the remaining bottles of his finest Madeira wine along with two silver goblets. Stems in hand, he blew into them—cleared dust and any dead roaches from the bottoms. Filling both, he handed one to the Captain and then struggled to his feet.

"To His Most Royal Majesty, Manuel I, by the grace of our Lord Jesus Christ, King of Portugal and the Portuguese Empire!"

Sebastián repeated the toast, sipped from his cup, then raised it again. "To the enduring bonds of friendship between your family and mine."

"Amen," da Gama said and drained his cup.

His subordinate snapped back to attention.

Da Gama placed his goblet back on the desk, subsided into his chair and remained thoughtful a few minutes.

After an agonized search of heart and mind, he decided no other recourse remained than to impose a terrible sentence. He was quite certain the officer standing in front of him had already arrived to the same conclusion.

For the first time in his life, da Gama felt conflicting emotions. Captain Sebastián's family and his had held firm ties of friendship for close to a hundred years—even during acrimonious relations between Spain and Portugal. If he pronounced a harsh sentence on the captain, an ignoble death of this officer would surely follow. Would the bonds of age-old friendship break between their respective families?

Idly tapping his fingers on the desk, da Gama stared unblinkingly at his subordinate and wondered what thoughts ran through the young man at this fateful moment.

Sebastián shifted his weight again. He heard the cheek plates of his helmet clank against the dagger on his belt—the sound, he thought, loud in the ominous quiet. His chest armor felt heavier than usual in the hot, narrow confines of the cramped cabin. From the age of sixteen and for years after, on the field of battle alongside his father, he had worn the protective covering. But he still hated wearing the cuirass, though he reminded himself the discomfort weighed little compared to the fate, he was convinced, awaited him. All because of his lust and insane weakness in falling for the wiles of that obnoxious, and *married* Lupiana. More than two years had passed, but visions of his foolhardy acts still haunted him.

He gazed at the silver goblet on the desk. His reflection pulled at him as though he had stepped into the tarnished metal and his past.

TWO

On a dreary, humid Sunday afternoon in early June and under a sky gray with scabious clouds, Lupiana arrived with her husband, Don Rodrigo de Montes, on an impromptu visit to the de Avíles estate in Southern Spain, three leagues from the city of Seville.

Two hours earlier, a messenger astride a mule lathered with sweat announced to the de Avíles household the impending arrival of Don Rodrigo and his wife.

Sebastián, along with his parents, changed into more formal attire—his mother in a gown of black silk but without hoop skirt, father and son in stiff lace ruff, doublets—moss green for Sebastián, ash gray for his father. Swords and daggers hung from sashes and belts on both men—as custom dictated.

The family now stood in the courtyard ready to greet the uninvited guests, watched dust clouds of red earth bloom in the distance as the carriage negotiated the long, curving road leading to the estate. The crunch of gravel pierced the silent countryside echoed through wheat fields, olive trees and grapevines; all part of the de Avíles estate.

The coach and its passengers drew nearer.

An unsmiling Doña Caterina Luisa de Avíles, Sebastián's mother, her back straight, fanned herself in furious strokes with an embroidered black fan.

"What does that pompous ass want?" Don Francisco de Avíles grumbled under his breath, stroking his pointed black beard. "We did not invite him or his whorish wife." Sebastián raised an eyebrow at his father's remarks, knew from childhood what his mother's reaction would be.

Doña Caterina snapped her fan shut and faced her husband. "Francisco, you are no longer on the battlefield with brutish men. I must ask you to please watch your language, at least while Don Rodrigo and his wife are our guests. Although rumors saying that woman is morally reprehensible continue to circulate. In spite of those rumors, they remain close friends of the court and Her Majesty, Queen Isabel."

"Yes," Francisco said. "Because that fat pig, Don Rodrigo, financed part of the queen's campaign against the Moors. And I detest his ever-present boast to the purity of his blood. 'I am an hidalgo, *hijo de algo*—a person of some consideration—and a member of the nobility. Not one drop of the cursed Moors, or the Jews, or any other foreign blood flows in my veins,' he proclaims to one and all. The idiot. Why does he persist? I sometimes wonder if all this posturing is to hide secrets about his birth. I also wonder if his mother patronized taverns—"

"Francisco! By all the saints—" Caterina fanned herself faster.

Her husband patted her hand. "Fine. Fine. Do not fret, Caterina my love, I will be polite and hospitable as befits my station. But why does Rodrigo insist on the use of Don before his name. Was it officially granted?"

"This title, *De Origen Noble,* is reserved only for the special class with a history of great service to the throne. Even if it is official, he is still a pig." He winked at his son.

Sebastián nodded. His father would hide personal dislike and be the perfect host as the rules of hospitality demanded. *If I could do only do the same and hold my tongue where other matters are concerned.* Sebastián was already in trouble with the church. Two months before, he had dared question the parish priest, in public, the granting and selling of indulgences for the forgiveness of sins. Soon after, he ran afoul of church authorities again.

"Are you reading the Bible in your home without the presence of clergy?" the village priest had asked. The practice of studying holy scripture by oneself strictly forbidden to the laity by the Church.

"I read the Catechism," Sebastián said in a half-truth, disbelieving the prevalent idea that priests were endowed with supernatural powers after ordination. Turning on his heel, he left the sacerdote fuming, He wondered if a passerby had seen him with the Bible or reading in the orchard. Only the reputation of his father—and a pouch full of gold coins to the local church—saved him from more serious charges. What if someone also found out Sebastián read tomes from the proposed *Index Librorum Prohibitorum*? Flames and the smell of sulfurous fumes had crossed his mind in the aftermath.

Wheels clattered on gravel, horses neighed and, amid the clink of harness, the ornate black and gold carriage rounded a curve in the serpentine road and jerked to a halt.

Two footmen leaped to the ground. One ran to hold the reins—to prevent the horses from prancing, rearing, rocking the carriage—the other rushed to open the coach door.

Lupiana exited first, lifted her skirts as her foot touched the first step.

Sebastián, a few paces behind his parents, drew his brows together in puzzlement at her action of exiting the coach first, but dismissed it with a shrug. What did it matter to him? Custom dictated men should leave the carriage first then help any lady passengers down the steps.

A strong, damp wind gust suddenly blew from the north, lifted dust and a portion of Lupiana's skirt. Underneath, with fewer skirts and petticoats current fashion decreed, an immodest amount of pale and *naked* calf exposed itself.

Caterina de Avíles gasped at the indecency and hid her face behind a partially closed fan.

Women, other than the peasant class and even in hot weather, wore full-length hose.

Lupiana reached the last step on the folded rungs. For some reason, the step lay stuck. The footman scurried to release the step. Her face reddened and she raised her folded fan to strike the hapless man across the face. "Move quickly, you dolt."

The step released, the man bowed and shrank back out of her reach.

"Servants," she said with a toss of her voluminous hair, "even in the best of times, they can be most tiring."

Sebastián looked away. The servant was doing his best. *She insulted, humiliated him in front of us and almost struck him across the face with her folded fan.* Why did she expose her lack of civility in front of hosts? The man was a servant, not a slave.

During the wars against the Moors, he and his father had practiced manumission, freeing dozens of Christian slaves held by the Muslims. Ruefully, he recalled, Catholics also enslaved Muslims. Some of the Muslim captives ended as galley slaves—for most, a slow torturous death, a few of the other captives given as gifts to the pope.

Sebastián watched his father paste on a smile, stride forward to greet his guests and bow low to kiss Lupiana's outstretched hand.

"Good afternoon, Doña Lupiana," Don Avíles said. Sebastián noticed his father had not used the customary and more cordial, "I am at your service. Welcome to our home."

The carriage rocked, creaked and groaned and her husband, a sweaty Don Rodrigo, with the help of two footmen, wheezed down the steps and onto the ground. Corpulent, in his mid-forties and owner of vast estates, the hidalgo had married twenty-five-year-old Lupiana three years before. Queen Isabel attended the wedding ceremony, held near the royal court at Valladoid in Northern Spain.

"Good afternoon," Don Avíles said, then, with a stiff arm, shook Don Rodrigo's hand and quickly proffered his arm to Lupiana. Her husband offered his to a stone-faced Doña Avíles who returned a slight nod and snapped her fan open again. Guests and hosts strode forward; Sebastián followed, off to the side of his father and a step to the rear.

While Lupiana strolled in front of Don Rodrigo with seemingly careless abandon, her husband, ornate walking cane in hand, pointed and struck the ground with each step. His face carried an expression hinting something rotted nearby. He motioned with his cane for Sebastián to draw near.

"Ah, Captain, I understand many young men of the aristocracy are taking ship for the New World. Will you someday serve Her Majesty and the empire in the same manner?"

"With my father's permission, I will go." Sebastián lied. If he sailed to the New World, he would volunteer only as a garrison officer, not in his usual position as Field Commander.

The hidalgo nodded. "Yes, yes, of course. On another matter. It is unfortunate the queen has listened to spineless advisers and ordered a stop to the slow poisoning of our blood."

Sebastián shook his head. "I beg your indulgence, Don Rodrigo, I do not understand."

"Foul unions between Spaniards and female savages in La Espanõla, Bermuda, Jamaica, the island of St John The Baptist, Cuba, other islands and lands under conquest to the west and south in the New World have produced offspring—mongrels. We must not have this mixing of races. We must have a *limpieza*—a cleansing. The offspring were being mercifully put to death by soldiers in the field, but Her Majesty—"

"Please excuse my interruption," Don Avíles said. "We will go to the garden at the rear of the house. It is cooler and there is a canopy to provide shade over the table." He nodded to a servant. "Refreshments." The man hurried off.

Sebastián excused himself and stepped back to the rear of hosts and guests. He had heard rumors of the slaughter of the infants by sword or garrote. In battle, he had killed without question or hesitation, but the thought of piercing the throat of a helpless, newborn child—All of a sudden, his stomach felt queasiness.

Don Rodrigo went on. "I sincerely hope Spain's trade relations with Bartolomeo Marchionni and Amerigo Vespucci do not falter and—"

Before his parents could stop him, Sebastián burst out, "Yes, the largest slave traders in Portugal and Spain. I saw their 'merchandise' during the Battle of Granada, black Africans, Canarians, Russians, Greeks, forced to dig and haul—"

Don Avíles raised a hand, interrupted Sebastián. "Please forgive my son. He is high spirited, does not know when to silence his tongue, and holds certain views on slavery."

Don Rodrigo spoke through tightened lips when he turned toward Sebastián. "What are those views, captain?"

"A slave always seeks to escape. He obeys reluctantly. A man treated fairly will serve you during peaceful times and in war has often served as a soldier, as have townspeople that reside on our lands. A slave knows if he is crippled or reaches old age, he will be thrown into the street like refuse—"

Don Avíles raised his hand again. "Enough!"

Sebastián noted the tightened lips on Don Rodrigo's lips had formed into a snarl. "I beg your forgiveness for our seeming haste," Don Avíles said. "My wife and I are preparing to visit relatives in the north of Spain."

Sebastián smiled inwardly. His father had exaggerated, presumably to hasten departure of unwelcome guests—the planned visit to Sebastián's uncle not scheduled for another two months. Also, he wagered, his father's apology was offered to lessen the hidalgo's anger at Sebastián's breach of civility to guests. Later on, his mother would take her husband to task and make him atone for the sin of almost lying by begging Don Avíles to use the 11th bead of her rosary, the one reserved for the Lord's Prayer. In addition, also ask him to recite the Pater Noster and a Hail Mary or two.

"Of course. Of course," Don Rodrigo said, and went on. "Here in Castile, thank Heaven, the Dominican and Inquisitor-General, Father Tomas de Torquemada and his Holy Office diligently pursue Maranos and Moriscos and their false pretense of conversion to Mother Church. We Old Christians must be ever vigilant."

Maranos, Sebastián knew, were Jews forced to convert under threat of auto da fé. Moriscos were Moors forced by the sword to convert to Catholicism. Old Christians called the converts New Christians, who in turn found themselves under constant suspicion for their sincerity of belief

16

Several Maranos had lived in the *alhama*—the district reserved for them in one of the villages governed by the de Avíles estate. One day, the villagers were taken away by the Inquisitor's Office. When Sebastián, under his father's request, inquired about the disappearance, he was told to watch his own faithfulness to the Church. The villagers disappeared, never to be seen again.

Servants served refreshments of wine cooled in a nearby stream along with grapes and slices of oranges. Glasses raised, he joined his parents and guests with toasts to the queen's health and long life. Conversation ebbed, turned to polite but desultory discussion about the weather, and continued expansion of the Spanish Empire.

Don Rodrigo, Sebastián noticed, had not mentioned the conversos—Jews who voluntarily converted to Christianity. Was it because Queen Isabel chose several conversos to be among her highest advisors and the don feared reproval and perhaps dire consequences by the queen for daring to question her choices? He thought so.

"Let us go into the garden," Don Avíles said, "My dear wife has planted some lovely arrangements of exotic flowers." Sebastián detected a slight softening in his mother's manner.

Don Rodrigo waddled alongside his hosts; Lupiana lingered behind while Sebastián took up the rear.

Rectangular in shape, the garden possessed two dirt paths; both converged to a bubbling fountain. House servants walked down one path, arms and hands filled with trays of cut fruit and flacons of wine, hosts and guests took the other path.

"As you can see," Doña Caterina said to Don Rodrigo, "we have planted cypress and Myrtle trees on one side…"

Sebastián slowed his pace, as did Lupiana. She turned her face to the side to look at him over the rim of her fan. He averted his gaze. A moment later he heard her whisper, "Sebastián."

He glanced her way.

From behind her fan, she fluttered her eyelashes at him.

Expressionless, he lowered his glance to fiddle with the sash holding his sword before raising his head.

"…on the opposite side," his mother was saying, "we have laurel and box trees…"

Lupiana stooped over a bush of purple bougainvillea, hid her face from the others with the open fan and winked.

Sebastián swung on his heel and chose the other path toward the fountain and the waiting servants. *Why the devil is she behaving this way? What if her husband catches her?*

"I've also planted lilies, irises and jasmine," Caterina continued, "I love their fragrance in the evenings."

A few minutes later, after effusive comments on Caterina's gardening skills by her guests beneath a darkening sky, everyone left the garden and entered the manor.

Inside, the group strolled through the cavernous banquet hall and its twenty-foot high ceilings with tattered battle flags hanging from poles at either end. At the room's center, Lupiana paused to admire tapestries depicting the triumphs of the kingdoms of Castile, Navarre and Aragon over the Moorish princes.

Alongside the cloth tableaus, hung several paintings: bucolic landscapes of windmills and fields of wheat bending before the wind. Above the landscapes: portraits of Sebastián's parents.

"I do not recognize the work," Lupiana said. "And I am thoroughly familiar with the Court's painters."

At a respectful distance of two paces in the rear, hands behind his back, Sebastián kept his gaze on the walls, still mulling over her actions in the garden.

Doña Avíles, with pride in her voice, said, "My son painted them. Someday, God our Lord willing, he will be commissioned by our gracious Queen Isabel to paint a portrait of Her Majesty."

"Indeed?" Lupiana turned, crooked her finger to beckon Sebastián. "Well, we must make sure he is prepared to present Her Majesty on canvas in a most professional manner. To that end, I will help. Rodrigo?"

Her husband lumbered to her side "Yes, my love?"

"Commission this young man to do a portrait of me. As soon as the painting is complete and this dreadful weather of rain and dampness permits more comfortable traveling, we will take a holiday. Perhaps to France."

"Yes, my dearest."

"At the present time…" she said, addressing the de Avíles family, "our home is filled with carpenters and such persons tracking dirt and dust throughout the house. I hope, dear God, they do not steal anything. In the meantime, my dear husband and I must struggle in a hovel of only nine wretched rooms until the redecorating is finished to my satisfaction." She pressed a hand over her heart and spoke to Sebastián's father. "May we have the sittings in your home?" she asked, eyes widened, eyelashes fluttering.

His father bowed. Stiffly and formally, Sebastián noticed. "Of course. At your service."

Sebastián felt flattered by her effusive compliments, although still puzzled by her recent and open display of crudeness to a servant—especially for the wife of a hidalgo. But he found himself drawn to Lupiana—the lure of something exquisitely evil about her. He crossed his right arm across his chest and bowed. "I accept." From the corner of his eye, he saw his mother widen her eyes and vehemently shake her head. At once, Sebastián regretted his reply.

While Lupiana and her husband viewed other paintings, Sebastián drew closer to his mother and whispered in her ear. "Mother, you disapprove. Flattery hastened my decision. But I have given my word. It is too late to retract my acceptance."

"She is a shameless woman," Doña Avíles whispered back. "No good will come of this. At vespers this evening I will light an extra candle. I feel grief in my soul."

THREE

Finally, over a period of two weeks, Don Rodrigo agreed to arrangements as to dates, time of day and payment of commission for the painting—the messages sent by mounted messengers. Lupiana's sittings began in Sebastián's chambers.

This afternoon of the first sitting, with a swish of brocade and silk skirts, a black shawl with red roses stitched into the lace covering her head, Lupiana sailed into Sebastián's studio located at the end of a long corridor.

"Good afternoon, Captain." She placed a gloved hand on her cheek. "Oh, that sounds so formal. May I call you by your given name?"

He nodded.

She clapped her hands. "How wonderful. You may call me Lupiana."

"Good afternoon. Please sit on the bench." He pointed to a wooden bench in front of a draped wall.

"In a moment. May I look around your charming studio?" She offered a beatific smile.

Sebastián waved a hand. He found her polite and well mannered at this time. Could his parents have been wrong in their judgment of her? Could *he* have been wrong about her coquettishness in the garden? Doubts grew in his mind.

Walking around his workplace, she examined several paintings stacked against a wall. Most of the canvases depicted landscapes of peasants gathering harvests, the golden yellow of wheat fields and blood red of sunsets; others represented still life in brilliant colors.

Without comment, she moved on to pause next to a plank table. Hands on hips, she stared at a slanting wall of glass windows. At this hour of the day, bright sunlight drew squares on the gray stone floor.

"I have never seen such a window. Such a profusion of sun would ruin my delicate skin. Would it not?" She pushed up her puffed sleeve and struck her arm out at him.

He ignored her question *and* arm, turning his head away. "The window captures the proper light. My father had it constructed for me. Lean against the bench I've placed—"

"It is bare! I will not sit on an ugly piece of wood," she said, her voice harsh. The next instant, her voice softened, her manner apologetic, lips in a childish pout. "I thought I would be sitting in a proper chair."

"I am painting the upper torso only. A seated pose would spoil the symmetry. There are cushions over there." He pointed to a stack resting on a bed. "Pick one."

Lips now in a full pout, she snatched a thick, yard-long green pad with black tassels, handed her choice to him. "You are the artist, please arrange it for me." She tossed back strands of her abundant hair.

He glanced at her for a moment. *She is an enticing woman.* If she would only…

Exhaling a deep breath, Sebastián arranged the stuffed cloth on the wood while she stood close to his side. Her perfume wreathed the room like an unseen wraith. The scent seized his nostrils. He shook his head to clear the enticement and returned to his easel. From his workbench he picked up a pad and pencil.

"Today, I will make studies only. At the next sitting, I will start with my oils. Now, bring the shawl halfway over your head. Good. Don't look at me."

"Why not?"

"Look past my left shoulder."

"I would much rather look at you. Oh, very well." She followed his instructions.

"Sebastián, are you betrothed?"

"Do not speak. It breaks my concentration."

"How dare you…" Her eyes flashed anger, an inferno behind her look. The flare up vanished as quick as a blink and Lupiana lapsed into a sulk.

Struggling to maintain a correct relationship of subject and artist, and squelch rising desire for her, Sebastián sketched in furious strokes, breaking points of pencils. This painting out of all those he had conceived would take the shortest time, he would make sure of that.

"She is late again!" Sebastián glanced at the hourglass. Earlier, he had walked to the garden and checked the device against the gnomon of the sundial. Upstairs, he watched as the sand trickled. An hour passed and he turned the device over. Now the grains occupied less than a quarter in the top half of blown glass.

Soon, the angle of sunlight he preferred to paint by would pass. The loss meant another delay, *and* another appointment for completion of the portrait. Damn that woman!

This, the fourth day of sittings, would see the final application of oils to the canvas. He hoped. By the end of the next sitting the painting would be complete. Sebastián kept his subject away from the easel; his work lay hidden under a cloth, Lupiana unaware of the portrait's progress.

The door to his studio flew open.

A flustered Lupiana rushed in, almost colliding with him. "Oh, Sebastián, I apologize most profusely for my lateness. With this damp weather today, it is abominably impossible to manage my hair. My maid could not arrange it properly. I wanted to look prettier than usual for you, my *artist.*" She squeezed his hand and leaned forward, lips quivering, her mouth a finger- length away from his. "Please say you forgive me."

Sebastián shut his eyes, took a step back, looked away, then opened them, struggling to keep his rising base desires in check. "You're forgiven. Since you have complained of 'extreme' pain in the back from leaning or sitting on the bench, and the major work has been done, I have placed a chair for you to sit on." He pointed to a high-backed, ornate chair in front of a draped wall.

Lupiana swished her way to the chair, sat down, raised her skirts to the knees and crossed her legs. The entire length of a shapely pale calf greeted Sebastián.

"Now I am comfortable," she breathed. "You may begin."

"Lower your skirts. Turn your head as I have asked before."

"How about..." She pushed a billowy sleeve down to her elbow, revealed a bare shoulder and sensuous curve of her breast.

"No. Cover yourself."

"Why are you so mean to me?" She raised her sleeve back in place.

Sebastián, palms sweaty, feeling his neck flushed, stabbed at the dollops of oils on his palette, painted, stabbed and painted, again and again. Before the hourglass could be turned a third time, he ended the session.

At the door and about to leave, Lupiana said, "Oh, Sebastián."

He turned. "Yes?"

In a swift movement, she raised her skirts to her waist. Underneath, no garments appeared. Even in the subdued light away from the windows, he could see her bare thighs glistening with beads of perspiration.

Sebastián stared in surprise, speechless.

"Until tomorrow, my captain." She lowered her skirts and left.

The last grains of sand trickled through the hourglass as he stared at the door, lust coursing through his body.

Working at his easel the fifth day of sittings, Sebastián paused in his preparations and turned pensive. He should have stopped her at the first telltale signs of her loose morals. Day after day, she continued the exposure of her breasts and lifting of her skirts past her thighs while sitting on the chair until ordered by him to cover herself.

Her countenance bespoke innocence, but her swift changes in character from seductiveness to a rigidity of her body and a strange wildness in the eyes, removed the affected mask behind which lay hidden the darkness of Lupiana's true character. But what a rare subject for an artist!

Sebastián heard the rustle of Lupiana's silk skirts close by, first on one side of him then the other. He refused to turn, to look, or ask questions. He bent over a table constructed of rough-hewn planks. At their center, mortars, pestles, and a jumble of pots gaped—tongues of paint, some dried, some bright with newness—hung or dribbled over the lips.

He mixed a fresh batch of colors from crushed lapis lazuli, earth-colored ochre and powdered flowers of zinc, then poured linseed oil over them. When finished blending the mixture into a thick paste with a stone pestle, he scooped dollops with a spatula and scraped them off onto a wooden palette.

The heavy fragrance of musk from the pomander hanging around Lupiana's neck flooded the air.

These hollow, lemon-size containers of silver or gold and drilled with small holes, held a cloth soaked in perfume or scented water to hide the person's body odors—regular baths left to the fastidious or the eccentrics.

At this moment, the scent vied with the pungent smell of turpentine and paint oils.

Her perfume forced a sneeze on Sebastián, and he faced away for breaths of fresh air.

Why did royalty and members of the European aristocracy, men and women, prefer drenching themselves in perfume rather than take baths? From his tutor in Latin, he had learned ancient Romans built castle-size baths with hot water and steam for bathing and used them at every opportunity. Unfortunately, that welcome facet vanished along with the Roman Empire.

At home after weeks on the battlefield, often without even washing his face before rushing to meet the enemy, he spent hours in a trough-like bath he and his servants had built behind a stable to rid himself of filth, grime and vermin.

Palette in hand, ready to paint, he raised his head and found Lupiana, bodice unbuttoned almost to her navel. She drew closer to him. He stepped aside and in front of the easel, effectively hiding the painting from her view.

Her outstretched arms promised passion, but also warmth or tenderness? Her body, although bathed in expensive oils, offended the senses. Honeyed words poured like syrup from her lips—"dearest," "Captain of my heart,"—yet no sweetness touched his palate—her siren's song could lure men to foamy destruction on treacherous rocks.

Each day, he had cursed himself for giving his word and rash acceptance of the commission.

"Please stand by the drapes next to the wooden screen," he said. "Open your fan and hold it under your chin." He backed away from her reach and grasped his palette until his thumb and forefinger turned white. "And…button your blouse."

She gazed at him from under her eyelids and offered a saucy look. "Oh, very well. Do you not like me, Sebastián? Please look at me."

He found a momentary glance sufficient, her features well known to him. Lupiana possessed cruel, thin lips. When she spoke, they curved down at the ends of the mouth in a sneer. The effect marred the natural beauty of her long auburn hair, clear blue eyes and voluptuous body.

"Your husband commissioned me to execute a portrait of you. That is what I am doing. You are the subject, I am the painter, nothing more."

He heard her sharp intake of breath, the snap of the fan closing and ducked as she threw the feathered object with the force of an assassin at him. The crack of broken wooden ribs cut the silence.

A few strokes later, he stopped, paintbrush in midair. "The painting is almost finished," he said through a clenched jaw. "If you do not stand where I ask, I will put my brushes away, walk out of here and you may tell your husband anything you wish." He returned her broken fan.

Lupiana threw it aside and stomped to the wooden screen.

An hour later, he applied the final brush strokes.

"We are done," he said, rolling a cloth over his work.

"I want to see my painting."

At his workbench, Sebastián cleaned his brushes, oblivious to her requests. Later, he would check his work; make any corrections before the final unveiling. Be rid of this succubus.

She snapped her bejeweled fingers and motioned with her hands. "Bring it here."

"No. The portrait is not finished. There are some touches I will make tomorrow. The unveiling will take place in a few days."

"It is my painting and if I wish to see it, I will." She gathered the folds of her skirts above her ankles, and with an exaggerated swivel of her body, scurried to the easel and flipped the cloth off the canvas. Head tilted to one side, then the other, she viewed the painting while fanning herself furiously. "My dear Sebastián, you have not captured me properly. You will make another painting of me at once. It will be *very* personal."

Uneasy silence fell between them. He deliberately swished his paintbrushes inside a ceramic pot of paint remover.

The sound of the wood handles striking the sides of the vessel echoed in the lofty chamber. Her orders ignored, he arranged his paint jars and dried his brushes. Perhaps if he tarried, drained her patience, she might tire and leave.

Out of the corner of his eye, he saw Lupiana slip behind the screen. He heard the rustle of clothing, as though she made ready to depart. *Thank God! She is leaving.*

"Oh, Sebastián."

He turned his head.

Lupiana stood naked except for chopines—exaggerated platform shoes and the latest fashion rage in the courts of Europe.

"See? This is how you should portray me!" she said, her voice low and seductive. Hands on hips, she executed rapid, seductive half turns to either side forcing her breasts to swing provocatively. She advanced on him, the unwieldy chopines forcing her to take mincing steps.

Sebastián forced his gaze away from her body and to her head, his mind in heated struggle between rising lust yet dislike of this woman. "The commission called for a full length portrait of you fully clothed. Not two paintings, one of them nude."

Arms outstretched, fingers beckoning, she closed the distance.

Sebastián, about to leave the chamber, found her arms clutching his neck in an embrace of nightmare strength. She twisted herself around to face him, her plump breasts pressed against his chest as she kissed him feverishly, violently twisted her body against his.

Desires heightened, blood rushing through his veins, he picked her up and carried her to his bed—Lupiana murmuring with delight as she undressed him—throwing his clothing over her shoulder.

Kissing her raised pink nipples, he carefully avoided her mouth—she had already bitten his upper lip—the warm, saltiness of his own blood tinged his tongue.

With practiced hands, she guided his body over hers, arched her back and uttered cries of delight—his every surge provoked a breath from her heavier than the last, her heavy pants like an animal in heat.

Each time he rocked forward, he gritted his teeth as her nails dug into his back. Finally, she reached her peak of desire and a scream escaped her thin lips. Sebastián placed a hand over her mouth, which she angrily pushed aside.

After his own climax, he rolled over to the farthest side of the bed—nearest the stone wall. *This will be the first and last time I will bed with her.* With belated clarity, he realized her terrifying tenacity, her constant effort to control and bend him to his will. Rising, he searched for his scattered clothing.

"Where are you going, Sebastián? Come back to bed," she purred and cupped her breasts at him.

Her enticements to no avail, Lupiana clutched a coverlet to her chest, slid off the bed and shadowed him as he plucked his pantaloons and blouse from the stone floor. Although the room was one of the largest in the manor, he felt the walls shrink and a sudden, deep sense of foreboding gripped him.

"Has a bride been arranged for you?" She spit the words out.

He pulled on his pantaloons. "Get dressed. My father may step in at any moment."

"Without knocking?"

"He is master of this house and estate." Sebastián shrugged on his blouse. "Unless there is an overnight guest, he does not knock on any door."

"Has a bride been arranged for you?" she repeated.

The question was personal and none of her business, but anxious to be rid of her, he said,

"My parents are speaking to a family about their daughter."

"Which family? Which daughter?"

"Señorita Ignacia Matilde de Alburquerque."

Surprise and anger flashed in Lupiana's widened eyes. "Daughter of the Duke of Alburquerque?"

"A cousin." Sebastián slipped his boots on and stood.

"How many women have you brought to your bedchamber?"

His back to her, he said, "Your husband may pick up the canvas in two days." *And I will be rid of you, thank God our Lord.*

Lupiana hastily dressed, her questions left unanswered, her efforts for additional lovemaking ignored. She hurried to the room's entrance, chopines clicking on the stone floor and swung the door open.

Sebastián leaned against the table and watched, his face expressionless.

About to step into the corridor, she leaned over some of his paintings stacked against a wall. With undisguised delight, Lupiana reached out with her foot and deliberately sent several frames flying. "I will get answers to my questions," she hissed, "one way or another."

She slammed the heavy oak door behind her. The sound boomed, echoed through the empty arched, corbelled hallways.

What did she mean by "one way or another"?

FOUR

An exhausted sunrise had barely risen to chase blankets of morning fog away the next day when a household servant handed Sebastián a beflowered and perfumed note. "A messenger delivered this, Captain. He awaits an answer."

Sebastián studied the wax seal. Plain, it bore no coat of arms or family seal. Probably only drippings from a candle, he thought. He skipped the Spanish custom of touching his temple with the letter—a sign of respect to the sender. He broke the seal and unfolded the note. Brows drawn together, he struggled to read the childish scrawl.

> *My Dearest Sebastián,*
> *A terrible misunderstanding broke out between us yesterday. I promise I will remedy all matters, but there are many things we must discuss. I am in love with you and can do much more for you than any cousin of a duke. I understand she is a mere child of sixteen. I am a woman. Did I not please you yesterday?*
> *Return an answer with my messenger and I will meet with you at a place of your choosing.*
>
> *Until we meet, my love,*
> *Lupiana.*

"Will there be a response, Captain?" his servant asked.

"Tell the messenger there will be no answer," Sebastián said and dismissed the servant. The door closed behind the man and Sebastián threw the letter into the dying embers of the fireplace. Like the false words in the letter turning from black to gray ash on the grate, he would erase the dalliance from the previous day and his own miserable weakness. Determined to blot out the indiscretion, he decided to stroll around the estate, mull over another matter vying for attention.

Nearing the outskirts of the estate proper, he wondered what he should do about a statement his father had made the prior evening over supper.

"It is time for you to be married, Sebastián, produce some heirs," his father said. "We have arranged a meeting to discuss a matrimonial union between you and Señorita Ignatia Matilde de Alburquerque—a noble name, an honorable family. At present, the young lady is studying at a convent. Sometime in the future, the duke plans to travel to the New World, conquer lands farther west. With your military experience, I am confident the duke will welcome you to his expedition and offer you command over a body of troops."

"Father, may I have some time to think about this. I wanted to visit—"

"No. There will be no discussion. I have agreed to meet with her family. That is tantamount to a contract. At that time we will discuss each other's lineage.

"Later, I am sure, her family will inform me of all details for the wedding, then I will give my word of honor and the banns will be read in church."

His mother patted Sebastián's cheek. "My dearest son, I have heard she is a charming young lady, well-bred, versed in all wifely duties. I am so happy for you." Tears welled in her eyes.

Sebastián kissed his mother on the temple to hide the look of discomfort on his face at hearing his father's statement. Once his father gave his word, his son would *have* to marry Señorita Ignatia Matilde Alburquerque. His father's word a solemn vow, the vow of a caballero—a knight.

What did Ignatia look like? Only vague rumors of a pale, fragile, but pretty girl of sixteen. Or was she, in fact, the spoiled offspring of an aristocratic family?

Sebastián had nodded. "Yes, Father," deciding to take a walk around the estate to clear his head.

A bramble of roses in front of him rustled and a shadow crossed his vision, broke his thought.

Sebastián feigned casualness, gripped the scabbard of his sword and pushed up on the hilt with his thumb—a movement scarcely discernible to anyone—his weapon now ready for instant use. Pace slowed, each step firm on the ground, he strolled forward and unobtrusively scanned both sides of the path.

From the corner of his eye, he watched the shadow—human. A thief? Brigand? Whoever it was, they acted like a badger skulking behind the brush, paused when Sebastián paused. Why hadn't he struck before this?

He nodded. Whoever the miscreant was, he intended only to watch. Slowly, he lured the unknown skulker to a familiar, secluded area, every twist and turn well known to Sebastián since childhood. Once there, the trespasser would be trapped at a dead end.

At a turn in the path, Sebastián ducked behind a hedge.

The man passed by the bush and Sebastián leaped upon him.

Both grunted as they landed on a bed of leaves and dirt on the path with the trespasser on the bottom.

The man, shabbily dressed, gaunt, but wiry, squirmed from underneath and took to his heels. Sebastián, dagger drawn, bounded after him, caught the man, and after a brief struggle, threw him again to the ground.

In a trice, Sebastián sat astride the man's chest, knees bearing down on the man's arms, dagger pressed against the grimy throat.

He inched closer to the man's face. "Why are you following me?"

The man's pockmarked face grimaced in pain. "No. I will be killed." Rotted teeth and black gums filled the open mouth.

Sebastián turned his head away. A stench of decay, sweat and garlic from the man's mouth, almost overpowered him. The dagger's point pressed deeper under the scrawny, dirt-creased chin.

A trickle of red rolled down the grimy neck and the man cried out, "Enough, Captain! I was to see if you met any women!"

"You know who I am. Now I want the name of your master? Speak or I will drive my dagger through your worthless hide."

The man glanced briefly at Sebastián, then tore his glance away.

"Doña Lupiana! Mary, Mother of God, she will have me drawn and quartered if she finds I have betrayed her. I have a family. I needed the money, Captain. Spare me."

Sebastián lifted his weapon from the man's neck, struggling to hide his rage and hold his temper in check. Lupiana, that hellish woman, hired this spy. To what end? He stood and motioned with the dagger for the man to rise. Eyes on the naked blade, the man warily rose to his feet.

"What is your name?"

"Alphonso Orentes, Captain."

"Hold out your hand," Sebastián ordered.

Alphonso shrank back. "By all the saints, Captain, do not cut off my hand!"

"I am not cutting…" Sebastián loosened a small cloth bag from his belt and untied a knot. Sunlight glittered off a gold ducat as it tumbled into the open palm, several *maravedis*—copper coins—followed behind. Alphonso's mouth gaped, eyes widened.

"Tell your mistress you saw me. No women in my presence. If you relate what has truly happened, I personally will hunt you down and kill you in a slow and most painful manner. Understood?"

Coins clutched in his hand, Alphonso plucked the ducat, then bit the edge of the gold piece to test its genuineness. He smiled through blackened teeth.

"After you meet with Señora Lupiana," Sebastián said, "you will leave the village for a goodly while. Travel south. Enjoy the sunshine. If you take care of what I gave you there will be enough for lodging and meals for you and your family. Heed well what I said about hunting you down. Go."

Alphonso's head bobbed in response. He muttered his thanks and scurried away, quickly swallowed by the thick woods surrounding the estate.

Sebastián turned on his heel and marched back to the manor. Damn Lupiana! Witch of a woman not only a possessive schemer, but also careless in writing notes and hiring spies. Over a single and brief affair.

Within two hours, Sebastián had his servants construct a wooden crate and deliver the portrait—paint still shimmering wet to Lupiana. No message accompanied the portrait.

At lunchtime, when asked about his moodiness by his parents, he muttered, "The wedding with Señorita Ignatia…I must think…" and returned to walk and read in the garden.

Choosing his favorite stone bench facing a murmuring stream beside an orange orchard, he opened his book—a translation from Arabic to Latin of the Arabian Nights—a tome slated for the proposed *Index Librorum Prohibitorum.* Strong rumors of its readiness for publication had filtered through the ranks of nobility, including Sebastián's father, then on to Sebastián. Mother Church threatened all Catholics with excommunication for reading books on the list.

At a pause in his reading, he turned and saw one of his father's servants hurrying down the long path from the house. Sebastián hid the forbidden book under his cloak.

"Captain! Once we delivered the painting, Doña Lupiana loosed her dogs on us without any provocation. One of the servants was badly bitten."

Sebastián sucked in a deep breath and clutched the edges of the stone bench. She had set the dogs out of spite—his not replying to her letter, and most assuredly found out her spy had disappeared. His dalliance with Lupiana was causing havoc on those around him, all innocent of any knowledge of wrongdoing on his part.

"I will report this unforgivable affront to my father. Tend to your men. Send for the doctor if necessary. I will speak to you later." His servant bowed and ran off to the servant's quarters.

Sebastián marched off to tell his father. He found both of his parents sitting at a table in the study going over estate accounts.

"May I speak with you, Father?" he asked.

Don Avíles nodded.

"I had the servants deliver the finished painting. They were set upon by dogs owned by Doña Lupiana."

"Merciful Heaven!" Doña Caterina said, clutching her rosary.

"How badly were the servants bitten?" Don Avíles asked.

"Bites on legs and arms, one of them seriously."

"Why were they attacked?"

"Perhaps because I refused Doña Lupiana's request to see the painting before it was finished." He felt his neck flush. That was only a half-truth.

Don Avíles stroked his beard and stared at Sebastián. "That is nonsense.

Many painters refuse to show unfinished work. I will send a letter to Don Rodrigo demanding an explanation then visit the servants. I will see you at supper." He waved his son away.

During supper, in answer to his mother's questions about the painting, Sebastián offered brief explanations.

After supper, Sebastián accompanied his father to inquire about the servants' injuries, then asked to be excused and walked back to the orchard.

Long shadows played along the trees and orchards. The hour set for vespers. His mother would be at the family's private chapel and upset, he knew, not yet resigned to her son's continued absences from services. Sunday masses were the exception, attended by Sebastián only after strong coaxing by his father.

Night fell, blanketed the estate in cool darkness.

Sebastián stood. He scuffed up the stone steps to his room and climbed into bed. Through many hours, he scoured his mind of any thoughts about Lupiana and fell asleep with one thought.

At least the indiscretion was over.

He hoped.

FIVE

Through swirls of fog and splatter of mud, an ornate carriage with scrollwork on its sides and a black boar on a white shield painted on the door, leather curtains drawn, rolled to a stop at the de Avíles estate. Liverymen leaped to the ground and unfolded the steps of the carriage.

Daybreak had swept in with slate gray storm clouds scudding across the horizon. Humid air crackled with lightning.

Don Rodrigo heaved himself out of the door—alone, red-faced and agitated. He pushed his footmen aside. "I demand to see Captain Sebastián. At once!" he shouted to the Chief Steward of the manor.

Upstairs, through an open narrow window in his bedroom, drawn by the clatter of galloping hoofbeats and whinny of horses, Sebastián watched the don's arrival. What did this unannounced visit mean? He slipped on his boots, threw a cloak over his shoulders and rushed into the corridor. Always best to face whatever the emergency forthwith.

His parents appeared at the gallery overlooking the vestibule. Worry flashed in his mother's eyes.

"Father," Sebastián said, "Don Rodrigo is at the door. It is probably about the painting. I will take care of the matter with dispatch." A sudden thought brushed cobwebs of sleep away. No, this visit hinged on…

"But why is he here at this ungodly hour?" his mother asked, tucking loose strands of hair under her nightcap.

"Please, Mother. I will take care of whatever business Don Rodrigo has on his mind."

"I have always felt that man is not a gentleman," she said, "and furthermore…" Her husband cupped her by the elbow and ushered his wife back into their bedroom.

The bedroom door closed behind his parents and Sebastián, cloak flapping behind him, bounded down the stairs, boots thumping on the stone steps. Once the meeting with the hidalgo ended, Sebastián would follow his routine— riding, fencing, reading and painting.

In the center of the reception hall, Don Rodrigo paced the granite flagstones. "Don Rodrigo what is the—?"

The hidalgo interrupted, pointed with a gloved hand at Sebastián. "You, sir, have not done justice in your painting of Doña Lupiana de Montes, my wife. Madam is quite displeased and in a frightful state. She feels the painting does not in the least give true measure of her beauty. Most unflattering and insulting to her, and to me as her husband."

Sebastián retreated a step. "Sir,…I did my best." In spite of all her complaints, petulance and interference during the sittings, he felt his work had infused warmth to her eyes, turned unruly strands of her hair into flowing, radiant tresses, softened the cruel thin lips

Don Rodrigo's neck flushed crimson. "Your best could be duplicated by a stable boy."

Anger crawled up Sebastián's throat. *Patience, Sebastián. patience. Do not forget, he is an hidalgo, very wealthy, and with many influential friends, including the queen.*

He forced a deep breath to restore calm and clasped his hands behind his back. *Wait. That is not the true reason he is here.* Venom for Don Rodrigo's vehement outburst and the dark menace in the portly man's eyes did not rise from the painting.

Did Lupiana reveal the affair? Did she twist the details as to who committed the seduction? Perhaps even accusation of rape by Sebastián against her person?

He stared at the gray flagstones, desperate for time to infuse clarity to the chaos in his mind—grateful in a sense his parents, especially his mother, were out of earshot of the confrontation. He could feel cold sweat glisten on his brow.

Don Rodrigo peeled off a leather glove and threw it at Sebastián's feet. Sebastián gazed at the gauntlet for an instant, then kicked it aside.

"I demand satisfaction. I challenge you to a duel. My seconds will make the arrangements." The hidalgo turned on his heel, swung the door open and stormed back to his carriage. Cracks of a whip split the air, horses neighed and carriage wheels clattered against pebbles as Don Rodrigo left the estate.

Sebastián watched until clouds of dust from the carriage settled to the ground. Head down, he strode over and shut the door. Walking up the stairs, he felt his body shrink. He had been drawn into a duel. As the challenged, he had choice of weapons. That mattered little. At this time, calamity sat on his shoulder. Refusal to meet on the field of honor meant disgrace—his own and his family's name besmirched forever.

But most calamitous of all, Queen Isabel and the Church forbade dueling among the nobility and upper classes—Spaniards known for their tempers—quick to take offense at the slightest insult, real or perceived.

Years of warnings and advice from his father had tempered Sebastián's immediate recourses to the sword—to a degree.

In spite of battlefield experience with cold, heat, hunger and killing of men, revelation of a duel to his parents the worse experience of all. What would befall them if reports of the duel reached the queen? Admonition against all participants in the duel or receive severe punishment—banishment, imprisonment on a galley, beheading? Shivers rolled down his spine.

Upstairs, he stepped into his parent's bedroom as though visiting someone in the hospital. He found his father pacing in front of dying embers in the fireplace, each step echoing against the stone walls. His mother stood by the headboard, silent, rosary in hand.

Sebastián informed his parents of the ill tidings.

Don Aviles stopped his pacing and spun around. "Have you lost your senses?" his father said. "Don Rodrigo has great wealth and is a friend of Queen Isabel. He demands satisfaction over a *painting?*"

Sebastián tasted the lump of bitterness in his throat. Damn Lupiana to hell. "I believe Don Rodrigo's anger may lie with a single, brief…uh, affair I had with his wife."

Her mother clutched her rosary to her chest. "Oh, God in Heaven. Carnal relations with that dreadful woman." She bowed her head and murmured a prayer with each bead, the click of beads loud in the new silence.

"What was that?" Grave-faced, his father stormed forward to confront his son. "An adulterous affair with a married woman, whose reputation, at best, is questionable? Officers who served with me have revealed rumors about this woman, dislike by wives of the queen's courtiers."

"Father, I succumbed to a base emotion and committed an immoral act. For that I am contrite. I will not make any excuses. What happened between

Doña Lupiana and myself cannot be undone. But I must accept the challenge. It is a question of honor."

"Yes, yes, of course, your honor," Don Avíles said. "And your family's honor also. You are still a fool. The embarrassment you have caused cannot be easily erased. But you are my son and stood faithfully by my side during terrible moments over the years with the endless wars and I will stand by you. I will defend you no matter the outcome. I am confident of your skill. You have learned well with your fencing instructor, shown your mettle in battle. I will choose your seconds and make other preparations."

The rosary beads of Doña de Avíles clicked faster.

Per the rigid rules of dueling and the strictures of Queen Isabel against the practice, only the referee, the seconds and the duelists would be allowed on the field of honor. Any accompanying servants—chosen for their trustworthiness, were required to stand fifty paces away from the dueling area.

"Sebastián, you might lose your life," Doña Avíles said. Tears streamed down his mother's pale cheek and she wrung her hands, anguish in her look. "To satisfy some absurd ancient code of honor over a harlot! My dear son, please reconsider."

"I cannot, Mother. I have sent a mounted servant with word of my acceptance."

"Caterina," Don Avíles, said, "In spite of our son acting like an idiot, it is a question of honor."

Doña De Avíles tilted her head back. "Honor. Honor. That is all I hear." She grasped and raised the silver cross of her rosary over her head. "O Sainted Mother of Heaven, look after my beloved son. Please open the eyes of these men and let them see the foolhardiness of this duel."

Sebastián sank to his knees in front of Don de Avíles. "Father, please do not attend the duel. I beg of you. If Her Majesty hears of the duel, all those present can vouch for your absence at the time. Let all of the dishonor fall upon me."

His mother ran to her husband. "Francisco, you still have a wound unhealed for many weeks. The dampness will delay their healing. I do not want possible harm to fall on my son and my husband."

Silent, Don de Avíles nodded.

Sebastián embraced his parents then pulled away. Heart heavy with the pain he had inflicted on them, each step leaden, he retreated to his rooms. Closing the door behind him, he forwent lighting a candle and stared out a window.

Outside, the sky darkened and rain fell, obscured the landscape. If only he had controlled his lust. If only he had refused the commission to paint. If…if.

Five days later, low-lying fog blanketed the clearing circled by a stand of oaks. Morning coolness coupled with cold anxiety chilled Sebastián's face, hands and body, his neck colder than usual. Earlier, he had the removed the stiff lace ruff from around his neck.

Sebastián would try wounding Don Rodrigo—the man almost twice his age and grossly overweight. Yes, a flesh wound, no more.

All concerned in the duel, referee, seconds, coachmen and participants, he knew, would be sworn to secrecy, to prevent reprisals from the queen or the Church.

He reached out and shook the hands of his seconds, Juan de Córdoba and Rolando de Ventillas, both fellow officers of Sebastián in the endless campaigns against the fierce Moors.

"Watch the don carefully, Sebastián," Rolando, oldest of the three, said. "When he alighted from the coach, he waddled. Now he struts. People see his great weight and think of it as an infirmity. Do not be fooled by that ruse."

Sebastián only half listened and clutched his cloak tighter around him, watched the referee check the ground for rocks the duelists might trip over, or holes they might stumble into.

"*Caballeros*," the referee called out. "The ground is satisfactory. Let us begin." He folded a cloth back from two rapiers—Sebastián's choice of weapons.

Sebastián, Don Rodrigo and their seconds formed a half circle around the referee.

"It has been agreed to by all," the referee said, "this duel will be held in the utmost secrecy. No word will be spoken by those gathered here about this matter hereafter. Understood?"

All the men placed their right hand over their heart and nodded. "We swear upon our honor and before God our Lord."

The referee went on. "I will explain the *Código duello*. I have placed stakes on the outside limits of the dueling area. If anyone steps out of those boundaries, he will forfeit the duel and bring disgrace on himself. If anyone runs away…" He paused and raised a loaded and primed espingarda—a bulky matchlock handgun. "I will shoot him and he will be dishonored. You will stand ten paces from each other. When I drop a handkerchief, you may proceed. If one of the parties suffers a non-fatal wound, he may ask for an honorable withdrawal from the field of honor. If his request is refused, engagement will continue. Understood?"

Sebastián and Don Rodrigo nodded.

"Your cloak, Sebastián?" Rolando asked.

"Yes, of course." His second slipped off the thick, Fustian military cloak from around his friend's shoulders and Sebastián stepped off to count the paces. Under his blouse and jerkin his skin felt clammy and he shivered again, but forced his thoughts away from the cold. A quick thrust to his opponent's shoulder and all could return home.

"Gentlemen," the referee said. "Please unbutton your doublets and open."

Both men complied. The request reflected the possibility one of the duelists might wear padding or other protective covering underneath to ward off fatal thrusts.

"Thank you," the referee said. The duelists left their doublets unbuttoned.

A voice—at once strident and boastful, interrupted.

"Well, my young cockerel," Don Rodrigo said, "are you ready to die?"

Sebastián avoided contact of eye with the don and slapped his arms against his sides for warmth. He had forsworn gloves. In summer, perspiration lessened a grip on a weapon, in winter—unless extremely cold—a naked hand assured a firmer hold of the sword's pommel.

Why did he feel the chill this morning? Many times in past battles against Moorish troops, damp, often frozen ground had served as his bed. Now his body shook involuntarily. Because possible death hovered close by?

"Gentlemen," the referee announced, "choose your weapon." He laid two rapiers—guards facing forward over his forearm.

Sebastián and Don Rodrigo each drew one, wiped the ends with a cloth dampened with strong wine—a task to make sure the sword tips free of poison. Stepping back, the duelists checked the blades for balance. Quickly, the duelists took their places on the field.

"On guard!" The referee dropped a white handkerchief.

Sebastián and Don Rodrigo turned sideways, left hands crooked behind their backs. Both saluted each other with a sharp snap of their blades.

Sword held waist high, Sebastián stood still. He would let the hidalgo take the offensive. "Watch your opponent's eyes," his fencing master always warned.

"Why not watch the hands?" a student had asked.

"If a man wears a cloak, how can you see his hands?" the fencing master said.

That sudden flare, the widening of the pupils would announce the opponent's attack.

Victory rested with those sharp of eye.

Rodrigo sliced the air with his sword as though testing its strength—smiled at the keening sound of the blade. He slid his foot to the right then left; feinted. With each feint, he inched closer.

A bemused look crossed Sebastián's face. *He shrinks distance between us by his feints.*

For a corpulent man, Rodrigo glided lightly on his feet, his movements smooth as those of a thief. Or perhaps the movements of a bullfighter? *Admirable.* Was the don a student of *tauromaquia*, the art of bullfighting, a ritual restricted to the aristocracy? *Now, if Rodrigo turns his shoulder a little more toward me, I can inflict a scratch, and we can all betake ourselves to our homes.*

The hidalgo suddenly swiveled on his heel and lunged, slashed for Sebastián's torso. The tip of the don's sword cut through the blouse. A trickle of blood crimsoned. Sebastián forced back a grimace, ignored the sting from the slash.

He pivoted right as Don Rodrigo pressed his attack—from the left, then the right, then right, then left, again and again, thrusting forward, but Rodrigo's sword point struck empty air.

Pale sunlight struggled against wisps of fog, sent shafts of white columns through branches to form leafed patterns on the ground.

Though the weather was cool, sweat glistened on the hidalgo's brow, his every breath sounded heavy and forced.

Sebastián slid his foot along the ground for balance, and watched. Don Rodrigo's skills—much higher than he had expected. But he parried the don's next thrust with ease and stepped two paces back.

"Don Rodrigo," he said. "If you wish to rest, I will agree. If you desire to withdraw from the field, I will not consider—"

"You are a coward, like your ancestors." The nobleman's breath rasped, but the don noticeably took advantage of the allowed respite.

At his opponent's offensive remark, Sebastián tightened the grip on his sword until his fingers turned white. He narrowed his eyes into slits, but decided to extend the respite by talking.

"Don Rodrigo, during the crusades, my forefathers fought against the Moors in African deserts under the banner of the Knights Templar, and again, my family fought alongside El Cid. While my father and I fought against the Moors in Spain, your forbears sank themselves neck-deep in corruption and usury. Your titles and riches have been bought with the blood and sweat of others."

The hidalgo's face reddened and his eyes burned with hatred. He feinted, lunged again.

Sebastián beat his opponent's sword away, stepped back again and lowered his sword. "I apologize, sir, for any dishonor I may have caused. You have drawn blood. Let us retire. I will yield." He saw his seconds shake their heads, eyes incredulous at the unexpected apology.

"That is honorable, Don Rodrigo. Please reconsider," the referee said.

"We agree," Don Rodrigo's seconds said.

Don Rodrigo spat on the ground. "No! I will not accept. Stand and fight. The captain is a son of a whore!"

Sebastián's blood flooded his brain. He would have accepted any insult to avoid a killing, but not this most vile of insults. Any thoughts of a flesh wound, punishment by Queen Isabel, or damnation to deepest hell by the Church vanished.

Sword point painting circles, left hand upraised behind him for balance, he closed the distance.

Parries and thrusts by the don followed one another. Foam on his lips, Don Rodrigo struck at the young man's head, chest, in wild, desperate strokes, the metal singing with each missed thrust.

Sebastián riposted with ease. Then, in a silver blur, his own blade arced in the still air and its steel point plunged into Don Rodrigo's heart. Blood blossomed like a red rose on the hidalgo's spotless white blouse.

The don clutched his chest, gasped once and slumped to the damp, cold ground. His seconds and the referee rushed over.

From the ground, and, with frightened eyes, the referee stared at Sebastián. "Don Rodrigo de Montes is dead, Captain. We saw how you tried only to wound him, then offered to yield. All of us here have been sworn to secrecy, but if word filters to the queen…" He crossed himself. "God help us." Shaking his head, the referee stood, walked to his mount and galloped away.

Don Rodrigo's seconds—with help from Sebastián's men, hoisted the dead hidalgo's body into the carriage and the coach sped through swirls of fog—to his manor and the now widowed Lupiana.

Numbed, Sebastián regretted his final thrust, oblivious when Rolando took the sword from his hand and draped the cloak back over his shoulders. The don's insult, his own temper, a flammable mixture ignited by anger would now consume all of them. He grasped both of his seconds by the shoulders.

"I have brought great disaster upon both of you. I humbly apologize and—"

"Sebastián," Rolando said, "You have apologized enough today. Do not fret for us.

"The wars are over in Spain. Juan and I are tired being swords for hire; escorting cowards to meet with their mistresses or collecting debts for greedy landlords. Peace hangs heavy on us. Juan and I have already signed to take ship at Cadiz for the New World. There are rumors of fabulous cities and riches lying to the west and south of Spain's recent conquests. You were honorable and as chivalrous as the knight Juan Ponce de Leon to the end. If it were I in this duel, I would have killed the fat pig as quickly as possible. Why not come with us?"

Sebastián shook his head. "My parents wait to see if I ride my horse home or arrive draped over the saddle. My father awaits a report on the duel. Then I will decide."

"Well, then, goodbye and may God our Lord guide your steps. After we leave our families, we will pass by your father's estate and bid our farewells to your parents. Let us go, Juan."

Sebastián nodded, all three friends embraced and shook hands. How many battles had they fought side by side? More than he cared to remember. He watched as his seconds and companions-in-battle untethered their mounts and rode off.

Rolando leaned back and shouted from his saddle, "Perhaps we will see you in Jamaica or the Virgin Islands!" Laughter trailed behind him. Soon, the hoof beats of their horses died in the distance. Silence fell in the deserted clearing.

The idea sorely tempted Sebastián. Spain now controlled most of the Caribbean. Why not sail to the New World, see strange lands and peoples? No, he must first report to his father. Victory in the past tasted sweet, this victory over Don Rodrigo tasted like the sourness of defeat. He would ask for an audience with the queen, plead for the life of the referee and others.

Left alone in the glade, his mood somber as the morning, he strode to his horse. Above him, sunlight vanished, clouds darkened and droplets of rain fell.

Bareheaded, Sebastián denied himself the comfort and dryness of his cloak's hood; not caring if chills or fever seized him. He mounted. Grasping the reins, he stroked the white forelock of his horse, Aliento, named for the mare's vigor of spirit.

The animal, of the Frisian breed, known and prized for its great strength, stamina and broad hooves—highly desirable on the battlefield—had served Sebastián well during the wars. Aliento was always there. Always ready. Always faithful—even when wounded in its great chest by a Moorish arrow.

Aliento nickered, stamped the ground, as though impatient to leave. Sebastián heard the chuffs of his horse's breath followed by a flume of white in the cold moist air. He patted the mare's neck.

"Yes, yes, you understand as well as I. The day has only begun, but it has ended for me."

Aliento, clomping through puddles of mud and sodden leaves, Sebastián allowed the mare free rein towards home.

Halfway up a hill, the horse suddenly stopped, snorted.

Sebastián jerked his head up.

Fifteen paces in front of him a horseman, face and head covered by a hood, blocked the road.

Straightening, Sebastián drew his sword and pointed the weapon at the rider.

"Sir, stand aside. I wish to pass. If you do not, I will run you through."

The horseman reached up with a gloved hand and pushed back the hood.

Sebastián gasped. "Father! What are you doing here?"

"If my son were to die, *I* would bring his body home to his mother, no one else."

A lump formed in Sebastián's throat. He urged Aliento forward, leaned over and embraced his father. "Thank you, sir."

"Let us not discuss it now. Let us go home."

Droplets turned into a downpour, pelted men and horses all the way to the manor.

43

SIX

A flickering candle in her shaking hand and a fearful look in her eyes, Eugenia, Lupiana's personal maid, approached her mistress. Outside the windows, gray rain clouds trooped by, rain ceased, yet dreariness clung to the day.

"Señora, there are some men downstairs. They wish to speak to you most urgently."

"Who are they?"

Eugenia visibly trembled and sniffled. "The seconds of Don Rodrigo."

"Oh, very well. I will be down as soon as I can. Have a servant serve them wine and see to their needs." She dismissed Eugenia with a wave of the hand. Lupiana did not ask if her husband accompanied the seconds.

She strolled to the window, cooing to a bright green, red and yellow parrot inside a carved wood cage—one of hundreds of birds Columbus and conquistadors sent to Spain from the New World beginning in 1492. She stroked the bird's plumage.

"How are you my sweet Peregrina?" Pursing her lips, she fed the bird a slice of orange. Then she felt a smile form, recalling how by a quick tryst behind a wooden screen with an aristocrat, stealing some of his jewelry while he dressed, then followed with threats of blackmail of exposure to his wife, resulted in acquiring the rare exotic bird. She hummed, her humming sounding like a beehive.

"After weeks of planning, full success comes closer," she whispered to her pet. Lupiana had manipulated her husband into a jealous rage, accusing

Sebastián of indelicate remarks to a married woman, meaning herself. Don Rodrigo had stormed out of the bedroom vowing revenge.

Now, sighing happily, Lupiana checked herself from all angles in the mirror and danced out of the room.

Downstairs, at her approach, the don's seconds swept their hats off, snapped to attention and bowed. She recognized Don Felipe Sannazaro and Diego Porrás.

"Señora," Felipe Sannazaro said, "it is with great distress and sadness we report the most distressful news. Don Rodrigo is dead."

She gasped, pulled a handkerchief from her sleeve and pressed her hand, palm out, against her temple, as though about to faint. Her other hand clutched her heart.

Diego Porrás leaped forward. "May we be of assistance?"

She waved him away, her hand limp. "No. Thank you. I must be strong and carry on as best I can at this terrible moment. Please bring my dear husband's body inside."

The men bowed again and hurried out. Moments later, don Rodrigo's corpse rested on a side table.

Not questioning the men further and, hiding behind an open fan, Lupiana affected loud, mournful sobs.

"We remain at your service, Señora," Sannazaro said. Both men offered polite bows, excused themselves and retreated to their horses.

The door shut behind the men and Lupiana's sobbing vanished.

"Eugenia, come here. Have the servants bring your dead master inside. They are to clean and dress him. Then take him to the chapel. Have the carpenter build a catafalque and coffin. Next, have one of those lazy stable boys hitch up a mule to take you to the village. Fetch my seamstress. Tell her to stop whatever she is doing. I do not care whether she is plowing a field or giving birth to more brats. I wish to have a dress made for the funeral that makes me look more beautiful than ever as a widow—even in dismal black. And have a mounted messenger stand by. Can your small brain remember all that?"

"Yes, Señora."

"Come upstairs after that. And stop that stupid sniveling."

Eugenia curtsied, wiped her nose with the back of her hand and scurried away.

Gathering up her skirts, Lupiana climbed the stairs to her chambers—without waiting to view her late husband's body. A matter of higher priority awaited her—her new wealth.

In his bedroom, she sat at her dead husband's desk and rifled through the drawers, searching for any hidden ducats or jewelry. Finding none, she pulled out a sheet of parchment and scribbled a note to the family lawyers in Madrid.

> *Sirs:*
>
> *My beloved and dearest husband is dead of wounds sustained in an unfortunate accident. You are to forward to me with the greatest of haste, copies of all papers relating to his estates and my legal claims to such properties as his grieving widow and sole heir.*
>
> *Sincerely,*
> *Doña Lupiana Montes,* **viuda** *de Rodrigo de Montes.*

After addressing, she sealed the letter with wax and imprinted the ring with her late husband's coat of arms on the still-warm beeswax. Letter in hand, she fed the parrot a few seeds and waited for her maid.

An hour later, a breathless Eugenia entered Lupiana's bedroom.

"Did you bring the seamstress back with you?"

"Yes, Señora. She waits in the kitchen."

"I hope she does not eat everything she sets her eye on. Give this to the messenger. Tell him to hurry to Madrid." She handed the envelope to Eugenia. "And tell the footmen to prepare the carriage."

Eyes downcast, Eugenia asked, "Shall we prepare for the vigil, Doña?"

Spanish custom dictated that family and friends of the deceased meet for two or three hours of prayers for nine evenings running and be led in service by a priest or other person sanctioned to officiate by the Church.

"Yes, yes. Go away. Can't you see I am busy? *Idiota.*"

Eugenia plodded out, each step slower than the last.

Soon, the carriage clattered to a stop, Lupiana descended from her rooms and quick paced to the open door. She placed her foot shod in silk lined shoes on the first step. "To the de Avíles estate," she told the footman. "And hurry!"

Settled back against thick, red cushions, Lupiana cut into a pomegranate with her poniard—a slender lady's dagger, took a bite and spit the seeds onto the floor. The new widow smiled to herself.

"I now hold great wealth in my hands, I will exact my revenge on all those who cast doubt on my character. Especially, those fat, smug ladies of the court." She twisted her lips into a sneer. Also, she would now seek the arms of a young and highly virile man instead of the bloated, impotent former husband.

An hour later, a sickly, pale sun struggled for view between dark gray clouds as her carriage rolled to a stop at the de Avíles estate.

At the rear of the manor, seated on a stone bench fronting an orange orchard, Sebastián, chin cupped in his hands, raised his head when a polite cough drew his attention.

The Chief Steward, hands clasped behind his back, stood a few feet away. "Doña Lupiana de Rodrigo, Captain. She wishes to speak with you on matter of great importance. Will you see her?"

"Is she alone?"

"Yes, sir."

Sebastián sat silent for several moments, then said, "I will speak to her. Show her here." The servant nodded and with a dignified air, left.

Sebastián stared down the avenue of orange trees. What did Lupiana want? A widow paying a visit to the killer of her husband? Demanding justice? Retribution?

She entered the orchard behind the steward, a clutch of her billowing skirts in her hand, her walk purposeful.

"Doña Lupiana de Rodrigo, Captain." The steward offered a stiff bow to her and disappeared around a bend.

Overhead, an intermittent drizzle sprinkled the ground.

She sat on a bench opposite Sebastián.

"Why are you here?" he asked.

Lupiana ran her fingers through her thick hair. "I know what has happened. I forgive you. I will not report the incident to the queen on one condition."

"What is that?"

"I am one of the wealthiest women in Spain! I have orchards, livestock and a manor fit for a queen. Come with me this instant. I will hide you in a small cottage on my estate. I have friends at court that will notify me if the queen hears of the duel. Within a month, I am confident the news will be good. Then you and I will travel to France or England."

Sebastián raised his head as though an anvil rested squarely on his neck. "Are you mad, woman? Your husband lies dead in his house, his body not yet cold and you ask his killer to run away with you. God our Lord knows I regret his death by my hand. You, Señora, are without heart, without shame, without remorse. No, I will not go with you."

Lupiana shrank back, a look of surprise and shock on her face. Her manner flashed from seductive to terrifying. "You're refusing *me*?" she screamed, eyes widened with fury. "Damn you to hell!"

She turned as though to leave. Suddenly, in a swirl of skirts, she spun around, a poniard in her hand. Eyes deadly as the dagger, features furious as a demon, she thrust her arm straight ahead and with the speed of an asp, aimed for his heart. "No one refuses me."

"What the devil…" Sebastián raised his arm to ward off the sudden attack. The blade caught his upper arm, sliced through doublet and blouse. A trickle of red oozed from beneath.

Her poniard now against his chest, a hissing Lupiana pressed harder. Off balance, both toppled onto the wet ground.

He shoved her arm aside, seized her wrist and twisted her arm.

"Drop the dagger!"

"You are hurting me!" The weapon fell from her fingers.

"Lupiana. What is the matter with you?" For an instant, anger flooded his brain and he drew back his closed fist to strike her, but forced coolness of thought. In spite of her attack, how would he explain severely beating a recent widow no matter the provocation? Even his parents would disown him. He stood, drew a handkerchief from a sleeve and dabbed at the trickle of blood on his arm. "Return home. I will forget what has happened and never mention the episode to anyone. Leave."

"Bastard! First, you abuse me, now you toss me aside." She spit at his face, lifted her skirts with one hand and threw herself at him again. Between kicking, clicking her teeth, she clawed for his eyes, and struggled to bite him between each curse she hurled at him.

Sebastián spun her around to avoid her kicks, fingernails and teeth. With both hands on her shoulder blades, he pushed hard. Lupiana rolled over in a tangle of skirt, hoops, petticoats and flailing arms. From the ground, she spat her last words at him as he stomped out of the orange grove, calling for his servants to escort Doña Lupiana to her carriage.

Her voice echoed behind him. "Sebastián! You will regret this day! I swear this by all the saints!"

Leaving the orchard, and changing into a fresh blouse in his rooms, Sebastián sought out his father. He found his parents in the great room discussing the handling of the marriage of their son.

"Father, with your permission, I wish to speak with you."

Doña Avíles stood and touched her son on his cheek and temple. "Your face is flushed."

"Son, are you all right?"

"Yes."

"Caterina, let him speak."

"Son, are you sure you are all right?"

"Caterina!"

Sebastián's mother fell silent, snapped open her fan.

"Doña Lupiana paid me a visit—"

His mother gasped. "It is scandalous. A recent widow paying calls—"

"My dear wife, please. I will handle this matter. I know about her visit. The Chief Steward reported her arrival to me. What did she want?"

Sebastián repeated her requests and his refusal.

Caterina De Avíles burst into sobs, stifling them with a lace handkerchief.

"And she left without any further…action?" His father's eyes bored into his.

Sebastián turned his gaze away. "Yes." He knew his father had guessed what had really happened. If pressed, Sebastián would deliver the truth.

Don Avíles slowly rose from his chair. "Hmm. I have some thinking to do. There are estate problems your mother and I have to discuss. Go, dress for supper. We will see you there." He waved his son away.

An action, Sebastián knew, not intended to humiliate him, but to keep his mother from prying further.

Supper ended and after servants cleared the table, Don Avíles poured brandy for himself and Sebastián. His mother declined, instead, clutched her rosary.

"I feel…" his father began, "…Lupiana is a manipulative and scheming woman who will stop at nothing to exact revenge for whatever insults she perceived you inflicted upon her, or to gain ends unknown to us. She will use carnal relations, bribe Crown officials or press charges of heresy with the Inquisition. She is possessed by complete madness. I have written two letters…"

Sebastián's mother sobbed, her sobs echoing against the stone walls.

Don Avíles sighed and continued. "…one is for Her Majesty, Queen Isabel. At present she is at Valladolid. With the Crown's constant travel around Spain, the letter may take weeks to reach the queen. I have asked for a personal audience. I will tell her that I have banished you from this house. It is a half truth." He patted Sebastián's shoulder.

Doña Avíles's rosary clicked faster.

"I have sent the letter by special messenger."

"The other letter is to our longtime friend, Vasco da Gama. From his last communication to me, he is sailing from Lisbon in three weeks. Since discovery of the New World, Spain and Portugal are desperate for experienced military officers to serve on their ships and lead their expeditions. He will welcome you. In a year or two, you will return home. By then, this affair with Lupiana will be resolved, God our Lord, willing. Now, prepare yourself for the journey. You leave at sunrise."

Sebastián bowed his head. "Thank you, Father."

"Oh, one last reminder."

"Yes?"

"This evil woman may have pressed charges of one kind or another against you with the *Santa Hermandad.*"

Sebastián nodded. The Holy Brotherhood, sanctioned by the queen as provincial police, patrolled the roads throughout Spain. "I will take care." He kissed his mother, tore from her arms, embraced his father, and trudged up the stairs to his rooms.

SEVEN

In evening's declining light, Sebastián passed through a postern and stopped at The Inn of The Red Bull. Here he would rest his horse and mule. The mule carried all his personal belongings: extra doublet, two sets of cuirass, harquebus and a pair of espingardas—pistols and an English longbow. A veritable fortune rested on the back of the animal. Both horse and mule then would be sold when he reached Lisbon. Now he would eat and rest himself.

A barefoot lad of fourteen or so ran over from the stables.

Sebastián dismounted. "What is your name?"

"Ramón, sir."

Sebastián handed the boy a silver ducat. The boy's eyes widened.

"Listen to me carefully, Ramón." Sebastián leaned closer. "Remove the packsaddles from the mule. Store them in the safest place in the stable, far from prying eyes. Understood?"

"Yes, sir. My brother, Antonio and I will keep watch all night."

"Most excellent. Water and feed my horse and mule."

Clutching the coin, Ramón bobbed his head.

Sebastián continued. "If all is satisfactory in the morning, you will be amply rewarded."

"Right away, sir." Ramón took the reins of horse and mule and led them away.

It had been a long day's ride. Sebastián looked forward to a hot meal, then to bed. He entered the *cuarto bajo*—the lower floor of the inn. A quick glance revealed a blackened fireplace he could walk under without his head

52

touching the mantel. At the center of the hearth a fire crackled and spit embers on this cool evening. Above the flames, two pots, their bellies black and fat, bubbled with thick stews. The pungent aroma of onions, garlic and the aromatic scent of saffron wreathed the air. Several sconces on the walls held lanterns throwing flickering light over the patrons.

He chose a corner table. Hanging up his cloak on a nail and slipping off his gloves, he observed the guests with unobtrusive watchfulness. "Always be aware of your surroundings," his father had preached many a time. Both sword and dagger stayed on his person.

On one side of the fireplace, a group of seven, four men and three women, occupied the single long table. Long staffs of holly and a scallop shell sewn on two of the men's doublets, identified the group as pilgrims on their way to the shrine of Santiago de Compostela—Saint James—in northwest Spain. They picked at their food wearily. Another table held a middle-aged man and woman deep into a quiet quarrel of whispers, gestures and finger pointing. The other five tables sat empty.

Sebastián nodded, viewed the dining room. *About fifteen paces in length and another ten paces in width.*

He leaned forward and glanced at the kitchen and its open front, its back hidden now but also leading to the inner courtyard. Alongside lit ovens, a woman swung and chopped with a cleaver at the carcass of a cow.

Surrounding the darkened inner courtyard, he knew from prior experience at inns, sat the actual dwellings for patrons. At one end of the courtyard were the stables, above them, a gallery with banisters, a wooden roof and rooms able to accommodate two guests, three—uncomfortably on roughly hewn wooden beds and pallets of straw.

The inn's stout owner or *dueño* in an apron with a mosaic of red and black food stains, clomped forward with a wheeze. "Yes, señor?"

"Do you have fresh gazpacho?" The cold soup was a favorite of Sebastián's.

"Yes, señor. My wife prepared it this morning."

"Good. I will have a bowl. Do you have lamb, pork, chicken?"

"Lamb."

"That will suffice, also bread and a bottle of wine."

The *dueño* nodded and headed to the kitchen.

In the midst of his supper, Sebastián spotted the two men entering.

He tore his gaze away from the two, but stayed alert. The older of the newcomers was like hundreds of soldiers after the end of the Moorish wars, desperate, dangerous swordsmen without a cause, without a patron, without employment, on the lookout for easy prey whether on the streets of Madrid or the roadways. Ready to intimidate, frighten, force payment from those who wished to continue living. Like him? Sebastián wondered.

Of all the guests in the tavern, Sebastián was the best dressed with high quality black boots, spurs, gray pantaloons, black doublet, white lace at his cuffs and lace collar. Although, with sword and dagger, perhaps also viewed as dangerous by the patrons.

The younger one strutted forward like a peacock, cloak thrown back, thumbs stuck through his belt, displaying sword and dagger for all to see.

The newcomers passed by the arguing couple, who stopped their arguing and lowered their heads, then, with the older man lagging behind, the peacock swaggered by the pilgrims. The men at the table watched warily, the women crossed themselves or fingered their rosaries.

The pair passed by Sebastián once. Twice. *They are taking my measure.*

The older man wore his broad brimmed hat low over his eyes while a thick black beard and mustache shadowed his face. Though broad shouldered and barrel-chested—a bear came to Sebastián's mind—the man's step was light as he stepped forward leisurely, twirling the ends of his waxed mustache.

Sebastián continued to eat. *The man with the hat is the more dangerous of the two.*

The tavern owner walked out of the kitchen. "You gentlemen wish a table?" the owner asked, wiping his hands on his apron. His eyes darted nervously.

"Yes." The younger man pointed to where Sebastián sat. "We wish to eat at *that* table."

Sebastián raised his head. Under the table, his left hand lifted the pommel of his sword a notch, ready to draw in half an instant. "I eat alone," he said, his voice calm.

"Did you hear that, Cardona?" the young peacock said over his shoulder. "He *prefers* eating alone. Señor *Aristocrato* does not want us here. That is a *personal i*nsult."

"There are other empty tables," Sebastián said. He bit into a piece of lamb.

"We want to eat at *this* one!" The man slammed his gloved hand on the table's edge. The pewter dishes bounced.

"No," Sebastián said.

"Another insult!" Peacock said.

The tavern owner hurried forward, wringing his hands. "Gentlemen, Gentlemen, please. The Holy Brotherhood prohibits swordplay in taverns."

Cardona placed a hand on the peacock's shoulder. "Come, Grimoldo, we shall wait outside for the aristocrat, if he is not a sniveling coward, and we will demand satisfaction for his insults to us." Cardona offered Sebastián a crooked smile.

The tavern's guests turned their heads away as the two men left.

Sebastián finished his meal, drained his tankard of wine, plucked a handkerchief from his sleeve and carefully wiped his mouth. "The meal was excellent," he said to the owner. "I will stay the night." *If he lived that long.*

"Ah…I know the señor will win the challenge, but does the señor wish to pay in advance…in case…" The owner shrugged.

"I will pay for the meal…and the room." Sebastián pressed a ducat into the man's hand.

"Thank you, señor," the owner said. "These days…dangers everywhere…" Shaking his head, he waddled back to the kitchen.

Without comment, Sebastián stood, slipped on his gloves and drew his sword to the acompaniment of gasps from the three women at the table of pilgrims—all three made the sign of the cross. The sash and scabbard would be left behind, impediments to rapid movement.

He marched to the door, his boots loud on the wooden planks in the sudden silence.

The three women pilgrims crossed themselves again.

At the door, he paused. *What if there were more scoundrels waiting outside?*

What choice do I have? I must fight. If not, I am sure they will lie in wait for me, today, tomorrow…

Outside, the tavern the postern light threw a dim yellowish circle of light. The surrounding walls sat in shades of darkness. At the center of the courtyard stood the peacock, a smirk on his face. *Where was Cardona?*

Sebastián quickly stepped out of the cone of light. He scanned the outer courtyard; a figure huddled in the shadows to his left. *Cardona.* His gaze returned to the grinning Grimoldo. Sebastián groaned inwardly.

The peacock clutched both sword and dagger in his hands.

Four blades against two. His eyes must never veer from watchfulness of his opponent's dagger hand.

Drawing his own dagger, Sebastián waited.

Grimoldo feinted as though to test Sebastián's skill, draw him out, first to one side, then the other. When Sebastián failed to move, his opponent charged headlong.

A hiss from the shadows.

Blades met in close quarters. Face to face with Sebastián, Grimoldo's features displayed victory. Sebastián easily pushed the other sword aside and to the left while parrying Grimoldo's dagger to the right, then sliding his own blade up, he slashed across the man's chest from belt to shoulder. Blood spurted.

"Cardona! I am hit!" Grimoldo staggered back and clutched his chest.

Sebastián leaped to the side as a gleam of naked steel raked his arm, sliced through the puffed sleeves of his doublet, laid bare his shoulder and arm to the wrist.

Grimoldo shouted, "Kill him, Cardona. Kill him. Look what he did to me!"

"Shut up, you fool." For a split moment, Carmona glanced toward Grimoldo.

The slight distraction allowed Sebastián to parry both sword and dagger.

In an instant, Cardona brought his dagger up to protect his throat from being cut, but found Sebastián pressing the point of *his* dagger between Cardona's codpiece and pantaloons. Sebastián drove the point up a fraction.

Cardona's bloodshot eyes widened.

"If you twitch I will cut your balls off. Leave off, sir." From the corner of his eye, Sebastián saw Grimoldo stumbling, circling behind him, arm raised, dagger in hand.

Sebastián clenched his teeth, pressed the steel farther into the codpiece. "Tell your friend to step back."

"Grimoldo, leave off!" Cardona growled.

A clatter of horses behind them, then, a shout. "Hold! In the name of Her Majesty, Queen Isabel! The *Santa Hermandad* demands it." A constable and five of his catchpoles appeared out of the darkness. They reined in their horses.

Sebastián drew his weapon away from Cardona's groin and both opponents stepped aside.

"What is going on here?" the constable asked.

Grimoldo pointed to Sebastián. "Look what he—"

Cardona pushed his friend aside, offered a crooked smile. "*Constable, the gentleman and I were merely practicing fencing strategy. Is that not correct, sir?*" he asked Sebastián.

Sebastián turned the shoulder with torn sleeve away from the constable, hoping to hide his exposed arm in the dim light. "Yes, he is correct. Only friendly swordplay." If he told the truth, the constable might leave men behind to ask more questions and order a possible appearance before a *corregidor*—

the local magistrate to determine the facts of the matter. *That* would mean a delay of days or even weeks, perhaps spent in prison. Sebastián *must* reach Lisbon before da Gama sailed.

"We are in strong pursuit of several fugitives," the constable said. "Otherwise I would investigate further. Are all of you staying here?"

One of the catchpoles drew closer to Sebastián, Cardona and Grimoldo.

"These men are not who we seek, constable," he said. "The men we pursue are half naked, emaciated and with shackles on their feet."

"My friend and I were just leaving," Cardona said, pulling along a disgruntled Grimoldo who held his cloak across his chest. They headed to their tethered horses, and mounted—Grimoldo helped onto his by Cardona.

The constable shot a hard look at Sebastián. "We waste time here. Turn your horses!" Horses snorted and neighed, the men uttered curses and the Holy Brotherhood rode off into the darkness.

As Cardona and his friend cantered away, Sebastián heard Cardona say, "You whining idiot. We lost him."

Grimoldo groaned.

If the Holy Brotherhood had not appeared on the scene, Sebastián might be lying in a pool of his own blood. Shaking his head, he walked back into the tavern. Inside, he was greeted by polite clapping.

"Thank you, but credit goes to the Holy Brotherhood for intervening."

"We thank you anyway for ridding us of those thieves and murderers," the tavern owner said. "For that we offer you our best room!"

The next day, Sebastián rose early, shaved and descended to the *cuarto bajo* for a breakfast of ham, bread and wine in the empty room.

Curious, he asked, "Where are the other guests?"

"The pilgrims left before sunrise," the owner said. "The couple from last night plus others who arrived later still sleep."

Sebastián finished his breakfast and strolled to the stables. There, he helped a sleepy Ramón while a tired-eyed Antonio watched them lift the packsaddles onto the mule after Sebastián removed his other doublet. He checked the tightness of ropes. Satisfied, he adjusted the headstall over his horse, shook out the reins and left after rewarding Ramón and his brother with a few *maravedis*. The two boys grinned, faces dirty, tousled hair feathered with strands of hay.

Another two or three days of hard riding lay ahead. Cloak draped over his horse's neck, wineskin wrapped around the saddle's pommel, Sebastián chose an easy trot, one hand holding the reins, the other resting on his thigh, close to his sword.

Half a league from the inn, he chanced upon the group of pilgrims huddled by the side of the road. Drawing abreast of them as they parted, he glanced at the upper body of Grimoldo, face drained of blood, lower half covered with stones. Both of Grimoldo's weapons were missing along with his horse.

"He is dead, señor," a grim-faced woman said. "Bled to death. Even if he was a thief and murderer, we are giving him a Christian burial. We will not leave this misguided man as carrion for crows or wild animals."

The pilgrims crossed themselves and continued covering Grimoldo with stones.

"The nearest cemetery…" the woman said, dropping her stone in place and straightening her back, "…we have been told, is a league away. We have no horse and cart available to carry the body and no shovels. We travel on foot by choice to the shrine of our blessed Saint James."

Their only possessions, Sebastián knew, were a wooden staff, perhaps a loaf of hardened bread and goatskins filled with wine or water—and a strong dedication to their pilgrimage.

About to dismount, Sebastián asked, "May I offer a hand?"

"Thank you, sir," the women said, "You repaid us last night. Who knows what villainies that man and the other might have inflicted on us."

"May God repay your Christian kindness," Sebastián said, doffed his cap and rode on.

The sun reached its zenith and the warmth of the day fought to close his eyelids. By sheer willpower he forced them open, but his grip loosened on the reins in the silence of the deserted road.

A horse snorted.

Sebastián snapped his head up.

On horseback, Cardona rushed out from behind a hillock on Sebastián's left.

The swoosh of a blade swept off Sebastián's cap and raised the hairs on his head as he ducked to avoid decapitation. He drew his sword and turned in his saddle.

At a gallop, Cardona, short cape flying behind him, wheeled his horse and charged again.

Sebastián parried the strike, but unable to return the thrust. The loud clink when both swords met sent vibrations running through his shoulders. His horse, untrained for the violent twists and turns of a battlefield, bucked. He dropped the reins of both animals and leaped from his saddle to confront his adversary. Cardona, on horseback would have the advantage.

Feet apart, Sebastián raised his sword in both hands—he had seen the unorthodox stance used at the Battle of Granada by a soldier with great success against horsemen. He waited.

Cardona wheeled his horse again and bolted forward. This time he held his weapon to the right side, ready for a sweeping slash.

An instant before Cardona reached him, Sebastián leaped to the left and swung in an arc. As quickly, Cardona leaned away from the blade. Sebastian only cut his opponent's sword belt away along with dagger, and struck Cardona's thigh.

Twenty paces away, Cardona, his horse snorting, straddled the road. Sebastián saw him sheath his sword, rip apart hose on his leg, wrap and tie the cloth around the thigh and draw his weapon again—all within seconds. The man was adroit. Experience on the battlefield?

How can I reduce the advantage he has on horseback? Sword held to the side, Sebastián raised his left arm, touched his chest and swung the arm in a wide arc and nodded. Would Cardona accept his challenge to fight on foot?

Moments passed.

Cardona's laughter rumbled back to Sebastián.

Cardona dismounted. Loosening the cords, he threw away his cape, followed with his hat. He marched forward. At five paces, Cardona sprinted ahead, cutting circles and swirls in the air.

They met, grunting. Minutes rushed by and the two men fought without respite.

Sebastián tried every stroke, every move he knew, thrusted, parried, riposted, all to no avail. Dust raised by both men's footwork settled on their boots, their clothing, their faces.

Cardona blanketed by dust, looked like a *phantasma.*

Drenched in perspiration, Sebastián marveled at the other man's great skill. Not those of a common thief or murderer striking in the dead of night. But a man schooled in the mastery of swordplay techniques honed in the finest of fencing academies in Madrid. Despite Sebastián's strong defense, Cardona had opened a long, although shallow, cut on the shoulder, close to his neck. Blood trickled down his chest.

As though by mutual agreement, both men paused. They breathed heavily, each drawn breath hoarse. Beads of sweat dripped from the ends of Cardona's dusty beard and his mustache drooped, the waxed ends dribbling beeswax.

Cautious, Sebastián kept one foot to his right side and to the front to maintain his balance. He peered at the hatless Cardona. Veins of silver snaked back to the ends of long hair on his adversary's head.

"Whom…do I have…the honor of facing?" Cardona asked.

"Sebastián Alejandro…de Avíles. You abandoned Grimoldo. Why?"

"A pest. Begged to join me. Thought himself my equal. I could not do anything for him. Bled to death by false arrogance. I mourn him not. I am Cardona Arteaga de Rocha," he said with an exquisite flourish of sword.

Sebastián raised an eyebrow. "You are the son of the Count?" Sebastián recalled that at the Battle of Granada, the count, in front of his *tercio*— regiment, displayed exemplary bravery against the Moors and later decorated by the queen.

"Illegitimate. Despised by his shrewish wife and cowardly family. My only inheritance: fencing lessons that I embraced like a mistress and tutoring in Latin which I hated." Cardona circled. Sebastián followed, sword at the ready.

"You stare at my hair…" Cardona said, "wonder about my age. How old do I look?"

"You approach your late forties, early fifties."

"I am forty-one years of age. I have gambled until destitute, drank until senseless and fornicated with women until I howled like a wild animal. I regret nothing." Cardona laughed, his laughter the sound of gravel crushing under a boot. He sprinted forward toward Sebastián in an *Over* and *Under* maneuver.

Sebastián leaped beyond reach, stretched his left foot behind himself until the sole left the ground, bent his right knee forward and lunged straight ahead.

A hand span of steel entered Cardona's chest.

He heard the sharp intake of his opponent's breath as the sunburned face turned pale.

Red flooded Cardona's blouse and he collapsed by a mound of dirt in the road. One gloved hand staunching the blood, he raised the other hand and beckoned for Sebastián to step closer.

Wary, Sebastián approached from behind, in case Cardona attacked with a hidden dagger. When none appeared, he circled and stood in front of his opponent.

A wan smile crossed Cardona's face. "I am…tired of the life I lead…Age gallops closer to me. I have ruined…many. I am led to believe…" he rasped, "…you were…a former officer…in the queen's army…as was I. But I have fallen far from…grace. *Sic transit gloria.* I will die here. I do not wish to be ignorant of my death. I wish…to die like an officer…in the field. You know what to do."

"I will comply. I swear it," Sebastián said. During the Moorish wars, a mortally wounded Spanish officer on the battlefield expected a fellow officer to administer *misericordia*—mercifulness—a swift, merciful death to prevent capture and torture by the Moors.

"Thank you," Cardona said, tilting his head forward.

Placing his sword down, Sebastián drew his dagger, held Cardona's neck and drove the slim blade between nape and spine.

Cardona shuddered and slumped forward.

Sebastián removed the dagger, picked up his sword, stood and saluted the former officer of the queen and his adversary. How many times had he performed the ritual of *misericordia* on the battlefield? Too many. Far too many. He sighed with fatigue.

What a waste of life for this man, the best swordsman I have ever fought.

Exhausted by the encounter with Cardona, Sebastián, in fits and starts, dragged the leaden body under the shade of a tree. Folding his adversary's hands over the still chest, he debated whether or not to leave Cardona's weapons on the body as the dead swordsman and former officer of the queen deserved.

But thieves lurked on the roads. He would leave Cardona's body where it lay. The group of pilgrims would be along, offer prayers and burial, two forms of penitence for the forgiveness of sins, real or perceived, or declared as such by the Inquisition, penitent steps towards easier access to Heaven.

A few minutes later, after bandaging his neck wound with a handkerchief, Sebastián collected his foraging horse and mule and picked up his fallen cap.

Dusting himself off with his cap, he loosened the horse's cinch strap.

Removing his cloak, he wrapped both of Cardona's weapons inside and slipped the cloth under the strap, then retightened. With a loud, tired grunt, he mounted and continued his trip to Lisbon, peering ahead between the horse's ears toward a vague but hopeful unknown.

EIGHT

The port of Lisbon hummed with activity.

A week had passed since Sebastián left Estremadura. Now he sought out the port master to inquire the whereabouts of Vasco da Gama. The letter Sebastián's father had written sat inside a pocket of his new doublet—the one with sleeve shaved off by Cardona useless and left behind at the inn—the gift of fine material welcomed by the owner's wife.

As he rode down the cobblestone streets, the tangy lick of the sea touched his lips, the smell of brine filling his nostrils on this warm July day.

Ribs and keels of new caravels stood out like bleached carcasses of whales while shipwrights measured out fresh beams to fatten the ships' sides. Hammers and saws added to the din of hawkers selling their wares of corks along with coopers working on casks slated to hold wine or water aboard ships. Countless sailors sat untwisting old rope, the final fibers slated for caulking on ships. Behind canvas-covered stalls, chandlers poured melted wax into molds for candles.

"Where can I find the port master?" Sebastián asked a sailor.

The man pointed to an aged, weather beaten building a few paces away.

"Thank you."

Sebastián dismounted, tied horse and mule to a wooden stanchion and walked inside.

The room smelled of candle wax and age-old mustiness. Flyspecked, dirty windows permitted vagrant light to enter. Charts and books filled tables and desks. A crippled astrolabe sat in a corner.

"Commander da Gama…" Sebastián asked the port master, "…where may I find him?"

"Two hundred paces to your left when you step outside. The ship is the *São Gabriel.*"

Sebastián tipped his forage cap, left, remounted and moved on.

He rode past a tavern with flaking blue paint and wooden sign reading: The Happy Sailor. Painted in bold colors of green and white, the wood depicted a sailor entangled in the arms and tail of a siren. In front, harlots swung their hips saucily, winked at Sebastián.

One of them, buxom and with wild tangled hair swished her way to him, reached up and stroked his thigh, smiled through wine-stained teeth. Another of the group ran to head off his horse, stretched out her arms to block the mare's passage.

"Off to sea, handsome gentleman?" the buxom woman said. "I can make your last hours ashore ones you will never forget."

Other harlots moved forward as though to surround him. *Choose your words carefully, Sebastián.* He had witnessed harlots, who, after being rebuffed, heaped curses and flung horse droppings at those who refused their services. Should he refuse or try for gallantry?

He glanced at the smiling harlot stroking his thigh. "I am in great haste to take ship."

Her smile vanished, replaced by suspicion in her eyes. "What ship? And who commands her?" she demanded, one hand leaning on generous hips.

"The *São Gabriel* under Commander Vasco da Gama. Remove your hand."

At mention of the name, the harlot stroking his thigh removed her hand— reluctantly. Both woman nodded, stepped away and quickly ran to accost another horseman.

Sebastián heaved a sigh of relief. Da Gama came from a well-known naval family. He also knew the severity of da Gama's anger at anyone presenting hindrance or delay to King Manuel's plans for expansion of empire. But what if Sebastián did not know the ship's name? Would he now be splattered with horse shit? Present himself in such manner to a superior officer? Unthinkable.

Urging his horse forward, he scanned the area before he dismounted.

Reins in hand, he led horse and mule, wove around nets, stacks of coiled rope to where several ships rode at anchor, peering at the carved names on the bows. About one hundred paces later he stopped. In front of him bobbed a caravel. Foot high letters near the bow read: *São Gabriel.*

"With your permission, sir. Commander da Gama, where may I find him?" he asked a man shouting orders to seamen loading provisions of salted beef and other foodstuffs over the gangplank and onto the ship.

"What is your business with him?"

"That concerns only—"

"Who is that you are speaking with, Solis?" a voice boomed from the ship's deck.

"I do not know, sir," Solis said.

Sebastián strained his eyes, unable to recognize the face behind the thick black beard. He had not seen da Gama in over three years.

"Commander da Gama?"

"Yes."

"I am Sebastián Alejandro de Avíles, at your service." He swept off his cap and bowed from the waist.

Da Gama waved a hand. "Come aboard. Return to your duties, Solis."

"Aye, sir."

Tying horse and mule to a post, Sebastián strode up the gangplank.

Sebastián saluted, then shook hands with the commander.

"Welcome aboard, Captain. You look fit. How was your trip to Lisbon?"

"Hot and dusty, sir," Sebastián said. When on duty, da Gama dispensed with long discussions or explanations. The incident with Grimoldo and Cardona would remain unspoken.

Sebastián reached into a pocket, fished out an envelope. "Sir, I have a letter from my father explaining…"

Da Gama took the letter and shoved it into his pocket. "I will read the contents later. I wrote to your father a few months ago asking him to allow you to serve with me. Are you here to accompany me on this voyage?"

"Yes, sir."

"That is all that matters. I assume that is your personal property on the mule?"

"Yes, sir. After I remove my property, I will sell horse and mule."

"Solis will take care of that."

"With your permission, sir," Sebastián said. "There is also a cloak under the stirrup wrapped around two weapons—"

"I will remind Solis. Now, I will have a sailor show you where you can store your belongings. Let me return to welcoming the rest of my crew." Da Gama placed both hands on the railing and peered over the side.

Curious, Sebastián paused and followed suit.

Dockside, a warder busied himself removing the shackles from several convicts. As Sebastián watched, the disheveled, filthy men, all of them barefoot, stumbled up the gangplank.

When news of mounting deaths of sailors at sea on long voyages—from disease, sinking of leaky ships, rotting food and stagnant water—particularly after discovery of the New World, crews grew scarce. Courts resorted to offering three choices to prisoners: live in pestilential dungeons and walk ankle-deep in stews of urine and excrement with rats as company for years, suffer agony and a shorter life on a galley, or serve on ships slated for long ocean voyages and have sentences commuted. Soon, decks filled with crewmen again.

Once on board, seamen pushed the convicts toward mooring lines while orders rang out:

"Raise sail!"

On July 8, 1497, with sails raised, Vasco da Gama and his fleet of four ships set out for Africa and India as Sebastián watched the port of Lisbon slide by, recalling the unnerving sight of convicts herded aboard. He gazed at the cloudless blue sky. It had drizzled the day Lupiana stabbed him.

Because of Lupiana, will I be one of those wretches someday?

NINE

Almost two years had passed, yet the shrillness of Lupiana's voice and stridency of her words that long ago day in the orange orchard still rang in his ears as Sebastián stood before Vasco da Gama on board the *São Gabriel*.

"You showed exemplary bravery in my difficulties with the sultanates, led my men well," da Gama was saying. "And you are a member of a family that has served Spain in all her wars."

Then a rare look of puzzlement crossed da Gama's craggy face. "Why are you so rebellious against the authority of the Crown and certain dictates of the Church—such as the selling of indulgences for the forgiveness of sins? There are times you seem to me to bear anger at the world." Shaking his head, he sat back in his chair and stroked his thick, black beard.

Sebastián looked into da Gama's eyes. "Not the world, sir, just the incompetent nobles and others who are made officers not through merit but by wealth and position. Also, the greedy government buffoons and those who preach that men can erase their sins by purchasing indulgences. Then, the Inquisition—"

Da Gama sprang to his feet. "Silence!" The face that could wither common seamen or noble with a glance, moved closer to Sebastián. Da Gama spoke in guarded tones. "Your words border on treason and heresy. You force me to be most prudent in my speech. Who knows what ears listen? Whatever someone thinks about the Inquisition, indulgences or anything else he feels is wrong with the government or the Church, should keep a silent tongue. On the contrary, you have not done so." He waved a hand. "Enough of that." Da Gama sat back down and refilled both cups. He lifted his.

"You're the finest officer I've ever had." Sebastián's superior uttered the rare compliment over the rim of the goblet. "However, your vocal insolence to nobility, insubordination and disrespect to various clergy and rumors of unauthorized reading of the Bible, have come to the attention of the Church, in particular, the Grand Inquisitor, Friar Torquemada. Those accusations first and foremost." Da Gama paused, swallowed a long draught, then wiped his mouth with the back of his hand.

"If I take you with me back to Portugal, sooner or later I will have to turn you over to the Spanish authorities to avoid any political difficulties between Queen Isabel and my lord king. If the queen doesn't have you garroted forthwith, you will eventually end up in the hands of the Church. Which, incidentally, has performed the Bell, Book and Candle rites against you as a catholic."

"I beg your indulgence, sir." Sebastián shook his head. "I…have forgotten the details." Too many battles, hardship aboard the ship, had dulled, slowed his thinking.

Da Gama nodded. "The bell will be silenced, that is, the church bell, the book, meaning the Bible will be closed and altar candles extinguished—all denied to you. Excommunication."

Sebastián shifted his feet. Any thought of return to Spain now drowned before his eyes.

"And most probably…" da Gama continued, "…it means the rack and auto da fé—denouncement in public and burning at the stake as a heretic. Last, I do not know the details of your affair with Doña Lupiana and the eventual killing of her husband by your hand, and I do not wish to know. Suffice it to say that before we left Portugal word reached me the widowed señora had placed a handsome reward on your head—your person alive, preferably." An unsmiling Da Gama paused to clear his throat and went on.

"Apparently your treatment and leaving Doña Lupiana so unceremoniously—according to her—hurt her Spanish pride to quite a venomous extent. In view of that, I do not doubt there will be a hundred scoundrels anxious to collect that reward."

Raising his goblet, da Gama drained the contents. Sweeping a finger across his temple, he flicked the perspiration away with a sharp snap of the wrist.

Sebastián picked up his cup. "With your permission?"

"Granted."

Sebastián drew a long swallow of the warm wine. If he drank enough, drunkenness would dull his senses, blur thoughts about his sins—at least for the moment. That nightmare of a vainglorious woman. Even after many months out at sea, he could feel her fingers of hate and talons of treachery reach out to claw at him.

He forced back the knob of anger rising in his throat.

Da Gama took a deep breath, exhaled slowly and wet his lips.

Sebastián braced himself.

"I have decided to place you ashore," da Gama said. "You are aware of our desperate conditions, so I can only provide a pauper's amount of provisions—three smoked fish, a pouch of raisins, a few sea biscuits and some salted beef. All of your clothing, personal weapons plus whatever powder and shot I can spare is being placed in the shore boat as we speak."

Worry lines around da Gama's mouth deepened. "I have one fervent hope. That is, with the help of our Lord Jesus Christ, of course, and your extraordinary abilities, you will prevail over forest and foe. If not, Spain and Portugal, both in dire need of good, experienced officers, will suffer a great loss."

Sebastián felt the blood drain from his face. His thoughts raced to the past and then to the future. Would there be a future for him? The sentence da Gama just imposed was part of an unwritten, unofficial policy of Spain and Portugal along with official authority granted by the Treaty of Tordesillas in 1494, sanctioning both countries to expand their influence and empires.

To further those aims of empire, fleets of ships and armed men penetrated into newly discovered areas of the New World, Africa, India and beyond to open trading outposts, establish colonies or seize control by force of arms— on occasion, European women, wives or lovers of officers, boarded the leaky ships. When the ships departed, dozens of condemned men were also left on shore—a permanent exile.

Sebastián slumped. But his sentence terrified in its ocean of difference from colonists. All of the other accused men had other condemned men as company and left in villages, or near trading posts established by the Crown— whether Spanish or Portuguese.

He, on the other hand, would be totally alone on the western coast of Africa, more than fifty leagues from the nearest Portuguese settlement. Fifty leagues through dense forests filled with bloodthirsty hordes of heathens, ferocious animals and a land ridden with a host of unnamed exotic diseases. His certain death—would it be swift or slow and painful to the end? He brushed the disturbing thoughts away. God our Lord controlled his fate.

Da Gama rose with seeming deliberate slowness to his feet, the inner turmoil etched deeper furrows on his face. Coming to the front of the desk, he extended his hand. Sebastián grasped it in a warm handshake and wan smile, hoping his commander would not notice the tremor in his hand.

"Sebastián," da Gama said, his voice strained.

"Sir!" Sebastián snapped to attention, taken aback by the unexpected familiarity. Da Gama had called him by his Christian name. Since the start of the voyage Sebastián had always been addressed by "de Avíles," or "Captain." Close familiarity of this kind was reserved strictly for close relatives and intimate friends of long standing. This extraordinary gesture of warmth increased Sebastián's misery.

"I am of the opinion…" da Gama said, "…that when I deliver the report on my voyage to India, His Majesty, will desire to open more trading ports along East Africa, India and the land known as Cipango where those of the warrior class carry two swords. Trading rights accomplished, I hope, by peaceful means, if not, by fire and sword. But I digress. Let us continue. If it is the will of God, I will again pass by this bay in two years." A flicker of a smile crossed the weathered face. "At that time, I expect to have you pay your respects to me on board my ship." Da Gama stepped back behind his desk.

"Before we leave, I wish to present the goblet you used moments ago as a parting gift. It has been in my family for many generations." Da Gama slipped the vessel into a cloth bag, drew the strings tight and placed the bag in Sebastián's hands.

Sebastián choked out a, "Thank you, sir." He looped the bag over his dagger.

Bolstered by da Gama's gift of an heirloom and expressions of absolute confidence in his subordinate's ability to survive the extreme conditions of his sentence, Sebastián pushed his shoulders back, spirits lifted. But deep inside, he struggled to muster as much confidence.

"May the blessings of Almighty God and His son, our Lord Jesus Christ be with you Sebastián," da Gama intoned. "The sentence will now be announced to the ship's captain and crew."

Da Gama pushed a worn, black cap on his head, and, as Sebastián held the door open, stepped onto the sun-filled deck.

He and da Gama squinted as they emerged from the miasmic gloom of the small ship's cabin into bright West African sunlight.

On deck, Sebastián straightened and swallowed a deep breath, the open air a delicious respite from the smothering closeness of da Gama's quarters. An escape also, he thought, from the damp smell of rotting wood and the putrid stench of bilge water.

Chin lifted to savor a fragrant breeze of jasmine sweeping across the deck. Sebastián closed his eyes for a moment. The breeze a good omen? *Pray God, yes.* He sighed, watched the plumes on his helmet spring to life as though awakened from sleep and flutter in the wind. Adjusting the helmet, he buckled the faceplates.

"Captain Alvera," da Gama said to the ship's chief officer, "assemble on deck those crew members still able to walk."

"Yes, sir." The officer saluted and barked the orders.

Crewmen too sick to move from their resting places on deck, offered vacant stares. Remnants of the crew, a third of the original that sailed from Portugal, sallow-faced and gaunt, shuffled themselves into a ragtag line. Two of the men—one of them the friendly and helpful Canarian named Felipe Sidonia, who had escaped slavery by first joining Columbus, then signing on with Vasco da Gama, and whose life Sebastián had saved during a battle— offered Sebastián encouraging smiles. Others looked over his head or sneered.

Sebastián acknowledged with a nod to those offering encouragement. The others, he wondered, could they be aware of the handsome reward offered by Lupiana and now watched their share of the prize slip out of their grasp? He shrugged.

His gaze shifted and caught the eyes of Friar Justin. A scowl burned on the cadaverous face of the Church's representative. Sebastián smiled enigmatically. The angriness on the churchman's face dug deeper, and the friar tightened his rope girdle. Well, those glares of hate would end today.

From the beginning of the disastrous voyage, the friar had spread layers of bitterness onto Sebastián. Sundays, he refused service of mass and the Eucharist to Sebastián. The ecclesiastic always bent on a constant quest for an excuse to complain and subvert Sebastián's standing with da Gama. Unable to stare down his sworn enemy, the friar crossed himself, raised his chin and turned his head away.

Expressionless, Sebastián remained at attention.

A pace in front of him, Da Gama fished a rolled parchment from a pocket and handed the document to the ship's captain. "Read it."

The grizzled sailor unrolled the vellum, held it out in both hands and in a loud, gruff voice, read the contents to the ship's company.

"By the grace of Almighty God and His Catholic Majesty, King Manuel I of Portugal, Captain Sebastián Alejandro de Avíles, will be put ashore. There he will propagate the faith of our Lord Jesus Christ amongst the heathen peoples and work for the glory of Portugal and its empire. By order of His Majesty's navigator, Vasco da Gama, this Fifteenth day of June, in the year of our Beloved Lord Jesus Christ, Fourteen-Hundred and Ninety-Nine."

The ship's captain rolled up the parchment and handed the document to da Gama, who stuffed it back into his pocket.

From the corner of his eye, Sebastián caught the shaking of the tonsured head and the look of intense disapproval on Friar Justin's face. The friar's sunken eyes burned like hot coals.

Sebastián recalled the contents of a conversation overheard by the Canarian, Felipe Sidonia between the friar and da Gama two nights before. The next day, Felipe revealed the words exchanged.

"I wish to know what sentence you have determined upon for Captain de Avíles, that heretic and murderer of a courtier of the queen," the monk asked.

"With all due respect to your ecclesiastical office…" da Gama growled. "…I am the commander of these ships. I will decide what type of punishment, who is to be punished, where it is meted out, and when it is to be pronounced."

"Mother Church will demand auto da fé and—"

"Captain de Avíles has not been tried for those alleged crimes, brought about by hearsay and the twisted passion of an evil woman. His Majesty, the King of Portugal, whose subjects you and I are, has given me—"

"Then how about hanging the heretic—"

"Sir! Never interrupt me again. This meeting is over. Goodnight."

The friar stormed out.

At this instant on deck, the monk tapped first one then the other sandaled foot, his long, bony toes caked with dirt. In his Pronouncement of Sentence, da Gama, had failed to mention the mortal sins of his condemned officer, the scandalous affair with a married woman, the killing of a loyal subject of the devout Queen Isabel. The supposed blasphemous utterances against the granting of indulgences for forgiveness of sins by Mother Church, plus the rumors about the forbidden reading of the Bible by a layperson.

All these heretical omissions, Sebastián vouched, the bilious cleric would report in a letter to the Holy See in Rome.

Sebastián clicked his heels together, saluted da Gama, pivoted, saluted the ship's captain and crew, then threw a brief nod to the twisted, angry features of the friar. The church's representative, as Sebastián had forethought, denied final benediction to Captain De Avíles. The monk's worn leather sandals slapped on the wooden deck and he padded closer to Sebastián.

"Captain," Friar Justin said, *"Quia in inferno nulla est redemptio."*

His features expressionless, Sebastián answered, "If I am in hell and will not be redeemed, it is God's judgment and *bene quidem*, it is fine with me. Which means, Friar, if I am in hell we shall meet again."

The sallow face of Friar Justin scowled and he made the sign of the cross.

Steps brisk and filled with confidence, Sebastián crossed the two paces to the rail, climbed down the steps built into the side of the ship and stepped into the waiting shore boat.

He worked his way to the stern, adjusted his helmet, and sat motionless, gaze fixed straight ahead to a shore filled with the unknown.

The sailors pushed away from the ship with their oars and rowed for shore.

Above, fingers of clouds painted themselves across a blue palette of sky while a phalanx of gulls flew silently overhead as each oar dipped with a soft swish in the crystal-clear water.

Without a wave or backward glance to the *São Gabriel*—his home for two years, Sebastián glanced toward the shore—the beach seemingly rushing forward to meet the boat. He swung his gaze to the sandy bottom.

Think of something else, Sebastián or you will go mad this instant. An almost forgotten image of Christopher Columbus imposed itself on his mind.

Was this the scene that greeted Columbus?

Sebastián recalled the time when, at the age of sixteen, while visiting the Spanish Court with his father; he met the Discoverer of the New World and taken an instant dislike to Columbus.

Not only the Genoan grasping, overbearing and seeking that Spanish nobility be conferred upon him, but news surfaced that the Discoverer had abandoned his common law wife, Beatriz Enriquez and their son, Fernando, in Córdoba, because of his wife's lowly status: a commoner.

Sebastián swept the memory aside. A life in Spain had ended for him and a new life waited. Life. Was the word ill chosen? Would his struggle with death be long and tortured, or swift?

TEN

With a scuff, the boat's gunwales slid onto the white sand. The rowers shipped oars and two of the sailors crawled over the sides and dragged the boat to firmer ground on the beach.

Sebastián adjusted his helmet, stepped across the seats and hopped over the bow. He strode forward and a few paces later fell to his knees and crossed himself.

"I thank you, Almighty Father, for granting me another day of life. May I be worthy of Your mercy." His words drifted and died away in the silence of the brooding forest in front. He stood, and brushing sand away from his pantaloons, reined in any thoughts about his future and glanced at his stores.

All of his packets of meager provisions and personal belongings lay haphazardly on the beach—thrown there by the seamen. Sebastián held his silence. Why reprove them? Especially after so hazardous a voyage to all concerned. These men and he would never see each other again—the finality firm in his mind, so what did it matter?

Reproval would only add bitter aggravation to his heavy heart and clouded mind.

Felipe, the Canarian, assigned as one of the rowers on the shore boat, barefoot, his canvas pantaloons dirty and ragged, pointed to a tree. "Captain, earlier this morning, we were ordered by our commander, Vasco da Gama to carve an 'X' on that trunk. Two hundred paces east of the mark you will find a stream of fresh water."

Sebastián nodded a tired thank you.

Felipe extended his hand. "I thank you again for saving my life. *Vaya con Dios, Capitan.*"

"Gracias, Felipe," Sebastián grasped the hand in a firm almost desperate handshake—it might be the last on this earth. He would sorely miss the old sailor who had regaled Sebastián and other crewmen with outlandish tales, especially one about a fabulous and wealthy city somewhere in Northern Africa whose women possessed dazzling beauty.

The other seamen offered careless salutes, turned the shore boat around, pushed its bottom seaward until it floated in deeper water and rowed back to the ship.

For a brief moment, Sebastián turned to his right and gazed at the dark jungle and its violent green depths. But crushing anxiousness forced his shoulders into a slouch and he returned his gaze back to the flagship. The creak of tired wood and straining rope carried across the bay as the *São Gabriel*, its sails unfurled, raised anchor and eased its bulk out between the bluffs overlooking the turquoise bay and joined the *Berrio*.

From the wrack of seaweed thrown up on shore by the tides, he watched the two caravels slowly disappear into the horizon in a quivering image of clouds and sea.

When outlines of the ships dissolved, Sebastián's body sank onto the sand—the sudden full realization of his severe punishment had struck like the blow of hammer. All civilization denied him, comforts of home and family vanished, perhaps forever. The sudden silence stunned, overwhelmed. Internal desolation struck at him.

"I will not accept defeat," he said, rousing himself from the emptiness surrounding him. A hollow, nervous laugh erupted from his throat. "Well, at least I will not have to share dark, cramped quarters, eat bread with weevils, endure the smell of death. Or sleeping on deck with the cries of dying men ringing in my ears and killing rats lest they chew my leg off!"

He scratched at the full, black beard on his face—the thick growth detested by Sebastián. Scarce fresh water on board forced sailors to dip and fill buckets from the ocean, then using the contents for washing—use of scarce drinking water from casks on board for shaving brought flogging.

Sailors used seawater and its salt dried on the skin. Intense itching followed. Lice swarmed. To rid himself of the vermin, he had slashed at the facial hair with his dagger—only rain would allow his shaving soap to lather.

His clumsy efforts rewarded Sebastián with numerous cuts, attracted more parasites. Soon after, he abandoned the effort of shaving.

On board the ship, men picked lice from their clothing and bodies, and for amusement, watched for the flash when they threw the vermin into a dish of burning tallow.

Sebastián erased any further unpleasant thoughts. "Thank you, Vasco da Gama for your thoughtfulness about the stream of fresh water. Perhaps now I will not die of thirst and also grasp the opportunity to shave the beard and its unwelcome visitors."

He sat down on one of the packets and removed the dispatch case slung over his shoulder. From inside the case he fished out two small paintings wrapped in oilcloth; portraits he had made of his parents several months before he fled Spain. Heat, humidity and the salt air had ravaged the canvas. His parent's features were blurred and faded, almost unrecognizable, the cloth fragile to the touch. A lump formed in his throat.

"No matter what fate awaits me, it will not compare with the pain and dishonor I have caused my family. May God our Lord protect them."

Despair and solitude, foes more formidable than the sea and the disease-ridden *São Gabriel,* tugged at him as he studied the paintings—he had been away from his family for two years. Would he ever see his family or Castile again? Head bowed, he carefully wrapped the paintings back in their threadbare cloth and strode to a packet crudely marked in tar: "*ARMAS.*"

Untying the ropes, he slid the paintings inside and extracted a brace of espingardas—matchlock pistols—primed and loaded each with powder and shot. He tucked one in his waistband, secreted the other into his dispatch case. They would be close at hand and ready to fire against…savages? Wild beasts?

Fully armed, hand cupped over his eyes, Sebastián scanned to his right then his left—both sides of the beach were clear of man or beast. His strides slow and short, he crossed to one end of the tree line, then reversed course. Other than the footprints of the sailors and himself in the immediate area, no signs of human activity marred the pristine white sand.

From deep in the forest, a sullen gust of heat struck while relentless sun scorched the air; his blouse and jerkin quickly soaked anew with sweat. Plodding on, a dozen steps later he paused for breath.

How times had changed for him. Once, agile of mind, high in spirit, and fleet of foot, his feet now plowed through the sand, his mind flagged, his spirit fallen. Would he recoup those losses? Only the heavens knew. No more exploration for the present, he decided and slogged back to his stores.

"What time might it be?"

A quick glance to the sky revealed a sun past the midpoint. Around two or three o'clock, he guessed and he felt hungrier than usual. One of the bundles held his food—parting gifts from da Gama. Atop the food lay an oilskin. Sebastián opened the worn, yellowed package. Inside the protective sheet was a crude map of the bay and the surrounding area. An unexpected surprise from da Gama.

"Thank you for your thoughtfulness, sir." Now at least, Sebastián had some idea about the lay of the land.

He unbuckled his cheek plates, removed his plumed helmet and wiped the circlet of sweat on his brow with a sleeve of his blouse—the former white cloth now aged gray from sweat and grime. He slid the leather straps open and, with a heavy sigh of relief, slid off his chest armor.

Plucking a dried mackerel the length of his forearm from one of the packets and a bottle of wine—this would be his only meal for the day. He sat down to eat under the generous shade of a leafy palm. He took a bite, each chew long and slow. If game were unavailable within the next three or four days, his meals might be roots and berries.

Suddenly Sebastián slapped his forehead with an open hand.

"How could I have forgotten?"

Tomorrow was the anniversary of his birth, the Nineteenth of November, Fourteen- Hundred and Seventy-Four. He chewed the last morsel, drank half a bottle of wine—small swallows at a time before he tore open a small bundle. From its depths he extracted a dog-eared journal, a quill and a small ceramic pot of ink—its cork blackened by use. He paused to debate whether to use this source of paper, irreplaceable under his present conditions. But why be frugal when he might be dead on the morrow?

He dated the top of the blank, yellowed page and paused again. In the veil of still air, quill in hand he marveled at the silence, no boisterous sea, no howling wind. Touching pen to paper, he wrote, the scratching louder than the gentle lapping of the mild surf. Endless weeks of a precarious life amidst creak of timbers, the batter of the waves against the sides of the ship, the slaps of sails, the whip of ropes, and the cries of men in the throes of death, this eerie quiet sent a shiver down his spine.

He shrugged off the shiver like an outer garment that does not have to be worn until the next storm and glanced at the horizon. A vast sea of undulating emptiness lay in front of him, a forest of uncertainty to his rear. Shaking his head, he dipped quill in ink, gave life to the mute and blind pages.

"Tomorrow, I Sebastián Alejandro de Avíles, enter the twenty-fifth

year of my life. I have survived battles with Muslims and a terrible sea voyage filled with hunger, death and disease. It is only by the grace of God our Lord that I have lived until today. But, I have offended God, angered the Queen, displeased the Church and disgraced my family.

"As punishment for my sins, I have been abandoned in a strange and savage land to fend for myself. My only companions are this magnificent bay, the jungle with its mysterious darkness, unknown dangers, and a desert of solitude that more often than not is a bitter enemy. How strange! I've heard some say they ache for the glories of solitude yet they are unwilling to forego the trappings of the civilized world for a goodly amount of time. How many would forsake hearth and home to trade places with me on this stretch of sand? At this time, I speak only to the silence."

He laughed, his laughter strained. He wrote on.

"I know not if I will die on the morrow or live to welcome another sunset. Will I die at the hands of heathens, torn apart by the jaws of a wild beast or go mad and die by own hand? I ask God for a mercifully swift, if not honorable, death. I do not fear death, but I fear thoughts of it. My days are filled with anger and my nights are restless. Friar Justin said I was possessed by devils that could only be exorcised by fire. I did not pay him any heed then, nor will I do so now. At the break of day, I will begin my travel in search of my destiny. First and foremost, I must think of survival. If I am not successful and meet my end, this will be my last entry. I commend my spirit to God our Lord. I go now to prepare for the night. May our Lord Jesus Christ watch over my mother, Caterina and my father, Francisco de Avíles, a most noble knight of Estremadura, Spain."

Sprinkling grains of sand on the pages to dry the ink, he slammed the journal shut. The clap startled a flock of seagulls poking in the nearby sand—they lifted off in a flurry of feathers and caws as they scattered in flight over the sun-infused bay. He heard their long cries until the birds narrowed into specks on the horizon.

Sebastián felt a small smile curve his mouth, envious of their unrestricted freedom. He stood, drew his sword, rested a knuckle on his hip and raised the weapon over his head.

"I, Captain Sebastián Alejandro de Avíles of Castile, claim this beach and secluded bay for…" He paused. "That does not make any sense. I am the only one here! Claim the stretch of beach for Spain?" No. Portugal had already laid claim to this territory. "Myself? Ludicrous," he cried out, his voice lost in the vast emptiness.

He sheathed the weapon and stared out to the empty bay. Talking to oneself, might that be the first sign of madness? Growls of hunger cut off the thought. He dismissed them by impatient hand gestures.

Concentrate on a plan of action—for two purposes, to keep his mind from dwelling on his desperate situation; the second, to restore confidence in himself and offer a sense of accomplishment.

Brushing sand from the chest armor with a scrap of his ruff, he stored his best cuirass away in a packet and withdrew another cuirass from the same bundle. Unlike his best, this one's surface was dull and would not attract an enemy's attention by flashing its brilliance in sunlight.

From the same packet he fished out a visored forage cap and a pair of Moorish boots. He would leave the helmet off. Cumbersome, in hot weather the helmet, in spite of a soft cotton lining, caused his head to drown in heavy perspiration and constant usage caused hair to fall out around the rim of the wearer like a reverse monk's tonsure.

His second breastplate, leather straps frayed and darkened by heavy use, bore marks of spear and sword thrusts. Grooves from glancing points of arrows shot at him by Moors in Spain beribboned the metal.

Later, other Muslims in port cities off the coasts of Africa had added to the scars of battle on the armor. A deep indentation pointed to where a hackbut ball had struck. The shot dented the breastplate and almost ended his life. Sebastián had thanked and taken his father's advice to use armor of proof— steel tempered to a high strength to ward off arrows and lead balls shot from hackbuts.

He yanked off his military top boots, gazed at the far different Moorish boots and turned pensive. The exquisite footwear was found in the captured supply carts of a defeated Muslim force after a bloody battle outside the Moorish stronghold of Granada, Spain. Sebastián still marveled at their unique construction—comfortable for walk or march, shed water and pointed toes for extraction from mud—possibly, he imagined, made for a Muslim prince.

"Excellent," Sebastián said in admiration of the cobbler. He slid on the boots, stood, slipped the old cuirass over his head and buckled the leather straps. Forage cap placed at a rakish angle, he tucked both primed pistols into his waistband and marched inland with a confident stride.

One hundred yards into his walk, a tall tree with a wide girth and thick arms drew his attention. "Ah! Exactly what I need."

He retraced his steps to the beach, carefully examined the forest growth along the way—any familiar, edible vegetation would be a welcome relief. None appeared. Fresh vegetables the seamen had gathered must be farther inland.

Among the supplies, lay several coils of rope generously provided by da Gama. Sebastián pushed the packets into a straight line on the beach and lashed one to the other.

When finished, he tied the front end of rope around his waist. Then, like a plow horse, he dragged and pulled his caravan of supplies to the tree's trunk.

Slanted rays of sunlight speared across the tops of the forest when Sebastián finally accommodated all of his supplies in the crooks of the upper branches.

Several breaths of fresh air later, he attached his hammock—introduced into Europe by Columbus—the bed of knotted rope invented by Taino Indians and called *hamaca* in the New World, quickly copied in Europe and used on ships. He climbed down and circled the trunk, smiled with satisfaction.

"Unless prying eyes look straight up, nothing can be seen of my weapons or supplies," he whispered to himself. He lifted a *pellejo de vino*—a kidney-shaped goat skin filled with Madeira wine, tilted his head back and squeezed a stream of the warm liquid into his parched throat until only drops remained. When the bag empty, he tucked it into his belt. For his march into the interior, the wineskin would hold fresh water.

Sebastián completed another full circle of the tree and stroked his beard. His home on branches was a far better defensive position than sleeping on the ground. Of course, if attacked, he had no place to retreat. Death would quickly follow.

"Sebastián, the less apprehensive about death, the better," he sighed and trudged back to where he had landed.

From his place of concealment behind shrubbery, Sebastián scanned both ends of the beach again for any activity, an ingrained military response of caution born from the endless harrowing campaigns against the fearless Moors.

Unsheathing his sword, he disrobed completely, rested the weapon over his shoulder and waded into the bay until wavelets lapped at his waist. The warm seawater enveloped him like a welcome bath—a rarity for Europeans, including the aristocracy and royalty.

One hand cupped over his eyes for shade, his gaze raked the horizon.

"When surrounded by the unknown," his father always said, "cautiousness rules over foolhardiness."

The horizon was empty.

Sebastián quickly dipped his body down several times to the pommel of the naked blade. Layers of encrusted dirt and sweat from the long voyage peeled away as he vigorously swabbed himself down with his free hand.

"If I could only brush away my misfortunes as easily," he muttered to the retreating dirt. Many furious strokes later and satisfied his cleansing of body best under primitive circumstances, he shifted his attention to the bay's entrance.

Hulking bluffs on both sides rose twice the height of the tallest masts of caravels and lush vegetation smothered the crags. Both ran down to disappear into the bay's clear water.

The cliffs, wide enough at the water's edge to allow free passage of two ships side by side, narrowed at their pinnacles like two lovers reaching out to each other for a kiss. On one peak, silhouetted against the shafts of a late afternoon sun, he saw the silhouette of a *padrão*. Dragged uphill by seamen under orders from da Gama on his first trip to Western Africa, the stone pillar with a cross on top announced to all: this land is under Portuguese conquest.

"With a few men on each crest, an enemy force could be bottled up, or prevented from entering. Even vessels mounted with cannon may easily be held at bay."

He shrugged. "Of what consequence is that at this moment?"

Shaking his head, he waded back to the beach, wishing he could have taken a real swim and bath—with a special luxury reserved only for the wealthy—soap.

With another remnant of his old ruff—the clothing accessory yanked away from his neck by Sebastián once the ship left India—he wiped the excess water from his chest and arms. The pleasant warmth of remaining sunlight would dry the rest of his body. He dragged a stump of driftwood over and pressed the bleached trunk into service as a seat, the unsheathed sword resting on his naked thigh.

Eyes widened, he watched as the sun's rays reached out, turned the sky into a palette of red and orange streaks over blue. A moment before the sun lowered itself further into the horizon, its fiery ball arrowed shafts between the cliffs.

The bay ignited into a shimmering lake of liquid gold.

"Ah! If there were only someone I cared for deeply by my side to share this magnificent moment." He cringed at the weight of his utter isolation, rose abruptly, and with a cursory sweep of his hand, swept the unpleasantness away.

"Have clarity of thought, Sebastián. Nothing else. Yes, yes, on the morrow."

Then he would begin his search for a watering hole used by animals. Fresh meat topped his list of priorities. He would travel at a prudent pace, cover the most distance physically possible in one day.

But, should he head for the nearest Portuguese settlement located about fifty leagues away?

From 1497 on, Portugal had established several trading posts along the Western coast of Africa—Sebastián was present at the violent opening of two of them in 1498. They would provide a safe haven—for a short time.

Eventually, his arrest warrant and possibly news of the handsome reward offered by Lupiana for his head would catch the ears of many. The final outcome: his forced return to Spain in chains and eventual auto da fé.

Visions of his body tied to a stake, consumed by flames in the public square, forced a shudder. He erased any further thought of walking to a Portuguese settlement.

Should he head to a Muslim city? Absolute madness. Sultanates forbade entry to Christians. Any "crusader" as Muslims called all Christians, captured on the outskirts of towns governed by sultanates was beheaded on the spot without pity or remorse.

Sebastián decided to travel the next day at a measured stride, reward himself with time to regain his strength lost with the nightmarish rigors of the sea voyage. He would carry, in addition to a pistol, powder, shot, sword, dagger, flint, one dried, smoked fish, a sliver of salted beef, the raisins, a pouch of water and another of wine. The hammock would be left behind; its added weight over a long distance was prohibitive—sleeping on the ground a necessary risk.

He clapped his hands once. Decision made.

South. His first foray would be in that direction using the crude map provided by da Gama as a guide. He dressed quickly, and, walked backwards, erasing his footprints with a leafy broken branch.

Confidence renewed, he marched back to his lodging in the tree, each stride lively as the sun dipped to a narrow arc over the horizon.

Retrieving a rope he had previously hidden under a bush, he threw the line over the lowest branch and hoisted himself up, drew the rope after him and repeated the action to climb higher. At his chosen perch, he pulled a familiar and favorite covering for the night: his fustian cloak with its thick, twilled cotton cloth. The garment, one of two sewn over many months by Doña Avíles, one for his father, one for him, boasted an embroidered scalloped shell on the left side—the sign of St. James—for the saint's own family of fishermen and Jesus Christ as "fisher of men." The cloak had turned into a true friend and refuge on board the ship.

On many nights during the voyage, Sebastián deserted the rabbit's warren below and slept on deck with the crew, including convicts—their permanent sleeping quarters, exposed to wind, rain, cold, the faces cauterized by the sun.

When evenings turned pleasant, he discovered the wooden planks preferable to sleeping below deck with the nauseating stench of unwashed bodies, rotting clothing, decay and dampness. During stormy weather on the *São's Gabriel's* return voyage to Portugal, Sebastián had anchored himself to the mast and rolled his body into a ball under the cloak—its tightly woven threads impervious to water.

An occasional strong wave would crash against the ship, slam him against the mast and he'd burrow deeper, brace himself for the next surge of angry sea or whips of rain. The once elegant, ankle-length hooded garment now bore stains from its harsh life on cold muddy ground, black color faded to gray by vehement sun, edges gnawed by rats. While wrapped in its familiar folds like a cocoon, somehow his own problems and the outside world were held at arm's length by the cloth. So many nights, so many dreams, hopes...

Around him tropical night fell in stages. First the empty ocean, the bay, then the forest, like a falling theatre curtain.

An inconstant moon rose, sent jagged silvery beams and Sebastián prepared for sleep. He spread his cloak over the hammock and smoothed out the wrinkles with his hands. Before stretching out—one foot draped over the branch, the other on a limb a foot higher—he reached for a small potion bottle he previously hung within reach on an overhanging bough. The oil inside the bottle had been bartered for after long haggling with the merchant in exchange for beads on the island of Trapobane, perhaps eight leagues southeast of India. Pouring a few drops into his palm, he spread the contents over arms and face.

Fingers of the pungent fragrance touched his nostrils. Nostalgia swept over him. The orange-like odor always reminded him of the orange groves of Southern Spain, the harvests, the lumbering donkey carts overflowing with the sweet fruit.

Spain...that also meant Lupiana. He shuddered.

It took the length of an "Amen" to erase any thought of her. He placed his brace of loaded pistols to his left, naked blade on his right—each weapon within easy reach. Content with his preparations for defense, he closed his eyes and intoned a short prayer.

"Heavenly Father, I will abide by your mercy and forgiveness. May your bounty extend to my family. Amen."

Sleep eluded him, his body restless, fragments of dreams appeared, disappeared, formless shadows and nightmares hovered over him. The discordant sounds of clashing arms, the jingle of harness, cries of dying men, screams of wounded horses, all crossed the rutted landscape of his anxious mind.

He was seventeen-years-old again, on a bloody battlefield, fighting alongside his father, pushing the Moors to the sea, expelling them from Castile.

Then a yellow fog rolled through the bad dream, the falling bulk of the hidalgo, Don Rodrigo, mortally wounded, disbelief written in the nobleman's eyes, bested by Sebastián in swordplay.

The angry, twisted face of Lupiana quickly loomed on the scene along with an entourage of demons of unknown origin—spitting her curses at him.

Twice during the night he woke with a start, swiftly reached for pistol and sword. Then he realized the origin of wakefulness—a nightmare—wondered if he had cried out in his sleep—a cry of such nature alerting the enemy, fatal on the battlefield. More so now. He fell back into the hammock breathless, his heart pounding in his ears, his blouse drenched in sweat.

Slowly, the perfumed jungle in concert with medley of chirps, clicks and other sounds unfamiliar to him along with a gentle sea breeze wafting through the trees lulled him back into sleep in this foreign, beautiful and dangerous land.

A dark night for the soul.

ELEVEN

A s was his wont, Sebastián rose at break of day, armed himself with sword and pistols, searched the beach again for any activity, and worked his way to the stream of fresh water reported by the seamen. The directions proved accurate. At its edge, he washed his face in the cool water, drank his fill, filled two small goatskins and mentally reviewed his plans. A shave to scrape off the beard? No. Anxiousness to leave tugged at him, Sebastián resolute in his quest to find a fair-sized watering hole where herds of animals gathered to drink. Such a place would provide a continuous source of food. Possibly.

Then with food, water and shelter assured, his next decision? Time hung heavy, time, time enough to give deep thought to the matter.

First, I'll move South, march along the coast, the next day, inland and East and finally North.

At rest stops of his own choosing, he would break his fast, eat his single meal of the day—unless his meager provisions bolstered by game.

After eating, devote a few minutes to write in his journal, fashion drawings and maps of the surrounding area. Those areas he thought suitable for an ambush carefully marked by an arrow as a reminder to exercise caution on his return trip.

If, after a week, and a watering hole was still out of reach, he would begin his search anew, increasing the distance covered in each direction by one day.

Leagues covered each day depended on his physical well being. Laden with pistol, sword, dagger, and other supplies, how much distance could he cover? Unknown at this time and severely limited, in spite of his experience with hardship in the field.

Sebastián would supplement his lean rations of dried fish by edible fruits and vegetables whose description and use had been explained on board the *São Gabriel* by the Canarian, Felipe.

Food mattered most now. Glimpses of wild game crossed his mind. Rabbits? Pigs? Turkeys? Perhaps. The landscape and its animals were unfamiliar to him. Use his hackbut for hunting? He shook his head—the weapon much too cumbersome and heavy for a long march, and, unless the prey stood only a few yards away, highly inaccurate. A smile carved itself through the thicket of his black beard.

Amongst his small arsenal, rested another weapon, much more accurate and deadly—the English longbow. But he lacked sufficient skill and experience in its use. He hoped mastery would come. How long would that be? Ruefully, he erased the smile.

Returning to the beach and climbing the tree, he lowered his travel supplies, hid the extra clothing and weapons in the crooks of branches and, with the same rope descended to the ground.

He took one last look at his refuge, uncoiled the rope he used for climbing and hid it under a thick bush.

Supplies loaded, he drew a dagger from its sheath and cut a branch with wide leaves.

From the edge of the beach and walking backward, he methodically erased his footprints from the sand and around the tree, throwing the used branch aside several yards away. Surrounded by a dangerous environment, extreme caution was an absolute necessity.

Lifting the pistol from his waistband, he checked the weapon for dryness. Would the weapon's accuracy bring down small game?

He chased away hovering doubt and crossed himself. God our Lord would guide his path. His stride brisk, he stepped forward into the unknown.

This, his second day with an easterly direction planned, Sebastian had not sighted a human soul all morning, save for the prints of animals pressed into dusty paths near shrinking waterholes. Other than the slight rustling of leaves in a hummock of trees, the sounds he heard were his labored breaths, the crunch of pebbles under his boots and the wind sighing in his ears.

Each step as heavy as wading through a swamp and disheartened by his slow progress, mounting exhaustion shortened his expectations of finding a sizable watering hole where herds gathered. Despite protests from his mind, he slowed his pace and munched on a few of his raisins.

It is due to all I have to carry; chest armor, weapons, water, and all else. I should have given myself more time to rest.

He pondered whether to return to the beach, exchange the cuirass for his hackbut. This would advance his luck for wild game—the gun's range more than thirty yards farther than the pistol. Would the vast increase in weight of weapon outweigh the firepower? What choice did he have?

About to step forward, he froze, widened his eyes.

A small deer-like animal with spiraled horns grazed among shrubbery. The prey, upwind and unaware of Sebastián's presence, nibbled at the leaves.

Sebastián drew his espingarda, placed the heavy weapon over his forearm to steady the barrel, aimed for the neck and fired. Without a sound, the game crumpled to the ground.

Skinned within minutes, the carcass roasted over an open fire—the cooked meat a good respite from constant hunger. While he waited, he reloaded his espingarda, placing the weapon by his side. Soon, with an occasional crackle of dying embers, his game now a golden brown, and filling the air with its aroma, he sliced a portion off the shank.

Mouth open, ready to take his first bite, clumps of nearby waist high coarse grass parted. A pack of spotted hyenas materialized like ghosts and slunk in a circle to surround him. He stopped counting their number after five.

Their leader, its length from snout to tip of tail two yards long, slunk closer, a ravenous look in the eyes, teeth capable of crunching bone, massive jaws dripping spittle.

If Sebastián stood his ground, he could kill two at most, before the other hyenas ripped his throat. In an instant, he shoved his cooked slice of shank between his teeth, snatched his weapon and waited.

"Come closer," he whispered to the predator. When fired at close range, an espingarda's round carved a hole the size of an empty eye socket.

The beast edged a paw forward, crouched its backside, ready to spring.

Sebastián shot the animal in its hindquarters.

It yelped and fell, the body twitching.

At the sound of the shot, the pack scattered, but as quick, swirled around.

Tucking the empty espingarda into his waist, Sebastián drew sword and dagger and backed away. He bit down on the slice, spit the rest away and watched as the pack turned on their luckless fallen member and tore into its flesh. Soon, shreds of skin and bones littered the ground. The scavengers next turned their attention to Sebastián's game on the spit. One of their number leaped and snatched the carcass from above the dead embers. His meal vanished in seconds.

"My first taste of fresh meat in months, gone!" Sebastián swallowed the coil of rage in his throat, cursing under his breath. When he thought the distance between him and the predators sufficient, he sheathed sword and dagger, reloaded the pistol and plodded forward—with frequent looks over his shoulder. Cursing his ill luck, he walked on…and on.

Daylight languished. By late afternoon, hopes of finding a watering hole, or game dashed, he returned to his base. By retreating streaks of twilight, he ate one of the two remaining smoked fish and the last of the raisins.

The night passed in restless slumber.

TWELVE

A rrow shafts of a tropical leaden sun pierced the canopy of leaves sheltering Sebastián, stirred him awake. He sat up, massaged sore leg and back muscles, picked up his wineskin of water along with a pouch of sea biscuits and descended—naked sword in hand. At the last branch from the bottom, he glanced around. Satisfied no enemy lurked to pounce on him, he dropped softly to the ground.

Pouring water on the wood-hard biscuits to soften them, he ate with deliberate slowness; this might be his only meal for the day. With the last morsel of cracker eaten, he made ready for his walk into the interior.

Now, on his third day of march, Sebastián halted mid stride. Earlier, he had decided to continue his eastward search for a source of food. He wiped his brow with a torn, dirty sleeve and peered ahead.

"Aha!" A bare stump lay a few paces from where he stood. The scent of wildflowers caught his nostrils. He inhaled deeply of the fragrance, then clomped forward, shaded his eyes and tilted his head back.

Almost directly overhead, the sun, sharper, stronger than he had known in Spain, glared at him with an unblinking eye. Sebastián nodded. He would rest and have his daily meal.

Today had proved more fortunate—in a sense. Earlier, a bunch of ripe yellow bananas level with his shoulder, had caught his gaze.

On closer inspection, he found most were overripe, invaded by a host of insects. Three at the top remained untouched. He pounced on them with wolfish pleasure, devoured two on the spot, ate the last of the fruit along his walk east.

Would his luck continue?

He dropped heavily on the stump and exhaled with loud, deep relief. His shoulders under his armor burned with pain. He rubbed the incessant throb with one hand and with the other removed a small cloth package tied around his waist. Couched inside—the last smoked dried fish. Starvation loomed closer.

Savoring each bite down to the last particle, he debated whether to return to his base at the tree, or march on. His strength ebbed. He had begun his quest too soon after the rigors of the long arduous voyage. Lack of sufficient food aboard ship had sapped his usual strong stamina; the weight of his supplies and weapons wore him down further. His meals, again were insufficient to replace his stamina. Under these adverse conditions, how many leagues had he marched? Two, three leagues? What did it matter?

Sebastián decided to make camp. A murmuring stream ran nearby—he had tasted the water, found it fresh and cool—a lift to his spirits. Thirst sated, he took pause to clean and reload his pistol.

Earlier he had shot at a small animal, but missed. Before he could reload, the game skittered into the forest.

The stream elbowed toward a grove of unfamiliar trees. The area would provide wood and, perhaps, shelter. From the depths of the worn dispatch case, he pulled out his journal and penned his thoughts.

"This is the third day of my search. What vexes the most is the necessity of constant vigilance. The demand of consciousness for that sudden blur of motion out of the corner of my eye, the rustle of branches in the brush. All this watchfulness slows my pace, limits my range. Later today, I will return to my base at the bay and rest four or five days, then, if it is the will of God, I march again."

He sprinkled sand from a thumb-sized shaker over the ink, blew on the page and shut the journal. Shaking off the sense of despair, he raised his head to absorb the surroundings.

"The view is extraordinary, Sebastián, if that is any consolation."

A vast *sabana* of scattered trees and undulating grass stretched to his left. In front of him, leagues away, craggy mountains rose majestically, their tops shrouded in blue veils of antiquity. Aloof, the peaks watched him in silence.

Then, thunderous pounding, rolling caught his ears. Sebastián shaded his eyes, squinted into the distance and leaned into the sound. A large herd of animals, perhaps hundreds, galloped across the horizon.

From their midst, clouds of thick dust billowed, kicked up by countless hoofs beating the ground. Snared by the noonday sun, the reddish-brown dust clouds turned golden in long shafts of sunlight.

"Too far away," he said in dismay, not able to make out what kind of animal or animals formed the onrushing tide.

Sooner than he expected, thundering receded and the herd quickly melted into the vastness of the land. He continued to look at the golden clouds of dust as large as sails until they settled to the ground, soon followed by a strange quietus.

He shifted his view to the right. Close by, the ground sloped to the grove of trees curving snake-like to the distant mountain range. How far away? Many leagues, he ventured. A refreshing breeze struck his cheek.

He drew several deep breaths, finished his meal and reached again for his journal.

Brushing the dust off the dog-eared cover, he scratched in remarks about the herd, a map and brief description of the area he had traversed since morning.

Piercing, high-pitched screams jerked him to his feet.

He flung journal and pen aside.

Another scream, from the grove of trees.

Lethargy in his body fell away. Every muscle sprang to life, all of his senses fully alive. He bounded forward with long strides, inserting powder and shot into his pistol as he ran—accuracy honed by years of practice on the battlefield. Loaded pistol in one hand, he drew his sword—Sebastián ready to defend or attack.

He crashed through brilliant ferns, snapped twigs, and circled trees, his eyes darting, searching side-to-side, naked blade winking in the beams of light.

The screams, more insistent, drew closer; vibrated in the warm, still air.

Trees brushed past him like shadows. He burst into a sunlit clearing and stopped. Swirls of dust rose around him.

Thirty paces in front of him, a lion snarled and leaped at a figure partially hidden behind leafy branches of a half-fallen tree. Sebastián cocked his pistol, raised both hands and weapons in the air.

Frantic, he waved to draw the animal's attention. "Here! Over here!"

The thick mane and massive head of the beast swung, mouth curled into a snarl, fangs bared. Its tail flicking, the tawny body wheeled and the enraged lion hurtled straight toward him.

Pistol held in both hands, he aimed and fired. The ball entered the animal above an eye—blood sluiced out. Wounded, dazed, the huge beast swerved for a instant, but quickly resumed his charge.

As swift, Sebastián tossed the pistol to the ground, grasped his sword in both hands, deftly moved to his left and slashed sideways with all his strength as the lion leaped.

The razor sharp edge of the blade cut through coarse fur and into the neck. The force of his thrust spun Sebastián around. Both man and animal tumbled onto the ground. Blood gushed from the lion's body. His sword had struck a large blood vessel. Part of Sebastián's shoulder leaned against a paw of the quivering, dying lion.

He scrambled to his feet and stood for a brief moment over the animal as the lion breathed his last.

"You are a noble animal." He bent down to pick up some leaves. Wiping the blood from the blade, he strode to the tree.

The elusive figure huddled in the branches, the face hidden from the viewer.

Sebastián stepped back from the tree, sheathed his weapon, and struggled to peer through the woven lace of branches.

Directly in his line of sight, a pair of finely wrought gold sandals peeked out. Delicate hands with slender fingers and a set of curious eyes gazed at him, but offered no further movement.

He took another step back, raised his hands and produced as pleasant a smile as he could muster, cursing his unruly, unkempt beard and its hint of menace.

He motioned for the figure to come down. *"Habla Portugés?"*

Silence. A few leaves fluttered in the slight breeze.

He touched his forehead, lips and chest with his fingertips. *"Saalam?"*

A deeper silence.

"Please, I do not mean harm to your person," he said in Portuguese along with a smattering of Arabic.

The branches parted and the face of a young woman emerged.

Sebastián blinked. "Those eyes…I cannot believe…" He leaned forward and extended his hand. Immediately, she drew back, only the top of her head visible.

She fears you, Sebastián, with much reason. She sees a bearded stranger armed with sword and dagger. He laid his weapons on the ground in front of her and stepped aside. He showed his empty palms, desperate to force calm into the situation.

He saw one foot slide down the trunk, then the other, and she came into full view. Head down and with utmost caution, she stepped lightly onto the ground. One hand clutched her chest.

In front stood the most beautiful woman he had ever seen

Air sucked away from inside his lungs, his jaw dropped open in astonishment, his eyes seized by her beauty.

He refused to believe this vision a trick of the fiendish Prince of Darkness to tempt him. Or was this bewitching woman a succubus, a demon in female form, ready to ensnare and lead him to the sulfurous pits of Hell. He shook his head. No, never.

In spite of the hellfire and damnation predicted for him by Friar Justin on board ship, he would not believe the clergyman's rants and threats toward him. Could he be in Heaven and she an angel?

He shook his head again. No. He never thought of angels as sensuous.

Sebastián wet his lips, struggling to unravel the turmoil in his head. Perhaps, his body wracked by constant hunger and dogged by exhaustion, his mind robbed of its sleep, rebelled, played tricks on him. Should he reach out and touch her exquisite, caressable skin to find it real or a maddening dream?

If this young woman were only a dream and he touched her, most assuredly he would surely wake up and she would be lost forever. But what if she was not a dream, but flesh and blood?

Then he would sink to his knees and thank the Almighty for his good fortune. Smitten by her beauty, he could only stare. He grappled to rein in tremors coursing through his body.

She was somewhere between sixteen and nineteen. Thick, long, lashes fluttered over almond-shaped eyes. The pupils glided beguilingly.

Speechless, he watched their languid expressiveness search him with fluid motion, as though they swam in a pool. Hands shaking, he wiped the perspiration from his brow and studied the striking eyelids.

From the bridge of the nose and extending a fingernail length beyond the lashes, silver blue painted the eyelid and ended in a small triangle. Where had he seen eyes painted in that fashion? Memory failed him.

Each time she closed her glittering lids, slivers of sunlight sent pinpoints of light in every direction. He squinted, unable to determine the color of her eyes, forced his attention away and to her cheeks.

Not a single blemish insulted her flawless skin. Black hair, luxuriant and shorn across the temple, undulated like deep ocean swells with every turn of her head and spilled over the narrow shoulders down to her waist.

He broadened his smile, then as quick erased it.

The young woman's frightened eyes had turned from fear to cautiously curious. Slowly a tenuous smile formed on a face indented by dimples. The lips of the bow-shaped mouth parted slightly—even white teeth shone against olive skin.

Reluctantly, Sebastián lowered his gaze, then felt his eyes widen in awe.

A crescent-shaped pectoral ornament shielded her chest from shoulder to shoulder. Torn, loose gold cords hung loosely over the arm held across her bosom. The cords probably tied the collar around her neck, and had pulled away when she desperately sought refuge in the tree.

Reflecting light from the sun's rays, the jeweled collar vied for attention.

Above and under the arm placed across her chest, thick, delicately woven gold threads on the collar gripped a dazzling array of emeralds, rubies and diamonds of different colors, shapes and sizes. All the stones had been worked into a partially visible image of…what? Was it the winged form of the Egyptian goddess, Isis?

"A king's ransom!" he murmured and quickly averted his eyes as a frown crossed her face, a line carving itself between her sculpted eyebrows. Enchanted, afraid his look might be mistaken for avarice instead of curiosity, he shifted his attention away from her bosom.

Her small waist curved to hips that flared sensuously under a white, form-fitting ankle-length skirt—torn in several places. And she possessed an…hourglass figure.

Sebastián rubbed his eyes in disbelief. "Merciful Mother of God in Heaven. Hourglass figure and painted eyes! This cannot be."

By the purest chance and divine providence and without the slightest doubt in his mind: He, Sebastián de Aviles, had stumbled upon a myth in the flesh.

Who is she?

Her eyes suddenly widened.

Sebastián flinched.

A spear point stung his rib cage, another jabbed his right.

94

THIRTEEN

A host of chills snaked through Sebastián's body. Rivulets of perspiration prickled his skin anew. He turned his head, first to the left, then to the right. Two men in sleeveless white tunics held spears against his ribs. A half dozen more had skirted around in front, one man held a spear aloft, ready to impale Sebastián. The men, almost as tall as Sebastián, olive-skinned and boasting fine features, glared at him.

Sebastián, you damned fool! He had let his guard down. He clenched his fists, enraged at his carelessness and realization of his impending death without honor. Impossible now for him to pick up his sword and fight before spears ran him through. He threw a pleading gaze at the young woman and steeled himself. Spanish field officers did not ask for quarter. They died where they stood.

Shoulders squared, he prepared to die. *I commend my spirit to Thee, O Lord*

At least her vision would feed his eyes for all eternity after he fell to the ground.

One of the men, their leader, he assumed, reached down for Sebastián's sword.

Shaking his head, Sebastián moved forward, spear points cutting into his sides.

He locked eyes with the man.

Sebastián lifted sash and scabbard over his head and turned. He addressed the young woman.

"Once, long ago, I took a solemn oath before God never to yield my sword while I live. But I will surrender my weapons to you." Twice he pointed to the weapons then to her and held out the sash.

Curiosity played on her face. She nodded, stepped forward and accepted his offer. As she placed her hands on a fold of the sash, her fingers, with thistledown grace, touched his.

A quiver ran down Sebastián's back. Her fingers felt cool, their smoothness like silk against the scarred roughness of his hand. Was that a tear at the corner of her colorful eyelid?

She fixed her eyes on the leader of the men, and uttered what sounded like a command.

The men handed Sebastián's sword and dagger to her waiting arms. She sheathed the sword.

Sebastián felt the spear points retreat from his ribs and he exhaled an audible deep breath of relief. His captors lowered their spears, but kept him surrounded. Were they soldiers?

At the center of her guardians, she clutched the weapons with her left arm, placed her right hand over her heart and offered Sebastián a reserved smile, her eyes serenely compelling.

A new wave of elation washed over him. Her intimate gestures, he felt, asked his forgiveness or understanding. He nodded. "Yes, yes. I understand." Those spellbinding eyes and sense of mystery brought forth a recollection of a few lines from a poem.

Her Eyes
He would steal, cheat, tell monstrous lies
For a glance from her eyes.

He would sell his soul and burn in Hell,
For a look from her eyes and their spell.

He would be silent and speak no more,
If those eyes were his forevermore.

At this moment he would sell his soul without regret and burn in hell if those very eyes favored him. *I am at her mercy. I cannot speak or move, my emotions ensnared in a whirl.*

Sebastián relaxed his shoulders then stiffened them again. Shrill, agitated voices broke the silence, drew near.

He spun on his heel. About to draw a sword no longer at his waist, Sebastián hesitated. The movement toward his weapon, now in the young woman's arms would be interpreted as hostile. Keeping his hands by his sides, he waited.

A group of women burst into the clearing. Their eyes wide with fear, they darted about, searched the area with great anxiousness. The soldiers stepped aside to reveal the young woman in their midst.

Upon seeing her, the group rent the air with piercing cries, waved their hands and arms wildly and ran to her side.

Immediately and in perfect order, the newcomers formed a complete circle around the young woman. The men with spears formed an open perimeter around the circle. The next instant, the group of women focused their attention onto Sebastián. In unison, the women reached under the folds of their ankle-length white skirts and withdrew daggers.

Their weapons, held at waist level, several of the cordon pointed the poniards at Sebastián, threatened him, others stabbed the air. The oldest of the six held her weapon over her head, fingers grasping the gleaming naked blade as though ready to throw the point at Sebastián. The other women shrieked at him.

Although the language was foreign to his ears, he deduced their meaning. He must not make any movement or declare anything but peaceful intentions.

No rapacious designs by look or gesture by him on the riches displayed or harm to their mistress, or whosoever she may be. Might they be her *menina,* women, usually young, chosen to serve a queen or other royal personage? With deliberate slowness he raised his hands over his head, and spoke. Which language should he use—Spanish, Portuguese, or Latin? He chose Portuguese, his voice calm, words soft.

"Please. I mean no harm to your friend or to any of you." He studied several of the group more closely. All wore the same design of collar, though not as richly decorated as their charge. Of the six, the oldest was in her late thirties or early forties; five perhaps two or three years older than the woman he rescued. A child of no more than ten accompanied them, being constantly reprimanded by someone in the group.

The youngster now stared openmouthed at Sebastián. She would emit a squeal, then hide behind the skirts of the women.

With exception of the child, all of the women displayed the small waist, curving hips, and painted eyes. Each of their eyelids boasted hues of gold, blue and green. Like a confection of rainbows!

Sebastián shifted his attention to the youngest then the oldest—favored each with an arresting smile perhaps he could ease their fear of him. *My appearance must frighten them. It certainly disgusts me.*

Blood covered one side of his blouse where the dying lion had brushed against him; his face and dark beard must be covered with dust and sweat, his clothing torn and filthy. And the last time he peered at his reflection in a stream, he looked more like a brigand than an officer of the Spanish Royal Army. Former officer, he reminded himself. He shrugged.

Slowly, the angry, suspicious looks on the women faded.

The young woman he rescued turned to face the group and spoke rapidly.

Her protectors lowered, then returned the daggers to their hiding places under the waistbands, but kept one hand close to the weapons. Bracelets jangling, she raised her arm, tilted her chin with a look of great admiration at Sebastián, and pointed to the body of the dead lion.

The oldest of the women—an imposing figure, detached herself from the circle and, hem of her skirt held above her sandals with one hand, she tiptoed to the dead lion as though the animal were still alive. The child let out a shriek and quickly hid behind a skirt. The older woman returned, offered the briefest nod to Sebastián and spoke to the others whose glances now turned to admiration and awe at the feat he had accomplished

Arms lowered, Sebastián smiled at every word and gesture, mind and body gaining composure.

Moments before, he had grinned when, along with the others, the youngster had pulled out a dagger the size of his small finger and threatened him with the point—ready to sacrifice her little body for her companion.

What a noble gesture! If someday he had a daughter…

Three of the soldiers stayed with Sebastián, albeit with spears lowered, the others kept the protective outer perimeter. Two of the women set to repair the torn gold threads of the broken collar of their rescued companion, whispering to each other in their tongue. The others watched Sebastián's every movement.

Soon, collar repaired, the young woman indicated for Sebastián to follow them.

She spoke a few words to the men guarding Sebastián. They bowed respectfully, he noticed and ran to take positions front and rear of the entire group. She paused and turned her head. Sebastián had not moved.

Indecisive, he debated the matter of his pistol and his journal. The espingarda still lay on the ground where he had thrown it aside. The weapon was irreplaceable—its twin back in the tree at his camp—both worth their weight in gold in Africa. If he went to retrieve the pistol, they might interpret the act as hostile. Why should he take the risk? Leave the weapon behind. He would do nothing to jeopardize his most fortuitous discovery of this fascinating, most alluring creature. He decided to pick up the espingarda and journal on his return. Return from where? Would he live long enough?

The group stepped forward. Sebastián circled closer than three arm lengths from the young woman. The oldest of the group immediately blocked his way.

In spite of his saving the young woman's life, he would not be allowed closer than three arm lengths to her person.

You are a stranger. What did you expect, Sebastián? "You protect her well." He offered a carefree wave to the group "Lead on!" He would go, not as a prisoner bound in chains, but a willing captive of those eyes and most enthralling of women.

Soldiers, rescuer, rescued and her companions stepped forward. Entering the grove of trees, they traveled in silence with only the footfalls of sandals on dirt and the crackle of dead leaves underfoot broke the still air.

At present, no doubt existed in his mind about who these men and women were. He, Captain Sebastián Alejandro De Avíles of Spain, had come upon the kingdom of Prestor John. He crossed himself.

"*In nominee Patris, Filii, et Spiritus Sancti.* O Mericful Father, I thank thee."

As he walked alongside the women, details of the centuries-old legend swept like a whirlwind across his enraptured mind.

For countless decades, an astounding tale spun by sailors, travelers and traders, circulated throughout Europe. The legend spoke of a kingdom somewhere in the Northern reaches of Africa, ruled by a white Christian king named Prestor John. This fabled country, spinners of the tale reported, boasted great wealth in gold, silver and precious stones.

Skeptics abounded.

"Show us the proof," they demanded.

Marco Polo, whom some skeptics called the biggest liar in Europe, penned the story in his travel pages.

The Genoan allowed that such a kingdom existed—somewhere in the Red Mountains, although his eyes never caught sight of the wonder. His words fanned the flames of the controversy higher.

In spite of lack of proof and verification of the existence of such a kingdom, rumors and believers roared louder. Finally, in exasperation, Pope Alexander III commissioned a special Papal Plenipotentiary to seek out Prestor John.

"Tell Prestor John," the pope said, "we wish to form an alliance against the Muslims and forge a crusade to free the Holy Land." With great fanfare and pomp the envoy set off for Africa.

The papal emissary never returned and no message from him ever reached Rome.

Doubters said marauding band of brigands infesting those vast reaches of sand and rock, along with scorpions and evil spirits that ruled over the wastelands, had captured the pope's emissary. These godless outlaws killed the papal envoy and his entourage, murdered in a fruitless quest for a non-existent kingdom.

But many cited another reason for the envoy's disappearance. "A great human treasure," the believers said, but kept secret: The women who lived in this kingdom caused the pope's envoy to disappear.

These ladies of Prestor John's kingdom possessed incomparable beauty. So much so, Arab slavers risked their lives and those of their tribal allies to capture one or two of these women. The maidens had never been seen in slave markets; purchased beforehand for enormous sums, by kings and princes.

One such woman entranced and bedeviled the pope's envoy, the defenders of the myth shouted with glee. Taken with her exquisite beauty, he forsook his Pope, his religion, his home and country for this entrancing creature.

The believers ignored the taunts. These fabulous enchantresses, the legends said were identified by two distinguishing features:

An hourglass figure and painted eyes.

Sebastián's mind returned from a distant past. His lips dry, constriction in his throat, tightness in his chest, he found himself unable, yet desperate to believe. Here before him stood living proof of the age-old myth. His mind reeled.

"Almighty Father, I thank Thee for sparing my life, allowing me to endure many hardships and granting my eyes to see this most glorious of moments. I also thank Thee for permitting me to be the most fortunate of men."

A thought occurred to Sebastián. All the reports and stories about these women placed them in North Africa. Neither of this group wore veils or *carcajes,* bangles or bracelets around their ankles as Muslim women did. She is not black African or Arab. Who is she?

Whatever the reason, he would follow, even to the gates of sulfurous hell.

FOURTEEN

Anxiety filled The Daughter Of The King Who Lives On The Red Mountain. She forced a smile to her savior, hoping to hide the despair running through her being. Without the slightest doubt in her mind, she knew the king, her father, would be extremely angry with her.

"My beloved daughter, you are to remain close to your companions and your guards at all times and not stray far from them," he had commanded, allowing her and her guardians to stroll outside the compound.

Never allowed to venture outside the gates, never allowed to cross the river, never to travel alone, she and her friends had begged, pleaded with the king for permission to step outside the walls—with guards, of course.

She had disobeyed him. Her friends, the four closest to her age, had persuaded her to play that silly game of hiding from her friends and waiting for them to find her.

"It's a childish game," she had said, but aware of the endless and strict restrictions on all of them, she relented and surrendered to their pleas—against the strong objections of Amanuet, the oldest and in charge of the group. The princess would take complete blame; not allow her father to punish the guards or her friends for her foolish and dangerous action.

This stranger walking outside her protective circle, this possible enemy of her father, stirred strong, heretofore unfelt emotions within her. His face and clothing were filthy. She found his full beard menacing. On his chest, armor glinted in the afternoon sun. Although his arsenal of weapons rested on her person, she witnessed the pride in his bearing yet melancholy resided in his eyes. His very manner, his alertness to the surroundings signaled a warrior of some kind. From what land?

From the moment they set eyes on each other, he awakened within her, desires, which she had only heard of, but never experienced. Feelings far deeper than she had had from any of her suitors. When his eyes touched hers, they spoke to her heart; *I wish to be with you, I wish to hold you in my arms…*raced through her mind, caressed her being. What would her father say of him? How would she convince the king not to harm this man? She shrugged. Only the gods knew.

She hoped he did not read the fear for his safety in her eyes, the despair deep inside her heart, the gravity of the situation this stranger found himself in.

The women, their protective, walking circle strictly maintained, engaged in good-natured banter among themselves, casting occasional, questioning glances at the stranger, more often then not with aloof disapproval. When he drew closer to their charge, all displayed anger on their faces. Alongside and behind, her guards kept a respectful, but watchful distance from the group, vigilant to their flanks, spears at the ready.

They also cast looks of suspicion at the bearded man in their midst. A few paces later, the oldest of the women drew closer to the princess and whispered in her ear.

"Princess, this man has saved your life, but he may be a sworn enemy of your father. Do not allow him to touch you in any manner. If he does, order your guards to kill him, or, if you wish, we will slay him. Our eyes will follow his every movement."

The princess nodded. "If he touches me, yes, of course." Her rescuer had already touched her in a most tender manner—in her heart. What may be his thoughts at this moment?

Off to the side and four arm lengths away, a soldier in front of him and one in back, Sebastián watched the women from the corner of his eye, enchanted by them and their beauty of mythic proportions. His thoughts wandered back to Europe and Castile. How far removed these ladies were from those in Europe.

What these women seemed to be born with, those of Europe went to great lengths to obtain; using stays of whalebones, cords and other devices for narrowing the waist, accentuating the hips and posteriors. All upper-class women in Spain ignored pain for fashion.

He smiled. Careful not to arouse more suspicion on his intentions, he kept his walking pace, but formed a habit of running his gaze in an arc. At the perimeter, the guards maintained their silence, displayed discipline. A few arcs later, Sebastián shot a slow, but long side-glance to the young woman in the center of the circle.

How sinuous her body! Those graceful movements of the limbs, the subtle motion of the hips. Deep in his reverie, he caught himself a moment before losing his pace.

With mounting qualms about what fate awaited him and frustration in not knowing her name at least, he decided to take a risk.

He waved his hands until he caught her eye. Hands cupped around his mouth, he called out over the protective, moving circle of ladies. "My name is Sebastián." He repeated his name once, twice, while pointing to himself.

At first, consternation played on the faces of the women. After much discussion from her group, an uncertain smile wreathed her features. Slowly, she said his name. "Se-bas-chan." She tripped over the syllables and laughed gently. The older woman shook her head as though she disapproved of the young woman's actions. The child in their midst giggled.

When the guards pointed their spears at him, the young woman he rescued shouted some words and the solders returned to pointing their weapons outside the circle.

Sebastián tilted his head back and let out a peal of laughter at her mispronunciation. "How wonderful the sound to my ears!" he said, shook his head and pointed to her.

"What is your name?"

She called out some words in her language.

Brows furrowed, he scratched his beard.

"Please, repeat your name." He again pointed to her.

She complied. He counted ten words. Her companions, possibly over the look of puzzlement on his face, joined in chorusing her name, as though he a simpleton.

"I am sorry. I do not understand." He spread his hands apart. "Your name sounds too long. I am going to call you Cebellina. When I learn your language I will explain what it means." He pointed to her again and repeated his name several times until she responded. The other women immediately took up the name. Finally after much coaching from Sebastián, they pronounced his name correctly.

How good the tinkling of their laughter sounded. When was the last time he had heard the sounds of joyfulness from women? Or, for that matter, laughed himself?

On the outward voyage to India from Portugal, vigorous heartiness prevailed amongst some of the seamen and officers for the most part, but certainly not on the disastrous return voyage. At the time, he had felt an almost numbness, perhaps due to unfolding tragedies around him. Perhaps also, because da Gama, although a brilliant navigator, lacked humor. Da Gama, Sebastián felt, was a storm cloud of a presence.

Sebastián inhaled a deep breath, pushed all painful memories of the voyage aside. "Ah, how beautiful and heavenly the sound you make." Those sounds birthed a peace—perhaps short-lived, but he would savor every note—settling within him at this blissful moment. The crushing weight of loneliness had lifted. New life vibrated through his body.

A question pushed itself through the jumble of thoughts. The kingdom of Prestor John practiced Nestorian Christianity—those who believed in two distinct persons in Christ. Neither Cebellina, nor any of the other women wore a crucifix, an almost obligatory part of the dress of any Christian woman in Europe. Also, he hadn't seen any of them make the sign of the cross, also a common everyday custom for Roman Catholics in Europe.

The absence of veils or long-sleeved garments on the circle of her watchful guardians meant none of the group was Muslim. The followers of Mahomet despised Christians. The guards would have speared Sebastián the moment they saw him at the clearing.

Only one answer existed. Cebellina and her companions were pagans. This heartbreaking beauty, a pagan! Sebastián forwent making the sign of the cross, as other Christians would have done, especially in Spain. He did not care.

He harbored neither fear or hated them for their beliefs. He would not force Christianity on this pagan woman. If such thoughts blasphemous in the eyes of the Church, let him burn in waves of flames. What mattered most to him and which he hoarded like a miser: each gaze he received from her. The richness of feelings for this woman increased with each step he took.

The group entered a dark thicket of heavy brush, the path, a fugitive from the eye, lay hidden beneath bowed, waist-high ferns. Dense vegetation deadened sound, especially if ambushers lay hidden.

In silence, the guardians tightened their circle; the soldiers moved closer and increased their vigilance.

Instinctively, Sebastián reached for his sword, touched empty space. For the first time in his life, he would have to rely on someone else to protect him.

In spite of his sense of naked defenselessness, all his senses snapped into alertness. He peered into the bushes, ferns and overhanging branches of the surrounding trees for lurking shadows or sudden movements. Later, he would draw a map of this area—the site excellent for an ambush.

He turned toward Cebellina. They shared a smile and she passed a hand through her hair as though immersed in thought. About him? Someone else? A pang of jealousy ran through Sebastián. Might she have a husband waiting? He thought not. Betrothed? Possible.

Suitor or suitors? Quite conceivable as Cebellina of marriageable age—sixteen or so. Unsure of anything, he marched forward.

Guards, companions, the princess and Sebastián proceeded in silence, the only sound, the snap of small twigs and swish of dead leaves as they passed. One of the group of women offered a coquettish glance at Sebastián but it quickly vanished at an immediate frown from Cebellina.

Shortly thereafter, the forest thinned out and the give and take resumed.

In the center of the moving circle and silent, the princess pushed a wayward tendril of hair back into place and resumed thoughts about her rapidly approaching meeting with her father. She would do her utmost to persuade him not to punish anyone, especially her rescuer.

What about her people? Would they voice any opinion? Her father allowed them to vent grievances. But in this case they would side with her father, of course.

From childhood, she knew the populace—after experiences and countless battles with slavers and others—distrusted all strangers. Uninvited outsiders who wished entry without plausible reasons or tried to force their way in were killed at the gates. She shook the unpleasantness away.

For now, a part of her reveled at Sebastián's open admiration of her. And why shouldn't he? Was she not a direct descendent of the famous Queen? Along with a light step, she marched forward.

According to the old narrative among her people, two famous generals of the mighty Roman Empire, upon setting eyes on their most beautiful Queen Cleopatra, fell in love with her.

When one of them was assassinated by jealous senators, the other one left his home, his family and his country to be by the queen's side. For a time, the empire stood on the brink of collapse. A battle followed.

Both the Roman general and the Queen died by their own hands rather than be captured. The tale had been told and retold by the descendents of Alexander's legions through the ages.

Cebellina glanced at the ever-watchful stranger, the beat of her heart quickened, then fearfulness over his life returned. Would tragedy follow her own footsteps?

Another silent prayer to Isis, the mother goddess rose from her lips, a fervent plea she was not leading this man, her rescuer, to his death. It would destroy her. She lowered her chin to her chest.

"If he is slain, I will kill myself."

FIFTEEN

Eagerness written on their faces, sparkle in their eyes, the women quickened their pace across a wide, open clearing. Sebastián lengthened his stride

Across the open field, several hundred paces away, he spied the wooden walls of a compound. The wind carried the fuming of many small fires from behind the palisade.

The group neared the structure and reflexive military training within Sebastián awakened. He glanced to the left then the right. A palisade, fashioned from sharpened, unpeeled logs about three yards high, ran for several hundred paces in both directions. A double gate sat at the center of the enclosure. Immediate disappointment crossed his mind

Those walls can be easily breached. Not a good posture for defense. Images from his past of moats, three-yard thick walls with heights twice of this fence rolled through. Shaking his head, he forced the images away.

Also as quick, any thought of escape. Why should he run? Where? At most, he could run a few paces before half a dozen spears brought him down.

At his back stood a thick forest that scorned weakness and stretched for leagues. At the bay no ship awaited him, no troops to aid in an attack against the palisade. Escape? Idiocy. Most important of all: he would never see the heavenly Cebellina again.

Behind the palisade, he could see the heads of men moving back and forth, spear points flashing in the sunlight. Sentries.

One of the gates swung open and a score of men armed with swords and spears poured out to form a file on either side of the entrance.

As Cebellina and her entourage passed, the men bowed their heads, stared at Sebastián from under their eyelids. The soldiers from the compound studied the forest for a moment—to see if anyone followed, Sebastián surmised. Once the group safely inside, two soldiers shut the gate and lowered a crossbeam across the center of the upright logs.

Sebastián swallowed hard, forced an outward appearance of calm. Surrounded by a dozen armed men, he was now under the complete control of whoever ruled this compound. Past the gate, the length and breadth of the town or village area lay hidden around a bend and out of his line of sight.

After seeing the wealth worn by the six women and their young charge, he expected to discover a fabulous city and wondrous sights. Only thatched huts greeted him.

Huts, yes, Sebastián, but regal compared to your solitude in the jungle and your sleeping quarters in the branch of a tree or on damp ground.

A few paces past the gate, another wall built of mud and stone about a yard in height confronted him.

The military man in Sebastián nodded approval. An enemy bursting through the gate would suffer additional casualties by defenders hurling spears or loosing arrows behind the second wall. Also, the invaders would quickly find themselves in streets with curving pathways, and hidden corners, easy targets for the populace to deliver deathblows to their enemies.

The huts, he noticed, for the most part were assembled from the interweaving of rushes and fronds. A half dozen displayed smoothly dressed stones.

"Of recent construction," he remarked, noting roofs being tamped into place.

Ancient chronicles about Prestor John had spoken of magnificence. Was this one of the smaller kingdoms under his reign? Sebastián shook his head in doubt. Who *are* these people?

Streets of packed dirt and thatched dwellings increased his disappointment. Did another, larger town exist nearby? Hopeful he would discover the answer soon, he turned his attention to the inhabitants.

Men and women had gathered along his path. In ranks two or three deep, they quietly viewed with calm surprise at the stranger in their midst. The children showed wonderment on their faces, their eyes a landscape of curiosity. Some children hid behind their parents, others boldly looked at Sebastián as did a young girl shepherding a flock of geese. Most of the adults showed suspicion, indifference or outright contempt by turning their backs as Sebastián passed by.

The hourglass figures on the women appeared after puberty, he noted, for the young girls under twelve or so were as any other child their age. Later, when puberty arrived, the women blossomed into the legendary figures. The eyelids on the women continued to intrigue him.

Without exception, all painted their eyes, as though headed to a ball, albeit with plain white skirts rather than silk gowns. His glance shifted to the older women.

An air of melancholy elegance surrounded these ladies, yet they carried themselves with a regal and haughty air. Around their necks they wore collars similar to that of the young woman he had rescued, but less exquisite in design and display of precious stones. The open display of great wealth forced Sebastián to hide his looks of astonishment.

Rounding a bend, he nodded at an incongruous sight. A woman with seamless beauty, gray hair at the temples, a gold band around her forehead, pulled on the reins of a donkey hitched to a wood-laden dray. *Incredible!* He smothered the desire to stare at the untold wealth around him, marched forward, smiled warmly at the onlookers even as some sneered or turned their faces away.

His guards approached a stone building of indeterminate size, its walls faced with dressed granite fitted together with great care. The ends of the walls rounded a bend, the outside painted in bright frescoes of red, yellow and green.

Sebastián paused.

"They look like paintings of Egyptian life and those strange symbols..." Sebastián, about to step closer, one of the guards approached and pointed with his spear to the entrance. Although disappointed at his inability to study the frescos further, Sebastián nodded and followed the others through the open doorway.

Several paces in front of him, Cebellina, though hampered by her form-fitting skirt, paced quickly toward a man seated on an elaborately carved chair of ebony wood.

She bowed, placed Sebastián's weapons on the ground in front of the throne, then padded to the man's side and sat down on once-opulent cushions, their cloth ends now frayed, colors of gold and purple faded.

At Cebellina's entrance, the man seated raised his hand to acknowledge her greeting with a half smile, then returned to peer at his unexpected guest. Or his prisoner?

She raised a slender finger, pointed at Sebastián and spoke in rapid outbursts accompanied by dramatic gestures with her hands and fingers.

Her companions from the walk, grouped in a semicircle along each side of Cebellina, nodded at her every word, but kept silent. Sebastián felt all eyes upon him—hostility in most.

Head erect, he pushed his shoulders back, and marched forward to the center of the room as though approaching the Queen of Spain—with half a dozen spears pointed at his back. A few paces away from the throne, he stopped.

Murmurings among those in the chamber increased. More than fifty of the inhabitants either sat on cushions or stood along the walls.

Smudges of incense from censers throughout the chamber threaded the air, filled his nostrils with scents of eucalyptus and jasmine. Dozens of oil lamps hanging from wooden-beamed ceilings threw flickering shadows on walls covered with metal shields depicting Greek and Egyptian signs. *Greek? Egyptian?* What did their presence mean? Under his present conditions, would he have time to ask questions? Or live long enough?

Sebastián swept his forage cap off, swung it in an arc in front of him, and bowed from the waist. Then he straightened and studied the man. Who was he to Cebellina. Father? Husband? Brother?

The man, in his late forties, boasted broad-shoulders and wore a plain, snow-white robe fitted at the shoulder with a gold clasp and flowed to his ankles. Leather sandals trimmed with gold shod his feet. His only ornament: a gold circlet of entwined cobras around his neck. Ringlets of dark hair curled around his temples and brow over an aquiline nose. An angry scar running from the man's temple to his beardless chin presented a fierce, menacing appearance.

Stern-faced, eyebrow cocked, the man glanced at Sebastián's weapons and listened quietly to Cebellina, who spoke without pause, breathless, her words tumbling over one another. After each word, her fingers stabbed the still air.

Sebastián watched her pantomime, curious about what she described. Perhaps the incident with the lion—oh, how it wished it so!

His mouth curved into an unconscious smile. He understood none of what she said, but he knew by the exaggerated gestures of her hands as if they held a sword—portraying Sebastián killing the lion, infusing greater detail than necessary.

Oh, God our Lord, how this woman enchants me! From the first instant she had stepped down from the tree and he set incredulous eyes on her. Never had he felt such depths of emotions.

Now, chin on his palm, the man seated on the black throne shifted his glance to Sebastián's worn, dust-laden, Moorish boots. Slowly the unblinking eyes studied the weather-beaten chest armor marred by dents, gouges and spots of rust.

He is trying to determine who I am by my Castilian chest armor and manner of dress.

Sebastián's cotton blouse under the jerkin, once new and white as milk, he knew was now a storm cloud gray. Circles of sweat stains and torn strips hung limply under his arm. What did it matter now?

The eyes returning Sebastián's glance watched with cautious curiosity, alert, bright and the color of port wine. A flicker of a smile crossed the face and a muscle quivered at the strong jaw. From the corner of his eye, the man turned his attention to Cebellina.

Sebastián pursed his lips. What thoughts hid behind those unflinching eyes? What fate awaits me? Is my life now measured in heartbeats?

SIXTEEN

Curiosity replaced anger on the face of Telemesus, The King Who Lives On The Red Mountain. He released the grip on the armrests and regarded his daughter.

She clasped her slender fingers tightly and pressed them against her chest, continuing to speak, with frequent glances at the foreigner. The king turned his head, caught the European's attention on the princess. The man's eyes, the color of emeralds, the king noticed, fixed themselves more on his daughter than on the throne and its occupant. Uneasiness coursed through the sovereign's body and he shifted in his seat.

His daughter and the stranger did not understand each other's language, yet messages of warmth and closeness more subtle than the spoken word crackled like lightning between them. Most unusual for her. He had never seen his daughter act like this with any other man.

Usually complaisant, she heeded his commands, but other times she displayed stubbornness and disobedience. Did this unusual behavior surface because of the incident with the lion?

Although the stranger might be an enemy, the king admired the man's courage. In spite of a half dozen spears pointed at his head and shoulders, the man's demeanor stayed calm, shoulders pushed back, eyes steady but watchful. *The young man shows no fear and is ready to die.* Also, this European had killed a lion to save his daughter—a remarkable feat for any man.

Was that why she spoke so highly of him? Those glances of…yes, affection, the king read in her looks and in her expressions were all due to his bravery? What else lay beneath the dust, ragged clothing, unruly hair and unkempt beard on this man's face? His armor, though worn, is etched and a faded coat of arms is still visible. This man is not a common soldier, but of higher rank. But why does he wear Muslim boots?

A sigh escaped the king's lips. This lion killer must be treated as a possible enemy. Like all others who lusted for the wealth of the king's people and the beauty of the women—not a single enemy had ever passed through the gates alive.

Should I grant him life or pronounce a death sentence? A difficult decision.

Cebellina ceased speaking, folded her arms across her chest, and lifted her chin. The Princess offered the European a polite smile.

Some members of the audience remained impassive or continued to throw scornful looks at the stranger in their midst.

The king kept his face expressionless and lifted his chin from his palm. True, this foreigner had saved his daughter's life at great peril to his own. But what did his presence in this country mean? Did others march behind him? At word of the stranger's arrival, the king had ordered extra guards at the gates and walls.

Finger curled, he beckoned a sentry and whispered in the man's ear.

"Take two of my daughter's guards, along with a runner. Search the trail she followed. Take care. If there are others of his kind or slavers, send the runner back at once. Go!"

The sentry dashed out of the chamber.

The king motioned for Kahun, the commander of the guards in charge of keeping watch over the princess to step forward.

"Kahun, why was my daughter carrying this man's weapons?"

"He refused their surrender to us. We were about to force him—"

Cebellina leaped to her feet, interrupted the soldier. "My Lord, my rescuer preferred to die before giving up his sword to our men. But he did surrender his *arms* to me."

The king nodded, studied her features. Was there a double meaning to her word *arms*? There were times her actions and words defied understanding. He shook his head. So, the stranger chose to be a captive and risk his life. *It may be of short duration.*

"I see." The sovereign pointed to the guard. "You are dismissed."

Visibly relieved, the guard bowed, scurried out the doorway.

A worried look on her face, the princess sat down.

The king rubbed his chin. If the guard had disobeyed a direct order from the princess, he might have lost his life and the king the service of a good soldier. The incident at the clearing with those concerned was, the king admitted to himself, most unusual.

The European in front of him. Should he be tortured for the truth? How would torturing the man affect his daughter?

The king watched the princess continue to cast too many glances at the man. How deeply the king wished for his departed wife. If only she were still alive—her advice through the years had been always valuable, always accurate.

With the back of his free hand, the king stroked the scar on his cheek. The old slash from a spear seemed to throb more than usual this day. He turned his head toward four men seated on his left. Alike in dress as their king— plain white tunics, cinched at the waist by a sash and reaching to their ankles— their heads closely cropped or shaven, they leaned closer to listen to their sovereign. Closest to the king and a head taller than the others was a black man.

"What is your decision regarding this man? Think carefully of all that has been said by my daughter and her companions," the king said, his voice laced with fatigue from constant attention to the safety and liberty of his subjects, he heard his own words sound harsh and demanding.

The advisers exchanged nervous looks.

His council conferred briefly, then the black man stood and bowed. "O King, we must not be known for weakness to our enemies. The man must die."

A piercing scream rent the still air.

Cebellina ran toward Sebastián, pushed the spears aside and stood in front of him, arms held straight back in a protective gesture. Tears coursed down her cheeks; the drops like crystals reflecting light from the hanging oil lamps. Her shoulders drooped as though in unbearable anguish. Quickly, she straightened, her shoulders straight as the walls of the chamber. She raised her chin.

"Please, Father, do not kill him. Spare him. He saved my life at risk of his own. Is this how we repay his courage? He placed his trust in me by surrendering his weapons. We reward his trust by treachery? He has done no harm to my person or of my companions. Let the first spear pierce me."

The room erupted in an uproar.

Stunned, the king fell back in his seat, disbelieving what he had just heard from his daughter.

Screaming, her ladies-in-waiting ran forward, prostrated themselves in front of the king, beseeching the king for mercy for the man who saved the princess. If the foreigner died, their beloved princess would die.

Women in the audience filled the air with shrieks, wails, moans and beat their chests. Men grumbled, shook their heads, raised their hands and looked at each other with helplessness. If this stranger were put to death and the princess carried out her threat, the kingdom would no longer have a future queen. All eyes turned to the king.

He snapped his gaze toward his daughter. Though tears continued to run in ragged streams down the beloved face, determination filled her eyes.

Would she carry out such a threat to allow herself to be impaled? Yes.

Once she had set herself on a course of action, she would not turn back. This time, her outburst no whim of a young girl, but an expression of…what? Affection? Or something deeper, stronger for a stranger?

The king gritted his teeth. If he had the death sentence carried out, his beautiful daughter might die. He would lose his only remaining child. If he let this man live, he would be defying the advice of his own council and his own inner feelings.

What should he decide? The king looked at his daughter. Another danger lay hidden in her clothing: Her dagger. Should he have one of the women forcibly remove the poniard tucked in his daughter's waistband? Prevent her from possibly using the weapon on herself or others? No. The forced disarming would humiliate his daughter in front of the entire court. He quickly threw a stony glance to the stranger before him. Their eyes locked.

This stranger in our midst man knows a death sentence awaits him, pronounced by the actions of my daughter and the other women.

The king raised a hand. "Silence!"

Immediate quiet smothered the uproar, save for the whimpering of the ladies-in-waiting.

The sovereign leaned back in his throne, grimacing as he rubbed a wound on one of his legs. Later, he would apply a paste of crushed peppers in unguent to relieve the pain. Moments passed before he viewed the European.

Ten paces away from the king, spear points pressed against his arms, his ribs and neck, Sebastián inhaled deeply from Cebellina's fragrance wafting over him, her sinuous body only an arm's length away from his. If he could reach out…He forced himself to glance over her head and toward the throne. He detected indecision and weariness in the eyes that held his.

This was no Christian priest-king sitting on the throne. Under those plain white robes sat a pagan warrior-king, dark eyes in a penetrating gaze, his body relaxed in posture but watchful.

Also, he wagered, by now the warrior-king fully aware of Sebastián's close attention to every gesture, every action, every word, Cebellina did or said—even if the words foreign to his ears.

In spite of the prisoner's visible attentiveness for the young woman, Sebastián had been condemned to death. Of that, no doubt existed in his mind. *I cannot reach my weapons. I know that I will die where I stand. I will not ask for quarter or beg for mercy. If it is the will of God, I am ready. I ask Almighty God to judge me as he sees fit. My only regret is not being able to declare my affection for this woman.*

With his right hand, he made the sign of the cross. "*In nominee Patris, Filii…*"

A commotion at the entrance of the chamber caused all heads to turn.

Sebastián ceased his prayer. The subdued wailing and sniveling stopped. Deathly silence filled the chamber.

Feeling the spear points pricking his body relax, Sebastián turned his head.

A wizened old woman had crept out of the shadows in the chamber.

A sudden chill ran through the room.

SEVENTEEN

Dressed in rags, the hag shuffled toward the royal chamber's center. In front of Sebastián, Cebellina stood unmoved though he detected a tremble in her shoulders while the women in the chamber hid their faces in their hands. Several children in the audience broke into tears. Except for the guards, many of the men lowered their heads or turned their gaze away from the frightening ghostly figure.

Who is she? Sebastián wondered.

No one knew whence the hag originated—and were too frightened to ask. Many years before, she had appeared soon after a pitched battle between the king and Arab slavers and their tribal allies. The king, bleeding profusely from chest and leg wounds and at point of death, found his retainers pushed aside and himself dragged away by the old woman to a dark cave and nursed back to health.

When his wounds healed, she told the king the gods had assigned her to save, protect and stay with him until his appointed time to meet them in the afterlife. Her own death would follow according to her gods' wishes.

Without being told, she was aware of the king's coming and going.

If the king needed her services, he would send a messenger to the hovel where she lived and she would appear, like a ghost conjured from the Great Beyond. She neither accepted payment or favor from the king. She made her predictions for the king and the king only.

Sebastián's body stiffened. Although alert for the slightest hostile movement, he found himself defenseless against any attack. From the corner of his eye,

118

he saw the king point to the old woman, then point at him. The king motioned for Cebellina to move aside.

She hesitated

The king frowned.

Reluctance on her face, she offered a slight bow and, head held high, joined her menina.

Her gait unsteady, the crone drew closer to Sebastián.

Only the sound of her scuffing bare feet on the hard-packed dirt floor and the loud wheeze of her breath broke the tomb of stillness in the chamber. She circled Sebastián once, then stopped an arm's length away in front of him. Her head barely reached the middle of his chest armor.

The emaciated head tilted back and her gaunt arm reached out. Long, gnarled fingers of the bony hand, splayed like a fan, landed on his forehead.

He flinched, shivered as icy chills ran down his spine. Cold, stark fear, he had never felt on any battlefield gripped his entire body at what he saw.

"Mother of God!" he gasped, "What foul demon is this?"

Her skin, thin as parchment, stretched itself over a skull-like head; eye sockets hollow and empty, her eyes a satanic glow of coals floating in the void. Sebastián's breath caught in his throat, his chest tightened, on the brink of bursting.

He could feel the color drain from his face and beads of sweat form on his forehead while streams of hot perspiration ran down his chest and back.

What was this apparition from the bowels of hell doing? His mind raced with twisted visions and thoughts. If he had his sword he would run her through. Should he try to flee? His mind ordered his feet to move, but for some reason he could not fathom, he stood rooted to the ground.

The shriveled gnome removed her hand from his forehead and slowly snaked a path with her bony fingers down to his armor. His breastplate burned and a terrifying, searing heat pressed down on his chest.

He saw her curl a finger and an image appeared to him that her appendage from the deepest bowels of earth, pushed itself through the hot metal, yet, her claw, as cold as a wintry blast pierced his flesh underneath quickly followed by her other fingers. He felt them probe, search, twist, touch his very soul. A scream crawled up his throat, but died on his lips. After what Sebastián thought an eternity had passed, she withdrew her hand. A sea of relief washed over him, the trance-like state over.

A deep, audible sigh fell from between his lips. His body trembled.

Raising his chin, he swallowed gulps of warm air until his composure returned. Cautiously, he reached up and ran his palm over his armor.

"I do not understand," he muttered. His cuirass was still strapped to his chest as it had been before she touched the armor. He touched the metal: warm, but not fireplace hot and without an opening where she had thrust her fingers. Through his flickering half-closed eyelids, his gaze settled on the dried-up old woman.

His very soul probed to its depths, bared by this witch, but to what purpose? By all the saints, what was she doing now?

Hunched over, her skeletal spine outlined under her threadbare covering, she untied a worn cloth bag from around her waist. Her bones creaking loudly in the funereal silence of the king's chamber, she squatted down on scrawny haunches. Opening the bag, she held it out in front of her and allowed the contents to tumble onto the ground.

"Seashells!" Sebastián gritted his teeth. Did his fate rest with seashells? God our Lord!

He had heard and read of witches using entrails, bones, both animal and human, but never seashells to forecast or cast spells. With fascinated intensity, Sebastián peered intently at the objects.

Leopard spots with a polished sheen curved over a rounded back and tooth-like projections ran along a creased opening. Recognition dawned.

"Cauris!" He had seen the shells, considered high in value, used as currency in other parts of Africa and India. He shot a quick glance toward Cebellina. She and the women, all wide-eyes, had channeled their attention onto the witch-foreteller.

Arms spread out like a bird of prey, the old woman hovered over the shells. The shapeless mouth would issue a cackle to one shell, offer a wheeze to a second, grunt to yet a third. All the while, unruly, Medusa-like locks on her head bobbed up and down.

Sebastián had counted sixteen shells. Apprehension over his imminent death surfaced again.

After she read the last shell, the witch lifted her head and turned her coal black eyes toward the king.

Sebastián straightened, his short reprieve over. What would befall him?

Close to the throne, seated on a cushion, Cebellina, hands pressed to her cheeks, moved her glance from the shells to the old crone, then to her father. Brows drawn tightly, eyes narrowed, the sovereign, she knew, awaited the divination by his soothsayer.

The spirit of the European had been exposed and would now be revealed. What did the shells foretell? Good omen? Bad omen? Fingers laced, then unlaced, heart beating against her chest, she watched Sebastián, turmoil in her heart, torture in her soul.

As though ready to lunge, she could see her rescuer's chest under the armor rise and fall with each heavy breath. His eyes darted now and then back to her, the hardness in them suddenly soft, filled with longing, reaching out to her, to gaze, touch, kiss.

Lips shut tight, she floundered in an agonizing maelstrom. Nothing she could do or say would change the outcome. Two of her older companions— by two years—but robust and tall—moved to Cebellina's side, watched her every move.

Ready, she sensed, to seize her arms, forcibly remove her dagger, prevent the princess from plunging the weapon into her heart or cutting her own throat in case the prediction called for death to her rescuer.

Sighing mournfully, Cebellina turned her head away and listened to the prophetess announce her revelations.

"O, King Who Lives On The Red Mountain," the old woman said, her voice shrill and raspy, "I have touched the heart and spirit of this man. He is not your enemy." A deep rumbling murmur of relief ran through the audience.

"Silence!" the king commanded.

Quiet fell.

The king's seer pointed a shaking, knobby finger at the shells. "I have also read and listened to the sacred shells, O king. They have told me how the winds of the Goddess of the Sea blew on the wings of the ship bearing him here to this land. He is looked upon with favor by the gods. With him, your enemies will see the sun rise, but on the morrow that follows, your enemies will see it rise no more. Their evil hearts will grow feathers and streams of water will wash their boot prints away. The shells have spoken."

The old woman wheezed a sigh, collected and carefully returned the shells to the worn cloth bag. Tucking the bag under a belt of frayed rope, she offered a slight bow to the king and plodded out. The audience, still silent, looked to their monarch.

Warily, Cebellina sighed away her weariness and watched the sorceress of the king leave.

Even after her father had assured his daughter his seer would never harm him or his family, Cebellina still harbored a deep fear of the old woman. In spite of his people's dread of her, the king believed in the woman's divinations; never having received any false information or revelation.

Cebellina's shoulders drooped, relieved at the favorable outcome of the shell reading and she gazed at her father. The final decision rested with him. What would he decide?

Also, what did the sorceress mean by "their evil hearts would grow feathers"? Cebellina shrugged her small shoulders. The witch never explained her prophecies. At this fortuitous moment, Cebellina felt utmost joy at the welcome prophecy. Her people were satisfied. And she would no longer sacrifice herself as the first victim of the spears aimed at her rescuer. Or any thought of plunging a dagger into her heart.

The king addressed the audience. The unblinking eyes scanned the chamber. "This man will not be killed and is free." He gestured to one of the guards as the princess hurried toward the sword and dagger. "Take the weapons to my bedchamber," the king said to the guard, sending a look of reproval to his daughter. "They will be returned to the European in due time. But he is not permitted to leave our city without my permission." Her father addressed an elderly woman, her hands folded in front, chin held high.

"Find quarters for him. Let it be known he is a guest of the king. That is my command."

The woman nodded and left.

The sovereign signaled for the tall black man to draw near and whispered in his ear.

The man nodded and stepped to the side.

"All of you may leave, except for my daughter and her companions and my Chief Scribe."

The chamber emptied save for the princess, her ladies and Sebastián in the center of the room. The black man stood by a side door, hands clasped in front. The king beckoned for his daughter to move closer to the throne.

"My beloved daughter, I see you are quite pleased. I will reserve my judgment of him. He must prove himself, in spite of what my seer has said. Go, arrange for food and drink for this man. I will assign my Chief Scribe to him. I must know more about this stranger." He tapped her on the shoulder and kissed her on the forehead.

"Heed these words. You are never to be alone with him." His finger drew an invisible circle around her companions. "All of you are to remain by her side at all times. If not, all of you will suffer the consequences."

Visibly trembling, the women bowed their heads. "Yes, Your Majesty."

His features softened "Do not disobey me, Daughter of the King Who Lives On The Red Mountain."

"Yes, Father." She offered a wide smile, tossed her hair back and marched to where Sebastián stood—but no closer than three arm lengths. She motioned with her open palm for him to follow.

EIGHTEEN

Sebastián slumped forward. His shoulders ached and burned from the weight of his armor. He grunted a deep, hoarse sigh. The look on Cebellina's face conveyed the message. His life had been spared. His fallen confidence and hope soared and he swiped a dirty sleeve across his sweaty face. Bringing his heels together, he bowed to the king, but remained in place. Most of the audience had filed out, engaged in animated conversation.

Finished gathering her shells, the old witch had shuffled past Sebastián, her skeletal head with its motionless black eyes tilted back and she offered him a toothless, knowing smile. He returned a nod and issued a silent prayer.

Pray God this sibyl and I never cross paths again and I be spared that demonic ritual of moments before. The most fearful nightmare of shapeless wraiths and minions of hell imposed on him that he could possible imagine, he ventured, hovered in her cadaverous body. A shiver convulsed his limbs.

Cebellina, about to turn and her group leave the chamber, Sebastián raised his hand.

"Please wait."

She arched an eyebrow.

Sebastián knelt with one knee on the ground and quickly drew stick figures, the palisade and footprints. He pointed to a stick figure, then to himself.

"This is me," he said then used his fingers to indicate walking away. He hoped to convey his desire to return to his base camp, retrieve his supplies. He drew a half circle and arrow to indicate his return to the king's city. He added a moon and sun to show he would leave the following morning. Cebellina and the king studied the drawings. She frowned at Sebastián as though reluctant to accept his request.

The king stood to glance briefly at the drawings. He called out to the black man who now knelt before a low table. The man rose to his feet, viewed with narrowed eyes at Sebastián for an instant before examining the drawings. While the king spoke and Sebastián watched, the man added four figures to those by Sebastián.

"I understand, sir," Sebastián said. This king, despite the reprieve and other tidings the witch may have said, would send men with his guest—assure himself the Spaniard had wandered alone in the forest and not in the company of treasure seekers and slave merchants. The king was exercising caution, acting like a true sovereign.

If slave merchants, or soldiers waited in the forest, the king's men had orders to kill the stranger in their midst and any others. But, if indeed, Sebastián traveled alone, the king's men would help him return. He nodded at the additions.

Accompanied by the black man, the king limped toward a back room with a door constructed of bamboo halves that shut behind him; the chambers were now empty save for Sebastián, Cebellina and her companions.

At the entrance to the chamber Cebellina paused and signaled with her fingers for him to follow her and her group.

He marched forward.

Tomorrow, after spending the night in the village, or city—he had not determined its size yet, he would retrace his steps in the morning to the stand of trees where he rescued Cebellina and pick up his pistol and journal at the clearing. The walk back with the king's men along, should proceed easier and faster.

What if they met other Europeans, or Arabs, or tribesmen? The thought mattered little now. He *must* leave for the beach. He needed other clothing to replace his torn blouse and pantaloons; besides, his best armor and his weapons would soon rust in the sodden heat. Upon his return, he would concentrate on communicating with her and make any other plans.

What other plans, Sebastián? He could not think of any. First and foremost, he needed a long rest. The king and his people—he hoped, had accepted him. A discernible and more favorable change in their looks, even several smiles toward him when they filed out of the chamber.

In long strides, he reached the women, but no nearer than the perimeter of the protective circle around Cebellina.

Soon, the women rounded a turn on the well-worn path of packed dirt and one of them pointed to a hut, then pointed to him.

"Ah! My new home," he said, offered a polite nod, turned and took a step toward Cebellina. The menina with her quickly shooed him away. Cebellina granted him a small smile, swiveled on her heel and left. The women rounded another bend and disappeared.

Perhaps another opportunity might rise for him to speak to her—with hand signals.

The hut, although covered by a thatched roof, boasted construction of well-matched stones jointed by mud. "They have expert masons," Sebastián whispered

Arms crossed, and about to enter, he paused in stride and gazed at the open doorway. On his way here, every dwelling he passed claimed a door. Why none for this one? He shrugged and entered to view his new quarters.

Inside, he stood still as his eyes adjusted to the cool darkness. Overhead, an unlit oil lamp hung from the ceiling. The room, about three paces wide and four paces long, led to an arched opening and another room. About to step through and investigate, a scraping sound drifted past his ears.

Sebastián spun around, reached for a weapon no longer at his waist.

In profile from a midday sun, the black man from the royal chamber stood in front of the entrance.

NINETEEN

After the stranger, the princess and the audience had departed from the Royal Chamber, Scribe Aton, the black man, followed the king back to the room after it emptied and sat anew, cross-legged on a faded crushed cushion. In front of Aton, a low table with legs a hand span in height held quills and rolls of parchments. Patient, he waited.

He saw Telemesus grimace as the king settled into his throne.

"The old wound, Sire?"

"Yes. I have to remember to rub that foul smelling unguent you prepared." A slight smile crossed the stern face. "But it works." He rubbed his chin. "First, I wish to know your thoughts regarding what my sorceress said about the stranger. Speak."

Aton paused before speaking, chose his words with care. "About her divinations, Sire. They have always borne the fruit of truth. There is no reason to disbelieve her. About the stranger. I observed the man carefully. His appearance points to an adventurer or mercenary.

"His clothing is torn and dirty, but of fine material not the coarse cotton of a peasant or lowly soldier. His feet are shod with Moorish boots. Why? I can only guess his own wore out or he killed an Arab for them. But there is pride in his bearing and manner. Although surrounded by a half dozen spears, he lacked fear. That alone shows utmost courage. I cannot speak about the sword, as yet unexamined by me. The dagger's sheath holds precious stones, the mark of a nobleman or aristocrat—"

"He may have stolen the weapon."

"Yes. If I am allowed to disagree…?"

Telemesus nodded. "Continue."

"Thank you, Sire. From all this I imagine the man a personage of substance or from a family of wealth. He wears a cuirass with an embossed coat of arms. I am unfamiliar with heraldry and am unable to decipher the origin. He may be a Spaniard or a Portuguese. I imagine the only words spoken were to the princess and her ladies—none of whom understand either Spanish or Portuguese."

The king nodded again. "I want you to question him further. Ask him to what purpose he has come. How did he arrive in Africa? Leave personal questions for later. I also want you to teach him our language."

Aton hid his discomfort at the command. "Yes, Sire."

The king shifted in his seat. "If he is a military officer *and* possess strong field experience, I want to use those skills. All of my best officers were killed in that last great battle against the Muslims. Epicydes is nineteen-years-old, willing and enthusiastic, but he lacks tactical battlefield knowledge. I want to know if the war between Spain and its four-hundred-year struggle against the Moors is over. If this stranger is someone I can trust, convince…to serve us." Telemesus stared into space. "First, of course, for my people's assurance of safety, I will assign a guard to watch him."

"I will do as you command, Sire."

"No, it is not command, but a request from a friend."

Aton stood and bowed from the waist. The king was taking him into the strictest of confidences and treating him as more than a scribe—especially after freeing Aton from slavery. For that and more, Aton would defend and sacrifice his own life for the king.

Leaving his table with pens and parchment behind, Aton padded out of the chamber and headed for the foreigner's quarters.

TWENTY

Lowering his head, the African passed through the entrance. He offered a perfunctory bow.

"*Loqui Latine?*" the man asked.

Sebastián took a step to the side. He forced a pause before answering, taken aback at hearing Latin from an African and surprised at the height of the man—a head taller than himself. The lean but sinewy black possessed questioning eyes with a penetrating expression. *He is in his late thirties, or forties?* The man's age difficult to determine because of the shaven head and smooth skin. A white tunic similar to the men in the chamber draped the African's body.

"Yes, I speak Latin," Sebastián answered in the Medieval form of the language. He ran a quick visual search over the man, eyes searching for weapons, saw none. Yet, from experience, he knew a potential assassin could hide a dagger behind his back.

Shoulders pushed back, Sebastián kept his arms by his sides, although instinct told him his visitor not an enemy. Could the man be a Moor? Many of the Moorish nobility spoke several languages.

A broad smile spread across the black's features, mouth displaying brilliant white teeth against the darkness of his face. "Praise be to the gods! You are…Portuguese? Spanish?" As quick, the smile vanished and the man's demeanor changed as though he had caught himself slipping into a too trusting a manner.

"I am a Spaniard," Sebastián said. "Formerly a captain in Queen Isabella's Royal Army. My name is Sebastián Alejandro de Avíles. Whom am I addressing?"

"My name is Aton. I am a scribe. Are your quarters satisfactory?"

"From the measure of this room, yes, quite."

"Food and drink will soon arrive for you. What are you doing in this part of Africa?"

"I was placed ashore as punishment after accusations of heresy by the Church."

"I see. Captain, where are the others?" The piercing black eyes bored in on Sebastián.

"I travel alone. I was hoping to find a suitable watering hole, then would set up a camp nearby."

"Are there others where you landed?"

"No. After leaving me ashore, the ship raised sail and left for Portugal. It will not return for me." Sebastián stared at the ground. *Will a ship ever come for me?*

"What were your plans after making camp?"

"I never reached that end. I heard screams. You know the rest."

"How long have you been warring against the Moors?"

"The wars are over. Spain forced the Moors out of the country. During those wars, I fought alongside my father and his *tercio*—regiment. I have been on and off the battlefield since the age of sixteen. I am now twenty-five. I spent nine of those years fighting against them."

Sebastián thought he detected a gleam of approval when he mentioned battlefield experience. But a veil quickly fell over the man's eyes.

"What are your plans now?"

"That depends on his majesty. Am I allowed to leave your city?" He had no idea of the size of this city, but decided against using "village" or "hamlet."

"You may walk around. Do not approach the gates. There is a river with a footbridge connecting both ends. You are forbidden to cross it."

"Understood. Scribe Aton, your king has spared my life and I thank him for that. I am beholden to him. I wish to say that I do not pose a threat to his people. I swear this on my honor as an officer and a hidalgo. I would like to ask for a favor from his majesty."

"What is that?"

"May I have my weapons returned to me?"

"Why?"

"I am a soldier. Experience and practice makes the swordsman. If I do not practice every day, I will soon lose my skill. Also, even though my sword and dagger are made of fine Toledo steel, they must be kept clean and dry or rust will invade the metal. It is one reason I must return to my base for other personal belongings. Since I am alone in this country, I use my weapons for survival, protection." Sebastián omitted reference to his other weapons. His life at the moment rested on sufferance by the king. Why raise more suspicion about his presence in the country?

Another matter Sebastián omitted. Perhaps due to his hunger and lack of rest, but he could have sworn someone had followed him to the hut as soon as he left the king's chamber.

"I will present your request to my lord king," Aton said.

"Thank you. May I say, your Latin is excellent."

Aton acknowledged with a wave of the hand. Sebastián thought he detected a slight relaxation of the former stiffness in the scribe's shoulders. A good sign; easing his own tension.

Both turned as a woman strolled through the opening.

"We will speak again, Captain." Aton nodded to her and walked out.

TWENTY-ONE

The woman held two small jars in one hand, an ivory-handled short blade in the other. For shaving, he assumed. A folded white garment and plain white cotton sash rested over the other. At arm's length, she handed them to Sebastián and shrank away. She pointed to his body and pinched her nose, lips pursed in a look of disapproval.

Tossing back glossy black hair flecked with gray, she raised her chin haughtily and marched out.

Sebastián smiled sheepishly. He hadn't realized how badly his body and clothing reeked of stale sweat and encrusted dirt; many months at sea had deadened his sense of smell by the surrounding stench of death, unwashed bodies and brine. The lion's dried blood added to the smell.

From the time he landed on the beach, a bath in fresh water and wash of garments crossed his mind, but with survival his primary concern, a clean body and fresh clothing rested at the bottom of his list.

Placing jars and tunic on a wooden shelf built into the wall, he decided to examine the rest of his quarters. The second room was the same size as the first and bare...except...wooden plugs hammered into the walls for clothing, a three-legged stool and...alongside a far wall, he spied an almost forgotten object from his life in Spain.

"A real bed!" Not the threadbare, filthy hammock on board the ship.

He ran over and passed his hands over the dark wood of the frame. Though scarred and gouged, the bed showed the markings of skilled craftsmanship. The artisan had sanded each piece of wood to the smoothness of glass. Planks lay lengthwise with crosspieces to support and hold them in place. Knee-high bedposts sat at the four corners, a lion's head carved at the top of each post, a claw at the bottom. No headboard existed. A bulky form draped the foot of the bed—straw, stuffed into a woven cloth sack.

"I haven't slept in a bed in over two years!" he murmured, unrolled the lumpy mattress and tamped the lumps into a reasonable flatness. Then he reached up and unfastened the leather straps of his breastplate, grunted with relief from the lost weight and allowed the armor to fall onto the straw mattress. Rubbing the sore muscles in his shoulders, he glanced at the bed, hounded by desire for sleep, yet perplexity of spirit drove him on. "Let us see what remains."

Save for the bed, a spartan bareness inhabited the interior. Suffused sunlight from two windows in the mud walls filtered through a painted cloth stretched over each opening. Reinforced holes stitched into the material, fitted over wooden lugs built into the walls held the cloth in place.

Curiosity drew him nearer. Figures had been painted on the coarse cotton fibers woven in such an intricate manner, pinpoints of light pierced the fiber, yet the pattern reduced heat, kept insects at bay and foiled prying eyes.

"It is wondrous," he said, observing the scenes on the cloth: domestic animals, women at household tasks, or infants at their breasts, and those strange symbols again. Closer examination revealed the artist had taken pains to show the hourglass figures and painted eyes of the women.

"Cebellina!" he uttered with a smile. He lifted a lug, lifted a portion of the curtain aside and peered out. A wooden footbridge spanned the glittering surface of a middling stream curving its way to the south. On the opposite bank, cattle grazed and oxen dragged ploughs. Also across the stream, behind a fence, he counted half a dozen horses.

"Arabians!" Even from a distance, he recognized the exquisite breed, having ridden them many times. What were they doing here? Part of their domestic animals? Captured from slavers? How he missed his mare, Aliento!

On the near bank, groups of men busied themselves with bathing—no women or children in sight. Separate areas reserved for women and children to bathe, he assumed.

A slight breeze filtered through the window, fluttered the curtain, enough to lessen the mid-afternoon heat and Sebastián shut his eyes. He took several deep breaths, drew the cloth back across the opening and pushed the lugs back in place. About to throw the new garment on the bed, and curious, he pressed the fresh white folds to his nose.

The clean, sun-dried smell of an early spring struck his nostrils. Spring! In Castile! The scent from orange groves after a rain, whitewashed houses…how very long ago it seemed.

He shook the homesickness off. Cebellina and her companions, he recalled, and other women who had passed by him, left a pleasant fragrance, an inviting ambience behind them.

Equally so, the woman who brought him the clothing. Did they bathe in perfume?

Forcing a deep exhale to erase the longing for a warm body next to his, he threw the new garment on the bed along with the jars. He shrugged off his blouse and tossed the torn cloth on the bed, sat on the edge and removed the Moorish boots and the torn, dirty, laddered hose. He would keep the pantaloons on. None of the inhabitants he had seen in the chamber or encountered on the street exhibited nudity.

Flipping his new clothing over his shoulder, he opened one of the jars and poured a few drops into his palm, rubbing it between his fingers. It foamed and felt like soap. His eyes widened. Liquid soap, the first he had ever seen— and in the middle of the forest!

The second jar held a fragrant oil—to be rubbed on the skin after the bath—he assumed, never having used the liquid. Both grasped in one hand, he marched barefoot toward the river.

Shortly before reaching the bank, he felt the hairs on back of his neck rise. He took a step forward, suddenly stopped and spun around.

Ten paces back, a man armed with sword and spear, also halted. He and the soldier exchanged stares.

The king has posted a guard to watch me. A precaution ordered by the sovereign to trace the stranger's movements. Sebastian shrugged and walked on past canvas-covered stalls with baskets of nuts, dried fruit, while others stalls boasted beads of lapis lazuli and semi-precious stones of varying colors. Buyers haggled with the vendors.

At the water's edge he paused and, scratching his beard, scanned behind him and both sides of the river. No one displayed any interest in him—as far as he could tell, only the guard watched Sebastián.

Several men nosily bathed, most cast him polite, cursory looks. Instinct told him to ease his caution. No danger lurked.

With a nod and polite bow to the onlookers, he tossed the fresh garments on a ledge and, pantaloons on, waded into the river, found the water warm, the current steady but lazy.

When waist high in the stream, he poured some of the liquid soap over his person and washed himself—watching crusted grime and dried sweat floating downstream. On shore, clapping and laughter erupted from several men drying themselves off. Sebastián smiled, continued with his vigorous scrubbing of body and pantaloons as his thoughts reverted back to the ship.

On board the caravel, once the supply of soapwort, a perennial herb common in Europe and used for washing clothing and bodies—a rarity by the populace—dwindled to a handful, another trusty sea custom surfaced.

A sailor would tie a rope around his bundle of dirty garments and throw the line over the stern of the ship. The movement of the bound clothing through the water, hopefully, removed the stench of disease, death, and also some of the vermin, lice in particular, infesting every fold of clothing, body creases, hair, beard, even the eyebrows.

Sebastián recollected an old sailors' tale.

"When you cross the equinoctial line, the lice will die!" sailors claimed. But the demise of the despised vermin never happened and the parasites lived happily on.

Hauled back on board, the seamen draped the wash over whatever limited space available on deck.

Once dried, blouse and pantaloons were shaken vigorously enough to remove the dried salt from the seawater. But grains of salt always wedged themselves in the fibers, eventually caused intense itch and rashes.

To avoid itching—the men battled enough vermin—most of the crew went months without bathing or washing their clothing. The rest of the seamen masked body odors by liberal use of scented oil brought on board in jugs for that use—until the oils also ran out.

Sebastián shook himself back to the present.

Body cleansed, pantaloons clean, he waded back to shore. Selecting a flat rock to lay his clothing down, he made ready to stretch out on the warm stone to allow generous warm sun to dry the wetness off his body.

Suddenly, a man ran out of the stream, picked up a spear from the ground and, weapon held at waist level, charged headlong at him.

"What the devil...?" Sebastián immediately wrapped his new garment around his forearm, left a portion of cloth hanging loose—to catch the spear point—and crouched, ready to ward off the attack. If possible, disarm the attacker and kill him with his own spear.

A figure on his right dashed past him—the king's guard. He lifted the man's spear with his own and held him at bay with the point of his spear.

135

Shouts erupted between the guard and the would-be assassin. Other men collected, joined the guard in what Sebastián assumed a berating of the man's unprovoked attack.

Two other guards appeared, grasped the half-naked attacker by the arms and led him away. The man, in his late thirties, muscular with close cropped hair, argued with the soldier and muttered loudly, cast angry glances at Sebastián.

"Thank you," Sebastián said to the soldier guarding him.

Face impassive, the soldier returned to a spot of shade under a tree and continued to keep his close watch over Sebastián

Why did the man attack? All the other men had either ignored Sebastián, or offered polite nods. Who was he?

Swallowing some deep breaths to restore calm, erase anger after a possible encounter with death, Sebastián thought himself sufficiently dry and dressed himself in his new clothing. The folds fit like a Roman or Greek toga he had seen in old manuscripts. Also, the fresh, clean clothing, he thought, eased the rising tension.

While walking back to his quarters, he asked any passerby willing to stop, words for house, river, trees by pointing to the objects. By the end of the day he had learned the words for husband, daughter and father. Also, by countless gestures and drawings in the earth later, he learned that the man in the large structure was the king and Cebellina's father!

TWENTY-TWO

Sebastián had assumed Cebellina a woman of high birth, but reality of her more exalted position more than he had dreamed. The young woman he rescued, a princess! His head swam. He thanked Providence for granting him the good luck on finding and rescuing her. Exhilaration set in and, with polite waving of his hands and nods to the villagers, he aimed his long strides toward his quarters.

Rounding a bend in the path, he paused. Several yards away, he spotted Cebellina under a thatched roof, covering a building three times the length of his hut. She sat in the midst of her menina and three older women. The covering over her was open on all sides and visible to any passerby. Sebastián slowed his pace and watched.

If prodded by his appointed guard to leave, he would comply at once and without argument or discussion. Nothing must mar his status as a guest.

The women spotted him and one of them bent over and spoke to Cebellina. She gestured with her palm down to the guard as though not to interfere and everyone returned to whatever they were doing.

Under the roof, mats woven from palm fronds or twisted vines carpeted the ground while low wooden stools and dozens of potion jars the size of those in his hand lay scattered about.

Out of the corner of an eye he saw one of the menina in the process of emptying a basket of its supply of fish. Deftly, she cut head and tail and prepared the catch.

Sebastián wet his lips enviously. A full meal had not touched his mouth in many months.

For most hours of the day after his abandonment, his life in the balance, hunger added to his misery. Over and over, he had ignored the urgent growls from his stomach. Now ravenous pangs clawed at his insides as a reminder. Thoughts of hunger forced aside, he continued his observation.

Preparations at another table surprised him and caught his curiosity.

Two of the older menina were scraping scales of fish off into a bowl. The youngster from the clearing collected the bowl and poured some type of oil over the scales. Then with a small stone pestle and in slow circular motions, she ground the ingredients in a mortar until a mixture the thickness of syrup formed.

Cebellina, back straight and steps graceful, walked over and sat on a stool.

One of her companions sat opposite her with the bowl in her lap. From the table, she picked up a narrow brush the length of an index finger and dipped its bristles into the liquid. Brush held like a quill, her companion delicately applied the liquid to the eyelids of the princess.

"Ah! So that's how they obtain the silver color!" Sebastián said in a mixture of amusement and amazement. He had seen the kohl used by Arab women and the henna brushefd the hands and feet of Indian women, but never witnessed their preparation or application for body adornment.

The princess picked up a polished bronze mirror and viewed herself from the front then the sides, turned and favored him with the hint of a warm smile. As she turned, a finger of sunlight pointing through a crack in the roof above touched her eyelids.

Instantly, bright points of light reflected from the lids. Sebastián imagined the languid eyes underneath moving in their slow, tantalizing rhythm.

"It's truly bewitching!" he whispered to himself, chafing at his lack of knowledge of the language. How would he tell her how exquisite she looked, how her eyes stroked his with a velvet glance? How her mere presence swept away his loneliness? Ruefully shaking his head, he picked up his pace and walked on.

Farther along the way, he spied two older, women, veils over their heads and faces, picking up several honeycombs from a stack of beehives. One of the women moved to a table, held a square of the wax over a small flame until softened and broke off a piece. She dipped the soft beeswax into a pot, withdrew the fragment and molded the wax into a cone. She eyed the workmanship, nodded and placed the cone alongside others on a burnished bronze plate.

A second plate held more of the collection. From this plate, the second woman picked up two cones, placed one in the middle of her head, the other on her companion's head.

From where he stood, Sebastián caught the scent of a medley of perfumes—perhaps jasmine, Egyptian musk, or some other fragrance unknown to him. He snapped his fingers.

"That is how the fragrance lingers and trails after them as they walk. Ingenious!" Under a hot sun, the thumbnail-size cone slowly melted and released the scents. Chin lifted, he inhaled deeply of the sweetened air and marched back to his new home.

Back inside, new clothing on, refreshed physically and spiritually after the cleansing bath he decided to explore the rest of the dwelling, then shave off his itchy beard.

At the end of a three-pace long hallway he happened on a door. It worked on a pivot and the latch could be opened from the outside by a cord. For inside security, a wooden bar was lowered between two sockets.

"Marvelous." Sebastián said. "But why is there a back door and not a front one?" Dismissing the question, he walked into a former garden; leaves of whatever had been grown now withered and brown among sprouting weeds. A waist-high fence of gnarled branches separated the area from his neighbors—none of which were visible at this time.

An obelisk three hand spans high sat at the center of the garden and served the household as a timepiece. The long shadow indicated four o'clock in the afternoon.

While shaving, he pulled his thoughts together, wishing he had his journal to note all that had happened.

Near the end of his shaving, the elderly woman from earlier in the day passed through the doorway. In each hand she balanced earthenware dishes. One held vegetables—he recognized lentils and onions—and a wooden spoon, the other, smoking meat. She handed both to Sebastián, acknowledged his profuse thanks with a slight nod, arched an eyebrow at his clean-shaven face and padded out, her waist-length white hair beauteous in movement. Even in advancing age, the innate beauty of these women defied the ravages of time.

Out of long habit from the battlefield and on board the *São Gabriel*, but for the briefest instant, he scanned the food for worms or swimming insects—a common occurrence on battlefields during the wars against the Moors and long months at sea. He saw none. Remorse at his action struck. He bowed his head.

"Almighty Father, these people have provided me with shelter and food. I have insulted their generosity by my unkind and ungrateful thoughts. I ask forgiveness. I thank Thee for this bounty." Without another glance to the food, he wolfed the fare down.

Soon, intensity of the previous days overwhelmed and yawns of unshakable weariness took control.

Pale shafts of sunlight still played through the window coverings when he sank into bed—after placing the small stool by his bedside to use as a weapon against an intruder or assassin—if he woke in time and in spite of the guard outside his doorway.

Twice during the night, awakened by barking dogs, or perhaps by sounds from the surrounding forest, Sebastián sprang from bed, grasped the stool, ready to defend himself. Outside, only the shadowy form of the guard crossed the doorway. Sinking back into bed, drenched in sweat, weighted by exhaustion, his eyelids finally closed near morning.

TWENTY-THREE

After a night that refused to die and restless sleep, Sebastián tumbled from bed, reached for an absent sword.

Dazed, as though failure of consciousness had occurred and unsure of where he was, Sebastián stood still. Gradually, he felt a smile crease his face. The chattering of children awakened him, not the screams of dying men or creak of ancient timbers.

Bright beams of white sunlight streamed at a low angle through the open doorway of the hut. The trills of songbirds filled the air. A new day challenged for him. He bowed his head. "Thank you, God our Lord, for granting me one more day of life."

He crossed himself, dressed and, about to strap on his chest armor— years of self-imposed discipline still held strong—he decided against its use. The appearance in public would be viewed as hostile. At the hut's entrance he lowered his head and viewed himself.

"I wear an Egyptian-like tunic, and Moorish boots." What would his parents in Spain say?

With the Church engaging in violent tirades against the remaining Moors or anything or anyone from North Africa and promulgating "purity of blood," his father, and especially his mother, would never have approved.

Outside the doorway, he greeted the impassive guard, and, intent on a long walk and cool deliberation on his present situation—a prisoner yet not a prisoner, he strode forward. A few paces later, he saw the scribe Aton approach.

When abreast of him, Aton asked in Latin, "You slept well, Captain?"

Sebastián forced a smile. "Yes, much better than on a rolling ship." He lied to hide the discomfort from a sleepless night. How many more before night granted him a peaceful sleep?

Aton waved Sebastián's guard away. "Would you follow me, Captain?"

"Of course." Sebastián sighed with relief, more comfortable with the scribe than with an armed escort. He searched the scribe's eyes and demeanor for any hint of what awaited him. Aton's face remained inscrutable. Each stride long, they made for the king's chamber.

Along the way, they encountered inhabitants up and about and Sebastián greeted all with a cordial wave—most of the women returned his gesture. Some of them still held their chins high, not for outright haughtiness, but out of normal character, a facet adding to their regal bearing. The children's mouths gaped, eyes widened in curiosity.

At a bend in the street, Aton and Sebastián passed a bakery, the enticing aroma of baking bread wafting through the air. The baker glanced briefly at the pair, ignored Sebastián's wave and returned to grinding grain.

They passed other men carrying animal hides draped over their shoulders and soldiers armed with swords in metal scabbards.

All nodded to Aton, but cast wary looks at Sebastián.

I am a stranger in their midst. If I were a resident of this compound, I would also be suspicious.

At the royal chamber, he hoped to receive permission to leave, perhaps have his weapons returned. Then bid farewell to Cebellina.

At the prescribed distance of three arm lengths from her and with only a wave of my hand, of course. The thought of seeing her again erased anxiousness on what awaited him.

Two guards with scarred metal shields and crossed spears guarded the entrance to the king's chamber.

At Aton's approach, they uncrossed the weapons and allowed the scribe and Sebastián to enter. Sebastián marched into the center of the room, and quickly erased the smile on his face. Although he found this court less rigid than the stiff and somber Spanish Royal Court, why chance a reprimand or worse by wearing a presumptuous smile?

Cebellina paced in front of the throne, agitation on her face.

Seeing Sebastián enter, she began to speak. The king raised his hand and angrily uttered a word to her.

Sebastián had heard the word used several times by mothers to misbehaving children. He knew it meant "No."

Arms folded across her chest, she shot Sebastián a look of helplessness and, with her menina trailing behind, Cebellina left the chamber. Were those tear drops he detected at the corner of her painted eyes?

He peered at the king. Was her disagreement with her father about him? If so, what did it regard? *Sebastián, what does it matter?* The time was not opportune to ponder the problem. The sooner he left, the sooner his return to this city.

He bowed to the king and waited for permission from Aton to address the sovereign.

"You may speak, Captain," Aton said. "I will translate for my lord."

"Your Majesty," Sebastián began, "I wish to thank you for sparing my life; for offering me shelter, food and clothing. If I am permitted to return here, I would like to make my way back to the beach where I landed. I have hidden my personal belongings there. Also, I left my journal and espingarda…"

Aton raised an eyebrow in question.

"A small harquebus…?"

Aton nodded.

Sebastián continued. "If it remains on the ground rain and moisture will render the weapon worthless. My journal will turn into a bundle of pulp." He cleared his throat. "May I have my weapons back?"

"No," Aton translated. "You will be allowed to retrieve your belongings. Any weapons must be turned over to the guards that will accompany you. I will also allow you to return here and reside with my people. My scribe has revealed all of what you said to him. I trust his judgment."

Elation coursed through Sebastián.

The king stood, gathered his tunic around him. "I have spoken. Aton will see to the rest."

Aton stepped closer to Sebastián. "You are to leave immediately—"

Sebastián raised a hand. "I beg your indulgence and apologize for interrupting. May I return to my quarters and strap on my armor?"

"No. Your armor is of much higher quality than those worn by the king's men. It will make them feel…inadequate…unworthy to protect you."

Sebastián swallowed his pride. "I understand."

Outside the royal chamber, Aton pointed to some of the king's guards. "Those men will accompany you."

Sebastián glanced at the men's armor. Lappets of leather over quilted cotton tunics underneath, they protected against native arrows, perhaps a spear thrust. But against hackbuts or espingardas they were worthless. If attacked by slavers or Portuguese with European weaponry, they would all quickly die.

He groaned inwardly.

Six men, taller than other soldiers he had seen, detached themselves from a ring of the king's guards and formed two on each side of Sebastián, one in front, one in the rear. Arms raised, the men saluted the king and the group exited the chamber.

Had Cebellina been asking her father to forbid Sebastián's leaving? Or, Sebastián hoped, she wished to accompany the European back to the beach? The thought moved him and fed his desire to speed his return. As much as he would have treasured her company, if he were king, he would have also refused her request. The forest held too many unknown dangers—even for six armed men. The question still remained on why she had wandered in the forest by herself.

He prayed the men with him were skilled in warfare and knowledgeable about the surrounding forest. If only the dispatch case with his maps had been returned…he would share the information.

Well, he would try to have them agree to a forced march to the beach and his base camp and back to the city; cut travel time in half. Her mere presence in his mind now enough to send his pulses racing.

The men stopped to pick up provisions for the journey. He watched the men kiss the women he assumed wives and embrace children in tearful farewells. Sebastián had always known what enemy he faced. These men ventured out not knowing whether wild animals prowled, blocked their path, hostile natives lurked, or collided with marauding Arabs on *razzia*—slave-hunting expeditions. He cast off the miasma, hoisted his share of food packets over his shoulders and he and the six guards marched past the gate.

A few yards outside, he turned and raised an eyebrow in surprise.

Cebellina stood by one of the portals, along with her menina. How did she know about his leaving? In quick strides, he shortened the distance between them.

Immediately, the same handsome and imposing woman, her height equal to Sebastián's, intercepted him, placed herself directly in front of him and crossed her arms, disapproval on her face.

"What damnation!" Peering over the woman's shoulder, he realized the futility of conversation with Cebellina. How could he convince her further of his deep sincerity to return?

His guards called out and motioned for him to follow.

"I know you do not understand my words, but if Almighty God wills it, I give my solemn promise to return to you," he said. "I pledge this on my honor."

He could feel the eagerness spread on his face. Chin raised, he drank in her fragrance of exotic scents and those of the women wafting through the air.

Fervent hope she understood lifted his spirits and Sebastián ran through the open gate to join the king's men.

At the edge of the forest he stopped and turned his head.

"Yes!" In the distance, beside the open gate stood the small figure of Cebellina. He waved with his free hand. She returned his wave. Her companions then hurried her inside and the gate swung shut behind her.

He shook his head, joined the king's men and after leaving the wide clearing, they plunged into the lush undergrowth. His mind apace with his long, marching strides, Sebastián wondered at all the incredible events in his life over the passage of only a week's time.

Abandoned in a savage, unknown land as punishment. By purest luck and the Hand of Providence had killed a lion, discovered the truth of a myth in the form of a woman of the most exquisite beauty. Finally, his life spared by a witch reading seashells!

"What living man could boast the same?" he muttered, passing under a canopy of trees. If he were to relate his adventures in Europe, people would call him a liar as they had called the adventurous Marco Polo. Well, no matter what happened to him in the future, his moment in the forest with her when she gazed at him with her liquid eyes would burn in his memory forever.

Determined to pursue this incredible dream and no time to waste, he strode forward, engaged the king's men.

"What do you call that?" he asked, raising his eyebrows in a questioning manner and pointing to a guard's clothing, then the weapons.

He must learn their language as quickly as possible. He must speak to Cebellina. So many words lodged in his heart he wished to say. Then a disturbing thought ran through his mind.

What if the king had ordered Sebastián disposed of while in the forest?

TWENTY-FOUR

Sebastián stopped pacing and glanced at the ground in front and behind him. A shallow furrow from the entrance of the hut to the window had formed from his incessant pacing. A fine layer of dust covered his Moorish boots.

Six weeks had passed since Sebastián returned from the beach—alive—with all of his supplies and settled himself into his hut. A permanent lodging?

The day after his return from the beach, Aton appeared at Sebastián's doorway. Cradled in the scribe's arms were Sebastián's sword and dagger, Cardona's weapons and the longbow.

"May I have permission to enter?" the scribe asked.

Sebastián waved a hand, hiding his elation at the sight of his weapons. He reached out for them. From the age of sixteen—other than at home in Spain—the weapons had never left his sight.

"His Majesty," the scribe said, handing them over, "has decided to grant your request for the return of your weaponry.

"You may practice with your sword or dagger but are forbidden to wear them on your person while walking through the streets or until my lord sovereign decrees otherwise. Also, the sentry will no longer remain on duty outside your quarters. In two days I will return to teach you the customs and language of his people." Aton turned to leave.

"A moment, Scribe Aton. I have been here many weeks and still do not know his majesty's name."

"His given name is Telemesus. But he is addressed as The King Who lives On The Red Mountain."

"Ah...one more question I have not mentioned. Soon after I arrived, I went to bathe...there was an incident at the river...without my weapons to defend myself...how will I...?"

"His Majesty has made it clear to all that you are his guest. The man who attacked you is called Sinumet, a former suitor of the princess and has been punished. He will not bother you again."

For a moment Sebastián thought about asking what happened to his attacker, then banished the idea. What difference would it make? In spite of the bodyguard, he would remain watchful during his walks around the city. How many other suitors lay in wait?

"I will return in two days." Aton spun on his heel and left.

Immediately, Sebastián set to fencing practice, deciding against asking one of the king's soldiers as a partner. His longer sword against their shorter Greek weapons would put the men at a disadvantage.

With a glance at the obelisk, he feinted and parried for three hours. Often during his swordsmanship, images of Castile wandered through the corridors of his mind. A few, those of his parents, harvest times and the festivals, bright as sunshine, others, like the burning at the stake those accused of witchcraft or heresy, cast a pall of dark clouds over him. The latter overcome by more strenuous fencing practice or thoughts of Cebellina.

True to this word, Aton, a low wooden table cradled under one arm and a rolled up cloth under the other, appeared on the appointed day to instruct the Sebastián in the language and customs of the sovereign's people.

At this time, intent on the lessons, Sebastián yet again shook his head clear and repeated words and phrases to Aton. The scribe knelt on the cloth in front of the low table. He had previously unrolled the cloth to reveal sheets of parchment, pots of ink with blackened corks and freshly sharpened quills.

"I am Sebastián Alejandro de Avíles from Estremadura, Spain and former Captain in Queen Isabel's army." He used Spanish words for those he could not translate, speaking in the language of The King Who Lives On The Red Mountain.

His appointed tutor nodded approval. "Most of your speech used Spanish words. Now, let us repeat the Greek word for speech—it is easier than Coptic Egyptian. For example, *épos*."

"*E-pos.*"

Aton shook his head. "No. It is not *e-pos*. It is *eh-pos.*"

"*Eh-pos*," Sebastián answered, "I thank you for your patience with me."

Aton, his baldpate black as polished ebony, and unsmiling, leaned back on his heels.

"When my lord sovereign commanded me to teach you his language as many hours as I thought necessary, I thought of this duty as punishment for some unknown crime I had committed against his majesty. You appeared to me as an uncouth, arrogant soldier, with the look and filth of a pig. I have reversed my opinion. As for your lessons. You pronounce poorly, mix words, but are an apt pupil. Continue."

"Please give me pause," Sebastián said. He squatted down in front of the scribe. "For three weeks, I have neither interrupted you nor asked questions. I know your name is Aton, but you are not of these people. Where do you come from?"

Aton smiled, his smile bright, teeth sparkling against the dark skin. The scribe settled himself more comfortably on the cloth. His words flowed smooth and precise.

"I am a Nubian. I was the servant of an Arab sheik and his slave merchants. No, I wish to correct myself. I was not a servant but a slave, subject to starvation and beatings whenever I displeased the sheik or one of his misbegotten wives. I was kept from being sold because of my natural ability for learning languages. I speak Portuguese, Arabic, Greek, Latin and several Bantu dialects and my lord sovereign's tongue—which mixes Greek and Egyptian."

"You are very learned," Sebastián said.

Aton shrugged. "Queen Cleopatra spoke nine languages. Extraordinary woman. Let me continue. My knowledge of Bantu dialects facilitated the slave merchants in their dealings with different tribal chiefs." The edges of Aton's mouth carved down and anger crossed the scribe's visage.

"There are some African chiefs more cruel than slavers. When they have no more captives to sell, they sell their own people for gold or European weapons! Horrible." He inhaled a deep breath and went on. "To explain how I came to be here with the king and his people. I was captured after a battle between Arab slavers and my lord sovereign. Brought before him, I spoke to the king in his own language—a few words, but he understood. I told him I was a teacher and scribe. He spared my life and gave me my freedom. But, alas, where could I go? My tribe is no longer; all are dead or sold into slavery. I am the last of my family. I chose to stay. Let us continue with our lessons."

Sebastián leaned forward. "Two more questions, if I may."

Aton sighed as though annoyed. "Very well. Proceed."

"Tell me about these people. Who are they? Where do they come from?"

Aton's stern looks softened. "Ah, a history lesson! In the year 331 before the birth of your Jesus Christ, Alexander The Great finished his conquest of Egypt and Northern Africa. But anxiousness fired his desire to return to Macedonia and engage Darius and the Kingdom of Persia in one last battle. However, he faced a difficult decision. From the many battles, several dozen of his finest officers and best men lay in their tents—many with grievous wounds, others with a host of ills. Should they risk a sea voyage fraught with storms and pirates? Or choose the endless leagues of a land route through burning deserts and hostile tribesmen?

"The men, mostly Macedonians, Greeks, a group of Persians and others, elected to stay. Alexander appointed Ptolemy, a Greek noble and friend, ruler of Egypt. Aristotle wrote that when Alexander bid farewell to his troops, tears ran down the young conqueror's cheeks.

"Eventually, he destroyed Darius and the Persian Kingdom. Many years later, the Ptolemy family gave birth to the Queen of Egypt, Cleopatra. These former soldiers of Alexander, a number of them skilled in working with silver, gold and precious stones, others, experienced in building roads and cities, prospered, married local women, both noble and peasant. Centuries passed. The unions produced the ancestors of those you see today. When Islam swept across North Africa, the offspring of Alexander's men refused to accept Mohammed and his teachings and fought the Muslims. But, greatly outnumbered, these people packed their belongings and moved to a range of mountains. They built a new city on one of them: The Red Mountain. Captain, my Lord Sovereign will relate the rest to you. Let us continue our studies."

"Please, tell me about the princess."

Aton peered into his pupil's eyes; the scribe's face unreadable. "She is my pupil as well as the young women who accompany her at all times. She is a treasure to her father and to her people. I have watched you. The features on your face soften and your eyes speak tenderness. You look for her...run after her."

Sebastián slapped the small table, shook the inkpots and quill pens. "My intentions are honorable! I only wish...Has not love ever touched your heart?"

Aton sat unshaken.

"Physical love," the scribe said, "is a deep sickness; temporary in pleasure. Carnal knowledge should be only for procreation. For many, it weakens the mind, tortures the body and consumes all in its path. I am a teacher, scholar and scribe as were my father and grandfather. My love is knowledge. I am content."

"Does she have any suitors or is she...betrothed?"

"Since the age of fifteen she has had many suitors." Aton paused. "One of them was Sinumet, the man who ran at you with a spear..."

Sebastián pursed his lips. How many more rivals waited, ready to stab him?

"...but she is not betrothed. She has rejected them all, in spite of the queen and the king's wishes. I have answered your two questions, let us continue."

Sebastián's heart beat faster. Cebellina was not betrothed. About her mother... "You mentioned the queen. I have never seen her."

Sadness appeared in Aton's eyes and his shoulders slumped. "The most gracious queen is dead. Shortly before her people arrived here, a battle ensued with slavers. During the conflict, her majesty and her ladies found themselves separated from the king. The queen, surrounded by Arab slave merchants and their African allies, and about to be captured chose death before slavery. She leaped over a cliff to her death. Her ladies held hands and followed their queen. The tragedy still haunts my lord sovereign. From that day, he smiles but rarely. I have answered your two questions with time spent away from your lessons. I must leave."

"A moment please." Sebastián bowed his head. How tragic for Cebellina, to lose a parent in that manner. Damn all slavers to darkest hell! "Two more questions."

Aton rolled his eyes. "That will add up to four questions. Continue."

"Thank you," Sebastián said. "The symbols I see painted on utensils and cloth, sometimes a bird, a hand, what do they mean?"

Aton stood. "The Greeks call them *hieroglyphikos* which means 'sacred symbols'. Their meaning has been lost over the centuries Even the priest cannot tell you. Next question."

"I...ah...will—" Should he ask Aton to act on his behalf, ask for a meeting between Sebastián and Cebellina? Act as a messenger? No, absolutely not. The request would humiliate the tutor. *That* was the real question he wanted answered. But Sebastián must seek his own way to meet the princess.

"It is a small matter. I can wait for another time."

"Then, until the morrow." Aton left the hut with Sebastián wondering how to overcome all the restrictions and obstacles facing him to meet the princess—by herself.

TWENTY-FIVE

In the midst of his lessons with Aton, a shadow crossed the hut's entrance. Sebastián whirled, reached for the sword laying by his side.

"Hold! I am Abydos, the king's messenger. My lord, the king requests the captain's presence at once." The messenger pointed to Aton. "Scribe, you must come also."

Sebastián welcomed the interruption from his lengthy lessons. What did the king wish to see him about? Long hours of tutoring left precious little time. Whatever leisure time remained, he practiced with his sword.

At the Royal Chamber, Sebastián stopped in the center of the room, crossed both arms across his chest in obeisance like Spanish courtiers at court, bowed his head and awaited the king's pleasure.

Telemesus sat on the edge of his throne, elbow resting on his knee, listening to a man covered from head to toe in a blanket of dust. When the man finished, the king called to a guard. "Have this runner be given food and drink." He dismissed both with a wave of the hand.

The monarch sat back in his chair and rubbed the scar on his face for a short spell, then said, "Everyone has my permission to leave," the king said, "Except my Chief Scribe and the Spaniard."

Men and women filed out of the chamber. Many of the men shook their heads, others stared straight ahead as though numb. Some of the women brushed away tears. The king motioned for both Aton and Sebastián to draw near.

"Aton, you will advise when asked and translate."

"Yes, my lord."

The king fixed his gaze on Sebastián. His voice, though hoarse and tired, filled the almost empty room. "Once we lived in a grand city with houses made of stone, our markets filled with bounty from the earth. Now we live in mud huts, dirt gathers on our feet wherever we walk and we eat only what we grow. Our fields boasted horses and cattle without number, my people as many as leaves in the forest. We felt safe in our mountain fastness and for countless years repelled the attacks of our enemies." The king's features hardened.

"Then the slavers came with cannon, harquebus and pistol. Their cannon balls breached our walls. We fought and won, but many of my people died." The king paused and stared into space.

Sebastián stood at attention and silent, waiting to hear the reason for the hasty summons.

Finally, the king broke the silence. "I sought advice from the gods and from my prophetess. I was told that we would be swept away like dust in the wind if we remained where we lived near the Red Mountains. We had to take what we could and leave the rest behind. I cannot recall how long we traveled or how many more of my people were lost. We have been safe until now because we have an arc of high mountains behind our backs, vast swamps infested with the poisonous vapors of Roman fever lying to the south, thick forest north and the great sea in front. How much longer we will remain at peace I do not know and the sorceress cannot tell me.

"I have just received word from one of my outposts located two days march from here. My soldiers in turn received the ill tidings from a friendly tribe that trades with us and provides information—for gold. A force of slavers is asking questions from the one of the other tribes.

They want to know where we are and how to find a path over the mountains to our city. I wish to know from you, Captain, what you can tell me about the harquebus and any ideas about defense against these weapons. Speak."

Sebastián felt this chest swell with pride. The king was taking him—a stranger and foreigner—into his confidence and asked advice in an area Sebastián could boast mastery.

"Your Majesty, I will give you the advantages first, then the disadvantages of harquebus also known as hackbuts and about pistols—known in Spain as espingardas. It applies to all. In an attack from a massed formation of hackbuts, these weapons wreak havoc not only with their power, but sheer intimidation. Individually, a hackbut is highly inaccurate, effective only with skilled marksmen.

153

In this climate, they require great care or rust before your eyes. In addition, any type of wetness renders the powder useless as sand. Last, hackbuts are costly.

"My advice, Sire, is to seek as much information about this group of slavers as possible, then use a posture of defense with tactics of secrecy, stealth and surprise. Majesty, if you will permit me the use of a dozen of your best archers, I may have a way of turning the knowledge of the hackbut and its limitations against this enemy." Hands held to the sides, Sebastián waited for the king's answer.

"Explain yourself."

The opening Sebastián had hoped for, prayed for, had arrived. Perhaps if he succeeded in this effort, he would ask the king permission to speak to Cebellina without a barrier of half a dozen women watching his every move.

The king's dark eyes studied his guest as though speculatively. Slowly, the sovereign nodded his acceptance.

"If I may return to my quarters, I will bring in to show you a—"

"I will send one my soldiers. What is it you wish brought here?"

"There is a package the length of a man wrapped in sackcloth hanging on pegs."

The king pointed to a sentry. "Go." The man trotted off.

A short while later, the sentry returned, the bundle held across both arms.

Sebastián cut the worn cords holding the threadbare cloth and pulled out an unstrung bow. "Sire, this is called a longbow and stands two yards high— taller than most men or any bow I have seen used by natives in Africa, India, or armies in Europe. The arrow is a yard long."

He splayed his fingers and measured the length of the wood. "Or as you can see, it is a bit more than ten hand spans—longer than most." He handed the bow to the king.

The monarch balanced the bow in his hands. "I have already seen your weapon." He handed the weapon back to Sebastián. "What do you propose, Captain?"

"A demonstration of this weapon's power."

Telemesus turned to his Chief Scribe. "Let it be done. Whatever is required by him should be forthcoming without hindrance."

Aton lowered his head. "As you command, Sire."

Only the semblance of a polite smile crossed the monarch's face. "I congratulate you, captain on your ability with the language of my people. Your lessons will be reduced so you can prepare in case we are attacked. I will send for you if conditions demand your presence."

Telemesus stood.

"The audience," Aton whispered to Sebastián, "is ended."

Sebastián, bowed, turned on his heel and left, head held high. Now, to prove his military knowledge.

TWENTY-SIX

Two weeks had passed since Sebastián's meeting with Telemesus in the royal chamber.

This morning, the king limped toward his carved chair—moved a few strides outside the gate of the compound by his guards. Cebellina, her menina and a number of inhabitants allowed to watch by her father, sat on cushions and mats on either side of him. Other inhabitants crowded the ramparts of the palisade. Aton stood to the sovereign's right.

Two hundred soldiers, a phalanx of two men deep, stretched from the gates to the edge of the forest several hundred yards away.

Sebastián, red and white plumes on his helmet fluttering in the breeze, polished breastplate agleam in the early morning light, strode forward, crossed his arms across his chest in obeisance to the king and pointed to the open field with his sword.

Out of the corner of his eye Sebastián saw the audience crane forward for a better view.

He said, "As you can see, Sire, during the last few days we replanted three young trees in a jagged line. Your men tied round wooden shields to each tree; all three shields then painted.

"The nearest one to us is the blue of the sky above, the next, the red of blood and the farthest and closest to the edge of the woods, a brilliant yellow." Unexplained was an indistinct object attached to the yellow shield. The ground, for several paces around the saplings Sebastián had had brushed clean. Only bare dirt remained.

"Sire, if you please. Have your best javelin thrower hurl the farthest he can from the line I have drawn on the ground." Sebastián gestured to a narrow furrow in the packed dirt.

The monarch barked an order. "Ibrim!"

A tall, lithe young man marched forward, stepped to the line, stretched out one arm for balance, drew back and hurled the spear. It arced silently through the air and landed beside the blue shield. A roar of approval rose from the crowd. The young man smiled and ran back to his post.

"That was one hundred yards or roughly one hundred paces, Majesty," Sebastián said. "Your best archer next, if you please."

An older, muscular man strode to the line, nocked his arrow, aimed and loosed. The shaft struck the red shield, dead center. The wood split with a loud crack. The crowd roared again, louder this time.

"Most excellent," Sebastián said. He beckoned with his hand to a young boy standing alongside another. "Start counting each breath you take as soon as I kneel. Like so, take a breath, that is one, exhale that is two. Understood?"

"Yes, sir," the boy said.

Sebastián tousled the boy's hair and nodded, then withdrew his hackbut from its canvas covering, ran to the line, knelt on one knee, then quickly poured powder into the bore, tamped it, loaded shot from a pouch, took aim and fired at the red tree.

"How long the count?" he asked.

"Twenty," the boy replied.

He motioned to both boys. "Remember my instructions?"

The boys bounded to the tree, dropped to their knees and started searching. After a few moments of restlessness from the onlookers, one of the boys jumped to his feet with a whoop, and dashed back clutching something in his hand. Breathlessly he handed the spent shot to the king.

"That was about one hundred paces, Sire," Sebastián explained. "The same as the spear. Note also the time it took me to load my weapon, aim and fire, and I have much experience with the weapon. During the time I prepared to fire, a skilled archer would have at least four arrows piercing my chest." He jabbed at his armor with a finger. The crowd joined in his laughter. "Without my armor of course! Now let us try something else."

From a bundle lying on the ground, Sebastián extracted the longbow and handed it to the same bowman. Previously, he had the man and several others practice endless hours with the weapon. Sebastián clasped his hands behind his back.

"Whenever you are ready," he said to the archer.

The man took careful aim. The bow creaked as it bent, then the loud twang of the string.

The projectile whistled through the starkly clear air and struck the object and yellow shield of the farthest sapling. A dull thud cut the air. The crowd leaped to its feet and rent the air with shouts and clapping.

Cebellina, face beaming, joined in with subdued, polite applause along with her menina. Sebastián glanced at the king and saw a smile curve below the scar.

The archer handed the weapon back to Sebastián who spun on his heel and in two long strides stood in front of Telemesus.

Weapon held aloft in both hands, he shouted over the applause. "That was two hundred paces!"

The king raised his hand for silence. The audience quieted and a soldier ran back from the yellow shield. In one hand he carried Sebastián's old, field breastplate; the other held the arrow point.

"Sire," the man said, "I had to break the arrowhead away. The shaft remains inside the tree." Bowing, he handed both broken shaft and arrowhead to the king.

"How thick was the sapling?" Telemesus asked, examining the hole in the center of the old chest armor.

"The thickness of a man's four fingers, my lord."

"You may speak, Captain," the sovereign said to Sebastián.

"As you can see, Your Majesty, the arrow penetrated my old chest armor and sapling!" Sebastián said, warmth in his chest increased by the joyous reception from the audience. "The arrowhead you hold in your hand has three edges instead of two.

"It is called a bodkin and will go through any breastplate, including the one I have on which is armor of proof—steel tempered to a high strength. This arrow will fly higher and farther than any spear, regular bow, or hackbut, and bring down the man firing the hackbut though armor clothe his chest."

Telemesus handed the arrowhead back and arched a thick eyebrow. "Then why do the slavers and others continue to use the hackbut with great success?"

"Arab and European slavers, Sire, are contemptuous of black tribesmen's fighting tactics. They deal with tribes who are superstitious. I have seen tribesmen in battle. Most of them present ferocious stances, shout, and charge in a massed group. But confronted with the clouds of smoke and noise from the harquebus, the battlefield rises to an unseen terror for the tribes. Disciplined, trained archers, however, using different tactics, can inflict casualties so heavy on an enemy, said enemy will retreat the field in complete disarray."

Sebastián gazed at the bodkin point for a moment before going on. "Majesty, with your permission, I will relate an event of some years back." Sebastián wet his lips and used the bow for emphasis.

"Two great armies met in field of battle; both armed with cannon, harquebus, pistols, swords and bows. One army was English, the other, French. The French outnumbered the English by four men to one. Suffice it to say the English slaughtered the French."

Sebastián raised the bow above his head again. "This weapon won the battle at a place called Agincourt! My Lord, with these bows, your enemy will fall at a greater distance. The arrows are swift and sure."

"You have done well, Captain." The king rose in stages to his feet—the pain visible on his features. He turned his head to Sebastián. "You have struck my curiosity. Why do the arrows whistle?"

The king's advisors, Aton and a few of the sovereign's subjects drew closer.

"A trick used by English archers in tournaments, Sire. It creates admiration and applause from the crowd. I do not know exactly how it works, but it is accomplished by the use of notches and a hole in the shaft. Your fletchers would know more than I do."

"I have skilled archers," the king said. "And excellent fletchers. Let the making of such bows be done as quickly as possible," he told Aton. Telemesus stood.

The audience rose and left, reentering the compound—at a respectful distance behind their sovereign.

Cebellina slowed her pace and approached Sebastián—as close as permitted by her menina—three arm lengths. "Captain, now that you understand my language, why do you call me Cebellina?" Her languid eyes stroked his.

Sebastián removed his helmet. "Please, if it is not too brash of me, call me Sebastián. Now, for the name I chose to call you. In Europe, it is a rare and beautiful creature of the forest. The animal's fur the most prized of all. Only princes and kings are allowed its use, all others forbidden use on pain of death. It is called sable."

Murmurs and nods of approval and pleasant surprise lifted from her menina. The ten-year-old clamped a hand over her mouth to control her giggles. The princess, a smile residing only in her eyes, waggled a finger in a mild rebuke to the young girl for impoliteness to their guest.

Sebastián inched closer to the princess, his chest brushing against an outstretched arm of the same woman—as always. She tilted her chin and glared at him as though challenging him to dare and push her aside.

He raised his hands and laughed politely. "I fear you more than any man. I know your other hand clutches a dagger under your waistband. I will not force my way. Cebellina, I wish you and your companions a good day. There is…I…"

"I must follow my father," she said and strolled away amidst a flurry of conversation among her menina.

Sebastián shook his head. So frustrating this inability of speaking to her without the constant vigilance of her ladies-in-waiting. But, at least now he could understand the language. He must be patient for the proper moment. Reveal his innermost feelings about her. With quick paces, he passed back through the gates along with the soldiers and searched out the king's fletchers. A sea of elation coursed through him at the success of the longbow demonstration.

The moment had arrived, he thought, to ask Aton and request a private audience with the king on Sebastián's behalf.

TWENTY-SEVEN

"Please wait in the other room," Cebellina said to Amaunet and the *menina*. "I wish to speak to my father alone."

Amaunet nodded and clapped to draw the women's attention. "Come, Aton awaits us for further tutoring in history and philosophy."

Groans and mutters followed her out of the Royal Chamber.

At the entrance to the chamber, Cebellina paused, glanced at familiar walls the height of three men. Affixed to the worked stones, shields battered and scarred, one, with a gorgon symbol painted on its face, glared at her; others boasted Egyptian hieroglyphikos—relics from long-ago battles. Dressed in her pectoral collar and other jewelry, head held high, she marched to the center of the room, bowed and waited for her father's permission for her to approach the throne.

After restless nights, days of lost appetite—in spite of Amaunet's prodding and her companions' pleading to eat—she now tightly clasped her hands in front of her.

Although she loved her father and the gods *knew* she tried to comply with all his wishes, *this* matter weighted most of any in importance. From conversations she overheard during the hours spent with her companions, she knew they and their families approved of the captain's presence in the city. Their buoyant answers erased any doubt in her mind. This morning, she felt determined to present *her* wishes on this matter.

"Oh, Isis, Mother Goddess, guide me," she intoned in a whisper as she approached her father.

The king raised his head, dropped a parchment onto a table, lifted a hand and beckoned her forward.

"Good morning, Father," she said, cheerfully.

"Good morning. What is it you wish to see me about?" He pointed to a chair to his right. "You may sit."

"I prefer to stand."

Silent, Telemesus gazed at his daughter. *She appears to have grown in the last few weeks.*

Children grow before one's eyes. There could be only one reason she would insist on observing court ceremony.

"As you wish. Speak."

"I have come on a matter of great importance to me. Much time has passed since the Spanish captain arrived here. I have not been able to thank him personally for saving my life. I wish to speak to him without others present."

"No."

"May I respectfully ask why not?"

He noticed his daughter kept her composure, although he imagined, agitation at his refusal roiled inside her. Good. Control of one's emotions, especially anger in public would serve well in future dealings with his…and her people.

"Are you questioning my decision?"

"Is it not proper for me to thank him?"

"Yes, but you must always bear in mind that your actions in public—"

"Then you agree I should meet with him."

Telemesus swept a hand across his brow. "You interrupt me. You twist my words."

Cebellina took a step closer to the throne, head still head high. "*Please, Father.* This is important to me."

Telemesus leaned forward in his seat. "Why are you so insistent?"

Cebellina bowed her head. "I beg your forgiveness."

"Why are you so desirous to meet with the captain? The truth."

She raised her head slowly. "I…cannot…describe…my feelings." Her glance darted from side to side. "They are…strange to me. I have not spoken to anyone about them, not even Amaunet whom I treasure as a mother. I lie awake at night with these thoughts…unable to…unravel."

The king saw tears well in her eyes, run down her cheeks. He paused, cleared his throat. *So, what I have been told by Amaunet and Aton is true. My daughter is taken* strongly *with the captain and he with her.*

Night after night, the king had wrestled with thoughts on what to say to his daughter regarding the captain. Her tears offered proof of her deepest thoughts. "How do you know his feelings are the same for you?"

"They reside in his eyes. There is delight when he approaches me; sadness when he must leave."

Her answer was one he would never accept from anyone, but he could not ignore the symptoms any longer. Sooner or later, his beloved daughter would find a way to escape the watchfulness of Amaunet and the young women. Well, *that* could be resolved.

The captain? A resourceful officer, who had already shown the soldiers new fighting tactics and deadliness of the longbow, *he* might find a way to meet secretly. *I will have him watched closely, especially at night.*

But, if in spite of the precautions, the violation of his daughter occurred, he would have the captain killed—in spite of the military experience the king desperately needed, and force the princess to marry a man he chose. And if she refused to obey and took her own life? Telemesus felt a sharp pain cross his chest.

After a deep breath to infuse calm, he said, "You may thank Captain Aviles in person—with the following conditions. Amaunet must—"

Cebellina smiled. "From my heart, I thank you, Father."

Telemesus shook his head in resignation. He pointed his finger at her. "Never interrupt me again, understood?" What good would his admonishment be? Soon, his daughter would forget and repeat her actions. Well, as long as her interruptions occurred in private…

She nodded.

"To continue. Amaunet must stand an arm length away, between or to the side of you and the captain whether sitting or standing. He may not touch you at any time. The meeting will be held outdoors for my people to see, but of course, they must keep a respectful distance. Agreed?"

"Agreed," she said, ignoring the tears on her cheeks. "Thank you, Father. After tomorrow, may I see him again?"

"No. That will be determined *after* you meet with him. Then I will decide what will proceed. Send Amaunet to me. I will repeat what I have said to her."

She dried her tears with a sleeve, bowed and backed out of the chamber, head held high.

Telemesus stood, stretched his arms and prepared for his day's work of listening to complaints and petitions.

"It is done. Let us see the response of my people," he said to the empty chamber.

Amaunet entered.

"Yes, my lord?"

"Amaunet, I have given permission for the princess to meet with the Spaniard. When they walk you will stand between them, the captain three arm lengths away from her. From tonight onward, you will sleep by my daughter's door, prevent any attempt by her to leave or escape without your presence by her side. You will assign, on my orders, two of the other women to keep watch all night. On the following nights, the others will take turns. They have my permission to sleep during the daylight hours but only equal to a night's sleep. As always, I know I can rely on you to be diligent in your duties."

"May I speak from my heart, Majesty?"

"Yes."

"I have known the princess since she was an infant. She is stubborn at times, but her stubbornness is of short duration. Maturity grows swiftly within her. Since the encounter with the captain in the forest she struggles, she is torn between two worlds. The captain is a fine young man, although he would be surprised to hear me say that. He is worthy to meet with the princess. I will do as you command, Sire." She turned and walked out of the Royal Chamber.

What, in spite of Amaunet's diligence, his own precautions, a calamity occurred? Telemesus rubbed a sudden dull throb hammering at his temples.

TWENTY-EIGHT

After instructing the king's soldiers on methods to thwart European weapons, Sebastián would return to his rooms to sketch the results of his training, hunt for weaknesses in his defense and attack postures, and offer suggestions to the king about changes in the city's walls.

For many weeks, he had followed the restrictions imposed on him by the king with utmost care. This morning, although unarmed, he would stroll through the city, take measure of its size and, perhaps number of inhabitants and their response to his presence in their midst. If attacked, he would defend himself as best he could. No other choice existed.

Shading his eyes, he glanced at the sky. "About ten o'clock," he said under his breath. Hands clasped behind him, he stepped forward at a leisurely pace.

At a stall selling necklaces and other jewelry, he paused.

"Ah, good morning, captain. May I interest you in something?" the merchant said.

"No. Not at present," Sebastián said, picking up an item made of lapis lazuli. "What is this?"

"That is a scarab, a beetle representing creation, new life." The man had recognized him and offered a cordial greeting. An auspicious beginning.

"Thank you." Sebastián walked on. Farther down, a stall with women stirring vats, the owner, he assumed, with the ubiquitous painted eyes, pointed to baskets of perfumed soaps in different shapes and sizes. Several women bartered over the prices. Over the weeks of his stay, he had noticed the people bathed *every* day. Unbelievable.

He walked to another stall selling jars of honey and pulled a gold ducat from his pocket. "I have this gold piece…" he said handing the coin to the merchant.

The man raised it to his eye and said, "If you wish, I will keep it. When you purchase again, I will deduct from the gold piece. I keep good accounts. You can ask the Widow Amanuet. Do you agree, captain?"

Sebastián smiled inwardly. "Yes." Elated at another recognition and welcome, he accepted two jars and resumed his walk. When he reached a rise, he stopped and gazed again at the sky. The sun glared past the midpoint. "Close to one o'clock."

Three hours. Back in Spain he would have covered the same distance through the three nearest villages governed by his family—villages holding a total of over a thousand souls. And he hadn't reached the outskirts of *this* town. He turned and retraced his steps back to his quarters. This city held twice as many. At a minimum, he estimated the inhabitants at more than a thousand, but more important, everyone he met recognized and greeted him at least with a nod.

Back in his quarters, hunched over his journal making entries, he heard a scrape against the ground outside his entrance. Sebastián spun around, reached for his sword resting on the table.

Amaunet framed the doorway.

"May I enter?" she said.

"Yes, of course." Sebastián backed away to allow her to enter, relaxed and drew his hand away from the weapon.

The woman entered, glanced around at the spartan furnishings of a chair and table, weapons, reed thin lengths of charcoal and open journal.

She paused by the table, viewed the sketches of spears, arrows and stick figures.

"Whom am I addressing?" he said, offering a polite smile.

"You may address me as the Widow Amaunet."

"Oh…my sincerest condolences…"

Her features hardened. "My husband and son died on the battlefield serving our king."

Sebastián pointed to a chair. "Would you care to sit?"

"No…thank you."

"I cannot offer anything but water." He spread his arms out.

"Captain, there is no need. Your offer of hospitality is noted," the unsmiling Amaunet said, but he thought he caught a softening of her features. "The princess wishes to speak with you."

His heart leaped. Finally! For two months he had driven himself towards the goal of acceptance by the populace—helping neighbors, *never* ogling any of the women—hoping, perhaps one day…

"Are you married?" Her gaze bored into his.

"No."

"Betrothed?"

"No."

She nodded. "You are to meet with her within the hour in front of the Royal Chamber." Her glance raked him from head to toe. She frowned.

She is looking at my dirty blouse and dusty boots.

"Dressed properly, of course," she said. Amaunet offered a slight nod, spun on her heel, and haughtily marched out.

Bemused, Sebastián shrugged at her visible distaste of him and his clothing. He walked out to the back garden to the obelisk to see the time—the angled shadow indicated close to five in the evening. Borrowing water in a wooden bucket from a neighbor's well, he washed and dressed. For an instant, Sebastián peered at his one and only doublet and other European clothing hanging on a wooden plug. He shook his head. The wearing of such clothes might stir unwanted, unfriendly stares from the king's people.

Instead, he chose the one clean simple tunic he possessed and replaced the boots with leather sandals purchased by bartering—he had helped the cobbler repair the roof and stall of the man's home. Finger combing his hair, he reached out for his weapons, then pulled his hand away.

"*That* is not what Amaunet meant by 'properly dressed.'" He laughed and strode toward the Royal Chamber.

When he reached a distance he thought proper for him, Sebastián paused outside the Royal Chamber. Although he had dreamed and hoped for this day to arrive, what would he say to her? Would this be the only time allowed for a meeting? Did a future exist for him as a suitor? What could he offer? Aside from a few gold ducats sewn inside his doublet, he possessed neither land, properties, horses or cattle. Absolutely nothing. Should he quash these unquenchable feelings about Cebellina raging through him day and night? The thought weighed heavily on him.

One of the sentries turned his head and spoke to someone inside the door.

Amaunet walked out of the chamber. Directly behind her were Cebellina and the menina.

Sebastián offered a slight bow.

"Good afternoon, princess," he said, hoping he spoke the words correctly in his newly acquired language of her people.

White sleeve billowing, she inclined her head gracefully

Although dressed in a white garment like her companions, Cebellina's boasted many pleats. Around her neck rested the pectoral collar and its depiction of the Egyptian goddess Isis. The half-kneeling figure's outstretched arms rested over wings of vulture feathers painted in banded shades of blue and green. On Isis' head, a silver disc representing the moon was shouldered by the horns of Horus, the cow god. Around her temple, a gold band held a cobra and a falcon. The collar boasted its richness in late afternoon brightness.

Respectful paces away, half a dozen curious women with their children had gathered to watch. *In Spain, they use one duenna, here they use a dozen.* Sebastián chuckled inwardly. The group of onlookers bowed politely to the princess and moved on.

Sebastián stepped closer to Cebellina.

Immediately, the imposing presence of Amaunet placed itself directly in his path.

"Captain, you may not approach closer than three arm lengths," she said.

"Understood." Although accustomed now to the restriction of keeping his distance from the princess—albeit with reluctance—he had decided to once again defer to the people's custom.

"We will walk to the river. It is peaceful and quiet there at this time," Cebellina said.

Amaunet said, "No. It is too far."

Cebellina reached out and touched her ever-watchful friend's arm. "I have you to protect me. My companions to watch over me, and I have the brave captain by my side. And, it *is* a pleasant evening."

"As you wish, highness," Amaunet said, grudgingly.

"Then it is settled," Cebellina said. "We shall all go."

Amanuet signaled with her hands for the menina to follow. In a semi-circle, and silent, the six women obeyed, whispering among themselves.

Sebastián clasped his hands behind his back and followed Cebellina with Amaunet sharing space between them.

"I know…" Sebastián said, walking alongside Amaunet, "…that I must keep my distance. But may I respectfully request you allow me to speak to the princess without having to lean forward?"

Amaunet narrowed her eyes at him, glanced at Cebellina who nodded, and Amaunet took two steps back to stand at an angle between Sebastián and the princess.

Several men fishing on the river's bank gazed their way, bowed their heads in deference to the princess and returned to their fishing.

Toward the west, feathered streaks of retreating sunlight sped toward an unseen horizon.

"In Spain…" he said, trying to open the conversation. "…twilight is called *crepúsculo.* "

Cebellina smiled, struggled with the pronunciation, then surrendered to the difficulty. "Captain," she said, "You are now conversant in our language It is time for me to speak these words."

"Yes?" He hoped his excitement at meeting with her was well hidden from the menina.

And Amaunet.

"I want to thank you for saving my life. I have waited until you could understand the language of my people and I could say these words properly. There are so many questions…I know you landed in Africa by ship. Tell me about your voyage."

Without gazing at her, he said, "Sailing out of Portugal we were blessed by fair winds and calm seas. On the voyage back from India, the winds unpleasant and the seas rough in nature. Many seamen died." He paused and looked at Cebellina. "In my daily walks around your city, I have looked for you, but have felt the sharp edge of your absence." *Was that a blush on her cheek?* She turned her head away.

"How long was your voyage?"

"About two years. Longer than I expected and care to remember." Was she afraid to look at him? Perhaps give herself away in some manner as to her feelings toward him?

"May you favor me with a glance?" he whispered.

Amaunet leaned forward.

Cebellina turned full face and smiled; a soft, caressing smile that erased all his doubts and cares.

"Will you return to Spain?"

"I cannot tell as yet. My future…is unclear. I left with disagreements between the religious authorities and myself. When may I see you again?"

Sebastián thought he detected a slight smile of satisfaction on her face. And those eyes!

Beguiling to the point of distraction.

"I cannot stay long. My father awaits my return."

"But…but, it has been only a short while!" He moved closer to her.

Again, Amaunet inserted herself between them.

He shrugged. If he lost his forbearance, he would forfeit even these few moments. "Widow Amaunet, please." He offered a beseeching look at her.

She stepped back.

Cebellina went on. "If my father allows me—"

"Forgive my rashness with the interruption. May I have your permission to speak to your father regarding future walks?" Was he endangering himself again? Was it not more proper to ask the father for permission to see his daughter?

He heard the sharp intake of breath by Amaunet.

"I will comply with my father's wishes. I must leave. I…" She shook her head.

"Goodnight." Cebellina turned, Amaunet followed, trailed by the menina, leaving Sebastián standing alone alongside the riverbank. He gazed at the last streaks of twilight.

She had paused. *What was it she wished to say?* "Well, it was a good beginning." Now, to seek an audience with the king. *How would that end, life or death for me?*

TWENTY-NINE

Finished with his language lessons for the day, Sebastián stood, stretched and clasped his hands behind his back. He wet his lips.

"Aton, I would like to ask if you can arrange an audience for myself with the king."

The scribe placed his quill down and rested his palms on his table. "His Majesty always demands the reasons why a petitioner desires an audience with him. It is my duty to ask."

Sebastián inhaled a deep breath. "I would ask his majesty if he might consider my request to be a suitor for the hand of his daughter."

"I see. And what will you offer in return?"

Sebastián felt the weight of the scribe's gaze upon him. "I cannot offer anything that is visible. All I can offer are my military skills and my loyalty which I value above all else to his majesty and the princess."

Aton rubbed his bald head. "I will speak to my lord sovereign and inform you of his answer for an audience. I will not see you for two or three days. There are matters about the harvests and trading with a friendly tribe his majesty wishes to discuss with me." The scribe gathered his quills and parchments, picked up his table and left.

THIRTY

Sebastián hugged a stone wall bordering the Royal Chamber, the stones still warm from the day's heat, fugitives on this cool night. Somewhere inside Cebellina slept. Guarded by Amaunet? By her menina? By others?

Four days had passed without word from the king or, when questioned by Sebastián, from Aton, the scribe telling his pupil to exhibit patience.

Over the four days, thoughts battled to be heard in Sebastián's mind. Caution warned of the extreme dangers involved, and most probable, death. Emotions pressed him to take action and risk. Hours passed.

Ahead of him, some thirty yards, he estimated, puddles of moonlight played shadows on the roof of the chamber, while slivers like sword cuts slid along the edges. The ground in front sat in Stygian darkness. He paused, waited for any sound, a footfall, a cough, anything to reveal the presence of guards. Nothing but the rustle of…what was that?

A *honk*.

A goose stepped into a spear of moonlight, followed by another member of the flock. They stared at him.

Geese! Those were the guards. In his haste, he had forgotten the birds' presence. The birds, he recalled, were famous for guarding castles, palaces, stately manors, alerting those who slept inside. What better guardians? One of the fowl always awake.

From behind, a large hand clamped around his mouth, another grasped his right arm and chest.

Sebastián struggled against the holds. His left arm tried to loosen the unknown attacker's unyielding grip. But the steel vise held, his desperate efforts to no avail. He awaited the thrust of a dagger into his chest or throat.

"Do not make a sound."

He recognized the voice.

Aton.

The scribe removed his hand. "I will quiet the geese. Do not leave."

Sebastián heard murmurings and odd clicking sounds, the shiny bald head of Aton appearing, disappearing in the shards of moonlight. Was Aton also a sorcerer, conversant with animals? He always marveled at the man's abilities. Soon, silence.

Sebastián started as a hand fell on his shoulder again. "Turn around, place your hand on my shoulder and follow me."

A couple of turns later, and in a dimly lit clearing, Aton faced him.

"What were you thinking?" Aton said.

Even in the half-light, Sebastián made out anger in his tutor's features.

"You don't understand—" Sebastián's own anger rose.

"Do not take me for a fool, captain"

Sebastián bristled, clenched his fists. "I never…it is my life—"

"Which I have saved. If you were able somehow to avoid the watchful geese, the guards inside would have killed you. If not they, then the women sleeping in the adjoining room. Or Amaunet who sleeps by the princess's door."

"I only wanted…" Sebastián said, voice hoarse, "…to speak to her alone. I meant no harm to her or the others."

Aton leaned closer. "I sympathize with your frustrations and anxiousness to meet with the princess. Your emotions clouded your judgment. However, as much as I am loathe to do it, I must report this event to His Majesty."

"Understood. I will accept the consequences and sincerely hope the king will not order punishment on you. I owe you my life. One question. How did you know I would be there this night?"

"During our lessons today, you were inattentive, your mind elsewhere, more than usual. This night *had* to be the night you would risk your life. So, I waited. Return to your quarters until sent for." He patted Sebastián's shoulder. "Only myself and the geese are witnesses and I will wait until morning to report."

"I will accept the king's decision." Sebastián plodded back home.

THIRTY-ONE

Cebellina sat combing her hair on a scarred black and gold-leafed chair adorned with lions' heads at the arms and claws on the legs. Once used by her father and his father, the chair bore witness to its sad travels from its home in the Red Mountain. Faded purple cushions eased the sitter's discomfort.

"When I meet again with the Spanish captain," the princess said, "we will take a walk to the river, it is peaceful and quite there and he and I will speak until the sun sets."

Amaunet took the tortoise shell comb from the princess and finished combing the long, thick hair of her charge. "Your father, the king, said, 'A brief meeting,' what you intend is longer than that."

"I cannot thank the captain properly in haste as I did by the river. I want to know more about him. That will require more time."

"You stretch the king's words like the gum of the acacia tree. He will be displeased."

"He will understand."

"No, he will not. He has instructed that I watch over and care for you. I will obey. When out of the Royal Chamber, I or one of your companions are never to lose sight of you."

The princess turned in her chair to face her guardian.

"Amaunet, there are so many restrictions on me. My father forbids me to leave the city. I cannot leave my chambers unless escorted by you and the others. I train with weapons in the morning, lessons from Aton in the afternoons, then to sit by my father's side while he conducts matters of our people. I refuse to be bound by this restriction."

Amaunet snorted. "Like you did in the forest when the lion almost took your life?"

"Well…perhaps that time also. I hope you understand. I have these strange feelings for this man. I cannot describe them. I cannot eat. I cannot sleep at night."

"I have noticed."

"At times at night, I fear those feelings…and him. Other times…I *must* see him. I *will* see him."

"I will also be there to guard against—"

"No. I will see him alone."

Finished combing, Amaunet stepped back, folded her arms. "*Alone?* That is impossible! The king has forbidden such a meeting."

The princess stood, embraced her companion. "And you will help me."

Amaunet raised her hands, palms out toward the beamed wooden ceiling in supplication. She closed her eyes. "Isis, Mother goddess, what have you done? Take me in your arms for I am dead. If this comes to pass, the princess and I will surely die."

Cebellina sat back down and smiled. "I have a plan."

Unmoved, Amanuet folded her arms. "I am listening."

"This morning, my companions had training in the use of dagger, sword and javelin. Then we partook of a scant meal of raisins and flour cakes—to prevent anyone from sleeping during lessons with Scribe Aton. When finished, they followed me to listen to my father handling court affairs. After the heavy evening meal and tired at the end of a long day, they hastened to their chambers. One by one, they have now fallen into a strong sleep, even those assigned to watch over me. I will leave now. Alone."

Amaunet raised an eyebrow. "*That* is your plan?" And how will you deal with the guards the king has placed outside?"

"I will leave by the back door in your bedroom that leads to a garden. There are no guards there."

"No."

"I can order you."

"No. I obey the king's orders."

"I will have you flogged."

Amaunet's features remained impassive. "His majesty will summon all those concerned and demand explanations. Very quickly, he will discover the truth. Also, if you try to leave by yourself, the king has ordered me to physically restrain and bind you. I do not wish to do that."

Cebellina sat back down, chin held high, but she trembled inside, hopes dashed, knew her plans were for naught without Amaunet's help. She would not beg help from her friend, she would never beg. She would rather die.

Amaunet reached over and touched Cebellina's cheek. "My dear princess. I know what you are struggling with. I will always remember the joyous times with my beloved husband since the day we married until he died on the battlefield." Her features softened and she sighed deeply. "But I cannot help you, will not help you."

Cebellina glanced at Amanuet. Although Widow Amanuet was in her mid-forties, she handled weapons with the best of any of the women, stayed trim and fit and feared no one. Impossible for Cebellina to overcome her guardian physically.

Amanuet turned to look at a thick candle set into a spike on a metal tripod. Blue bands on the taper marked the length of predetermined hours, the twelfth band wider than the others. The small flame would last five days. At this time of the evening, the light drew closer to the wide band.

"It is past the eleventh hour and a long day," she said. "I have prepared some water scented with cinnamon for you to wash your hands and face and you can prepare for bed." She waited until Cebellina washed, removed bracelets and armlets, placed them and the comb on a chest and slid under on a blanket on this chilly night.

Cebellina watched from under half-closed eyelids as Amanuet strolled out, dragged a narrow cot over to block the entranceway to Cebellina's bedroom and shook awake one of the women.

"Nephtys," the widow said, "Go and sit on the cot. I will be back shortly. Keep watch over the princess."

The groggy eighteen-year-old rubbed her eyes. "Why do *I* have to watch?"

"Because I order it to be so." Amanuet motioned with her palm. "Up."

Muttering under her breath, Nephtys nodded and stumbled forward to the cot.

Amanuet disappeared into an adjoining room.

An instant later, Nephtys' lids closed, her head lolled to the side and she collapsed on the bed, feet still on the floor. Snoring erupted from her lips.

Cebellina threw off the blanket and leaped from her bed. Swiftly, she plucked a dark cloak with a deep hood from a hook on the wall along with her dagger and sheath, picked up a pair of plain leather sandals and walked to the cot blocking the doorway. Careful not to touch the edges, or awaken Nephtys, she stepped over a corner of the bed frame and hurried to the stairs leading to the roof.

Sandals in hand, she crossed the roof to the one adjoining belonging to the king's architect. At the steps leading to the main living quarters and bedrooms, she paused and listened for movement, hoping no one was awake at this hour. She tiptoed to the bottom, one hand on the wall as a guide, bent herself into a crouch and aimed for the door. She found the wood frame and groped for the latch and lifted. A creak broke the silence. She grimaced and froze in place. The house remained silent.

Stepping through the open door, Cebellina paused outside, slipped on the sandals and tied the cords around her ankles. In the darkness, the houses so familiar in daytime now assumed shapeless forms in the blackness.

"O, Isis, guide me this night," she whispered, removing the dagger from its sheath, left hand touching the walls she stepped forward. Her mind struggled to recall the distance to the captain's quarters. Then a thought intruded.

On occasion, her father, along with two of his best guards, checked the safety of the streets. What if he discovered her wandering alone? What would she say to him?

Both questions dismissed with a shake of her head, she moved on. This brief freedom was a rare luxury from the strictures that bound her day in, day out.

A familiar smell struck her nostrils. "The bakery!" Her spirits lifted and in a sliver of moonlight, increased her pace. She passed one house, then another.

"I will be there soon!" she murmured as her foot struck a wayward basket in the street.

She slammed her palm against her mouth to smother the cry of pain shooting up her leg. Pausing, she bent over, briefly massaged her toes, straightened and clenching her teeth in determination, limped forward; stopping every few paces to ease the insistent throb in her foot. Her pace dropped to a disappointing shuffle.

Cebellina spotted a light coming from where she felt the captain lived. She hopped toward the entrance—then heard steps rushing behind her.

"Stop!" a voice hissed in the darkness.

Cebellina spun around, dagger held waist high.

"Amanuet! What are you doing here?" she whispered, tucking the dagger back into her waistband.

"Princess, why are you limping?"

"I tripped in the darkness. It is a minor annoyance." Cebellina pointed toward a rectangle of light outlined on the dark street. "I think that is the captain's quarters. We are almost there."

"It *is* the captain's quarters," Amanuet said. She studied the princess, noticed the jaw set in determination, the intense gaze in the eyes. If she bodily forced the princess back to the Royal Chamber, she knew her young charge would try again to see the Spaniard the next night, or the next. It would be far better to allow her to see the captain than extend this dangerous situation and its discovery by the king.

"You may see him…briefly. First, swear to Isis you will not attempt this again."

Cebellina hesitated.

"Princess, you place everyone in danger. Do it."

"I swear to Isis."

Both moved to edge of the brightness and the princess peeked. She drew back, eyes widened. "Wonderful news. The captain is awake!"

Before Amanuet could stop her, Cebellina hobbled through the opening.

The sandal with the injured toe scratched over a pebble and he leaped from his chair, grasped his sword from the table.

"Captain, do not…It is I." She pushed back the hood.

He blinked and drew back. "Wha…what are you doing here?" He dropped the sword back on the table and rubbed his eyes. Sebastián pointed to the chair. "Please sit." Forcing away the throb in her foot, she sat while he pulled over a stool for himself and sat eye level with her.

"My visit must be brief," she said.

"I will accept whatever moment I can have with you. Do you travel alone this night?"

"Sebastián…" Excitement ran through her body in saying his name, his question ignored. How good it felt! Reaching out, she took his hand in both of hers. The warmth and strength of his palm banished the coldness and fear she had felt moments before. She raised her head and glanced at him. Sadness etched his eyes.

"What is wrong?" she said, sitting forward in the chair. "You look troubled? Are you not happy to see me?" How she ached to run her fingers through his tousled hair!

He squeezed her hand. "You have brought brightness to this room, lightness to my heart and lifted my spirit." He smiled broadly, but she heard his loud swallow. "I wish I had enough breath, you take it away." *His smile though beautiful is forced. Something is deeply wrong. Is it a woman back in Spain? A woman here?* A sting of jealousy bit. He had told her he could not return to Spain. Someone in her city? No. Rumors surfaced quickly.

"Cebellina, our time together is so limited. I want to be your suitor and will do anything the king asks of me." Bringing her hand up, he gently kissed her fingers, moved to her palm.

"I will ask my father…"

A hiss from the shadows.

"Who is that?" Sebastián spun around, reached for his weapon.

Cebellina wrung her hands. "Do not be alarmed. That is Amaunet, my companion." She stood. "I must leave."

"Will I…see…you again?" Sadness again appeared in his eyes.

"Perhaps. I will try. Yes." *Why does he hesitate with his words? What is wrong? I must find out.*

Placing her hood back over her head, she glanced back once and, grimacing with pain, hurried out.

"I am over here," Amanuet said, stepping out from shadows as black as her cloak. "Now, place your arm around my waist, keep the weight off your foot. We must make haste before others become aware of our presence in the streets."

"There was sadness in his eyes, Amanuet," Cebellina whispered. I wonder—"

"We will discuss the matter when we return home. What path did you use coming here?"

"Through the architect's home and roof."

Amanuet nodded under her hood. "I must remember to close off that method for any of the women to leave without permission. Hmm. It is high in risk. But we will use the same method and pray none of the occupants are awake." Half-lifting her charge, Amanuet led the way back.

THIRTY-TWO

The flame on the banded candle neared the second hour when Amaunet arrived with Cebellina to the women's rooms. They were all asleep—including Nephtys.

The widow glanced at the sleeping form of Nephtys. Hiding her anger, she shook her head and moved the cot and Nephtys aside. "Princess, sit on your bed and I will examine your foot."

Cebellina hopped over and sat.

"It is not bad," Amanuet said, lifting the foot and running her fingers along both sides. She bandaged the ankle with a strip from a torn sheet then poured water from a clay jar—thankful the water was still cool—over the bandage. "Rest now. I will examine again in the morning. Also, tomorrow, when you enter the king's chamber, walk slowly."

Cebellina whispered. "Thank you for risking your life to aid me. I…there are so many things…I cannot understand…"

Taken aback at the change in the princess, Amanuet stared.

Over the last hour a transformation had fallen over the princess, the measured tone in her voice, the way she had stood erect in spite of the obvious pain, arms by her sides, seriousness written in her face, yet eyes filled with an exultant glow. The widow sighed, recalled her own youth, her own disobedience of her own parents in risking all to see Tatenen, her future husband. Still, Amanuet must obey the king's orders and report the incident of the young woman's secret visit to the Spanish captain.

Amanuet nodded. "Goodnight, Princess." She walked to where Nephtys slept and shook her awake. Clutching the arm of the young woman, she pulled her into an adjoining room.

"I ordered you to watch over the princess," she hissed. "You fell asleep. She left this room unattended."

"I only slept a short while."

"The candle flame nears the second hour and I have just returned with the princess. Therefore, what you say is a lie!" Amaunet reached over and slapped the young woman.

Holding her reddened cheek, anger in her eyes, Nephtys cried out, "I was tired! You drive us from sunrise to sunset." She snatched a dagger from a table holding everyone's weapon and held the naked blade in front of Amanuet.

"What is wrong?" one of the wakened woman said from the doorway, rubbing her eyes as the rest crowded around her.

"Nothing," Amanuet said without turning, grateful her back covered Nephtys. "Go back to sleep." The widow gazed at the banded candle. "It is now the second hour. You have four to sleep. I advise all of you to use them. I will watch over the princess."

Amidst groans and mutterings, the women retreated.

Noting Nephtys' distraction, Amanuet slid a cloak from a hook as the women scurried away from the doorway. Swinging the cloak in an arc, she caught the blade in the folds and yanked the dagger away from Nephtys.

"If you ever point a dagger at me again…" Amanuet said, "…I will take it away and beat you with it. If I discharge you from your duties to the princess your family will be disgraced. Do you wish that?"

Nephtys bowed her head. "No. Will you report this to his majesty?"

"I will give it thought. *Now* you can go back to sleep."

Nephtys shuffled off in tears.

Amanuet returned to the cot and sat on the edge facing Cebellina. A deep, tired sigh escaped her lips. *I must give thought to so much…the women under my charge, the princess…and the captain.*

At this, the sixth hour, Amanuet hurried toward Aton's rooms located next to the king's. She had left the princess sleeping and wakened two of the other women to keep watch. This early in the morning, she knew he would be preparing to meet with the king to discuss and advise the sovereign on court matters. She must meet with him *before* he left his rooms.

She knocked on his door.

Shafts of a new sunrise were striking the roofs of the city. Time, she needed more time.

"Enter," he said.

Inside, she paused and glanced around the room, surprised at the smallness. In five paces she could cover the width, add another three paces for the length. Scattered, open parchments, scrolls and books lay on a threadbare rug edged with faded weaving depicting papyrus leaves. A flickering banded candle stood by his bed.

She watched as the scribe methodically picked up the materials. Aton was always ready to answer the king's questions. Some of the rare volumes, she knew, had formerly belonged to the king and been given as gifts to Aton. Other tomes, in Arabic were captured after the king's defeat of Arab slavers in battle.

A narrow bed hugged a wall, its linen neatly folded alongside a wooden headrest. A bedside table held a parchment, a quill and pot of ink. Three oil lamps hung from hooks in the ceiling, their curls of smoke snaked out the room's single window opening.

"Good morning, Scribe Aton. I beg forgiveness for this early visit. I disturb you at this hour to discuss a most urgent matter."

"Good morning, Amaunet. Are you well? You look...distressed. There is redness in your eyes and dark circles beneath them."

She unconsciously touched her cheek. For many mornings she had washed the redness in her eyes away with a collyrium of diluted rose water and hidden the discoloration on her face with umber lightened with flour to blend into her skin. But in her haste this morning...

Aton, dressed in a Greek *chlamys*, a loose-fitting white gown draped over one shoulder and held in place by a gold clasp, pointed to a worn, backless chair of woven reeds. "Please."

Positioning himself in front of her, he sat on a floor mat and crossed his legs. "I am accustomed and more comfortable in this position," he said

Amanuet adjusted her long skirt and sat, back straight. "Thank you for your kind concern," she said. "I am physically well. My mind struggles with itself. After much thought, I have guided the princess to the captain's quarters this night."

Aton rubbed his bald head, but kept silent.

She wet her lips. Sleepless nights without number, events now ran at a faster pace than she could handle. Unusual pains pressed outward against her chest. "She is of fierce determination on seeing the captain. Perhaps even at the risk of her life. I feel strongly there will be a great tragedy for the king and his people if she is restricted further from the captain. This restlessness and anxiousness to see him has led to disquiet in the other women."

"His majesty has placed you in charge of these women and expects you to handle the situation."

"Scribe, these women may train with weapons but they are not soldiers, they are still women…young women." She clenched her fists. "You do not understand!"

Amanuet thought she detected a flash of anger in the scribe's eyes at her outburst. The flicker vanished as quick.

"Calm yourself," he said. "Agitation will not solve the problem. I will never achieve the knowledge and understanding of women you possess. But allow me some knowledge of human beings."

"Granted."

Aton continued. "This very night I have witnessed…" he said, "…the same determination in the captain."

Her heart beat faster. She felt dizzy. Shaking the lightheadedness off, she sat forward in her seat. "In what manner?"

"I intercepted him on his way to see the princess secretly."

Amaunet steepled her fingers. "Oh, Mother Isis, help us. We are approaching the edge of a cliff. Scribe, will you tell the king?"

"Yes. I will not lie to my lord sovereign about the captain's attempts this night. I advise you to do the same about the princess. If the king asks me about what you have told me, I will tell him. The young man's actions and those of the princess are those struck with that most conflicting yet most elevating of human emotions: love. What do you wish me to do?"

Amaunet inhaled a deep breath to calm herself. "It is too late for me to ask for a private audience with the king. If I appear before the court and babble, I will look like a fool. I came to you because if one of the women carelessly reveals what has happened this night…." The widow pressed a hand to her chest. "There is only one solution to all these problems, we must—"

Aton raised a hand. "There is no need to speak further. I understand and agree with what you propose." He uncrossed his legs and stood, surprising Amaunet with his agility. The scribe was able to rise from a crossed-leg position without using his hands.

"Thank you for confiding in me," he said. "I must now leave to meet with my lord sovereign. I pray he has not risen in ill humor. Then we will all suffer."

He led Amaunet to the door.

"I will do my utmost to resolve your problem," Aton said.

The flame in the candle hovered near the seventh hour.

THIRTY-THREE

Books and parchments in hand, Aton approached the king in the antechamber. The room, the same size as Aton's boasted rolled parchments inserted into cubbyholes. A slender table held two incunabula—rare, hand written books made before the invention of the printing press.

Aton bowed. "Good morning. Sire, may I have few words in private before you begin your day?"

Telemesus, in the process of placing a cloak over his tunic on this chilly morning, turned a stern face toward his scribe. "Speak."

"Amanuet paid me an unusual visit only moments before I arrived here." *The king is in ill temper. Perhaps the pain of old battle wounds? The untimely death of the queen haunts his nights? I must take each step as though I walk on dried parchment.*

The king adjusted the clasp of the cloak. "*Unusual* visit? How so?"

"There is exhaustion in her speech, eyes and step. The young women assigned to watch over the princess fall asleep. She prods them awake, which in turn forces sleeplessness in Amanuet. They also have fallen asleep during my tutoring."

"Why is Amanuet assigning them to watch my daughter?"

"The princess is restless at night. Wanders the rooms, wakes the other women with her wakefulness. I know Amanuet keeps order, but constant surveillance is trying on her and the other women."

"Widow Amanuet is strong. She has undergone much worse. She will recover from any lost sleep. As for my daughter's companions, you have my permission to punish them when they sleep during tutoring with two strikes to the shoulder using a reed. It will instill discipline." The king raised an eyebrow. "Does my daughter also fall asleep during your classes?"

"No, my lord, she is *more* than awake. I will explain in a moment. However, the constant watchfulness and loss of sleep has made those under her charge irritable and difficult to control. They complain to me on how little time they spend with their own families. What is happening is a slow, though quiet, contagion. It will spread to all the others. Amanuet is distraught and feels that in her present state of distress she cannot think with clarity and dares not approach Your Majesty with muddled speech. Sometimes, due to pressing problems we cannot see what is directly in front of us."

"You speak in riddles. That is not like you." The wine dark eyes of the king bore into Aton's.

"Sire, all of what I have said can be avoided and cured with simple measures."

"And those are…?"

"The princess lives in a highly agitated state, thus the reason for her intense wakefulness. This affects those around her. A calamity has taken seed. If allowed to grow, a great tragedy will ensue. This can be avoided."

"All this has come about because of the captain, is that not so?" The sovereign's intense gaze searched his.

Aton inhaled a deep breath. "Yes. If I may be of utmost frankness…?"

The king waved a hand.

"It was and continues to be the custom of your people, both Greek and Egyptian, to give women, of all levels in society to choose whom they will accept…Sire, allow the princess and the captain to meet more often. Their meetings will solve many problems."

The hardness in the king's eyes settled on Aton. He paused as though weighing his answer. Finally, he said, "Perhaps you are right about my daughter. I have paid too much attention to my people's problems, especially those of little merit. I will consider your suggestion."

"Majesty, I must report, last night the captain…"

A sentry burst through the doors of the chamber. "I beg forgiveness, sire. A messenger from one of our outposts has arrived. He bears most urgent and grave news."

THIRTY-FOUR

Dawn broke, sent shafts of diffused sunlight through the woven curtain of Sebastián's window.

He had lain in bed awake hour after hour, elated at Cebellina's unexpected and most welcome visit, but also running through his failures in Spain: disobedience of the Queen's edict, excommunication by the Church, disgrace to his family, and facing him today, possible execution.

Struggling out of bed, he washed and shaved carefully—to look his best when facing death.

"Captain," someone shouted.

Sebastián sighed. "They are here already." He strode to the front room, head held high, shrugging into his blouse.

"Captain!" Abydos, the king's messenger rasped for breath and leaned against the doorway to Sebastián's hut. "His Majesty commands your presence at once. Slavers march upon us."

"How far away, Abydos?" Sebastián pulled his top boots on. *A reprieve?*

"They will be here when the sun hangs over our heads."

"Hmm." Sebastián quickly calculated. "About three leagues. That gives us about two hours." He buckled on his cuirass, pressed the forage cap snugly over his head. "The princess and the other women. What is being done for their safety and protection?" He slipped sash with sword over his head.

"As we speak…" Abydos said, "…they are on small boats crossing the river or hurrying over the footbridge to the other side. The children and our older people go first."

Sebastián bolted for the door.

Outside, Abydos ran alongside the sprinting Sebastián.

"What about the footbridge...if the enemy...?"

Abydos smiled. "We removed the planks from both sides of the river and hid them. There will remain only the section in the middle of the river, which has the depth of two spear lengths."

"Excellent." Without an intact footbridge and lacking boats, the enemy would have to swim—under a hail of crossbow bolts, arrows and spears from the women soldiers. "How many men does the enemy have?"

"The scout counted seven Arabs and many tribesmen, perhaps two or three hundred."

Sebastián slowed his stride. "Two or three...?" *Why so many?* From prior knowledge, he knew slavers used at most a score of tribesmen for slave hunting expeditions.

How did they acquire information about the size of the king's city? Shaking his head, Sebastián picked up his pace.

"Their weapons?" He decided to leave his pistols and hackbut behind. The time was not propitious to reveal to the enemy the presence of European weapons. Most important of all, he lacked extra powder and shot.

"The Arabs have swords, hackbuts and pistols; each tribesmen carries a bow, a war club, or spear, and shield of cowhide."

Sebastián grinned. "Our cloth-yard length arrows will pierce those shields like parchment."

The messenger nodded.

"Cannon?" Sebastián asked.

"None."

"Good." Sebastián's grin broadened. Lack of cannon meant overconfidence by the slave merchants, who, ignited by greed, had, perhaps, forced a night march on their men after crossing over the mountains. The enemy would not be in peak fighting condition. The odds for victory brightened.

"I hate slavers, Abydos."

The face of Abydos turned solemn. "Our people have suffered much because of them."

"Well, we have knowledge of their approach..." Sebastián said, "...we fight on ground of our own choosing, the sun will be in their eyes and they are unaware we have a secret weapon. The day will be ours!"

He dashed around a corner and stopped. His mouth gaped.

Ten paces away, Cebellina stood with several of her menina.

"What…?"

Fitted armor blinking in the sun covered her chest and shoulders. A skirt of interlaced lappets of leather strips reached to her knees and greaves hugged her calves. Two belts girdled her waist; one held a short sword the other, a dagger. Amanuet, the menina and several women behind the princess stood dressed in like manner. Sebastián smiled, pleasantly surprised.

In Spain, women of the aristocracy shied away from personal battle on the field. At word of a Muslim approach, most of them ran into fortified castles. Peasant women fought back with rocks, kitchen knives and hayforks.

As Sebastián watched, Cebellina adjusted a helmet and its crest of stiffened horsehair over her head. About to step toward her, the stern-faced Amaunet blocked his path.

"Princess," one lady cried out. "The king commands us to leave for the bridge at once!"

Cebellina raised her hands in a gesture of helplessness but Sebastián thought she mouthed the words, "I will see you soon," before she accepted a javelin from one of her companions. The group, silent and grim-faced, tramped off in formation towards the river.

"Incredible! One moment she is a princess, next she is a Greek Amazon."

Abydos drew closer to Sebastián. "The princess and her friends know how to throw the javelin and fight with a sword. She is also skilled with the dagger."

"I have never seen them practice."

"Captain, you are still a stranger in our city. It is forbidden to you. Perhaps someday you will be allowed…The princess and the others are our last line of defense. If we are defeated, the enemy will have to swim—"

Sebastián spun on his heel and glared at the man. "We will not be defeated!"

Abydos stepped back as though unsure if Sebastián would strike out with fist or sword. Then a smile formed on the man's face. "Yes, sir!"

"Excellent!" He and Abydos hurried back to their positions.

Alongside a hut's wall, they found King Telemesus shouting orders and men climbing to the walkways behind the palisade.

Sebastián crossed his arms across his chest. "Majesty, may I have the men I asked for?"

The king pointed to a score of men. "Follow the captain. Obey his commands as you would mine. Captain?"

"Sire?"

"I am leaving two extra men with you. In case you need reinforcements, send one man to the east, another to the west to find me. I will be covering the right flank. Oh, yes. No prisoners."

"Yes, Sire."

Followed by a troop of his soldiers, the king limped away to the right.

Bows and quivers grasped in hand, the score of archers fell in behind Sebastián. Of all the king's men, he had found these the most proficient in use of the longbow *and* the Egyptian composite bow.

"Take your positions. I will repeat my instructions. Use your personal bows for the two nearest tree markers, the long bow for the farthest marker," Sebastián shouted.

The men scattered to their assigned positions on the palisade.

An hour passed unnoticed by Sebastian as elderly men and boys filled wooden buckets and gourds with water to douse possible fires.

"Damn the slavers to hell," Sebastián muttered under his breath. Six weeks had passed since the day of the demonstration with the long bow. Since then, fewer than three-dozen bows had been made by the fletcher and his assistants using lemonwood; the tree closest to the yew used by the English. Sebastián had ordered sixty arrows for each man—only forty now available. There were also a dozen crossbowmen. Not enough crossbows and accurate only for short distances.

The archers and crossbowmen must make each shaft and bolt strike an enemy.

At Sebastián's suggestion and under the king's command, the archers practiced using the new bows five hours each day plus additional hours at night—rain or shine. In wet weather, small leather hoods kept the arrows' feathers dry until used.

His confidence remained high in spite of insufficient longbows and arrows. He marched to the gates to check their worthiness against the imminent attack.

Many native villages existed without gates; those with fragile entrances quickly fell against a physical onslaught by dozens of tribesmen throwing themselves against the flimsy barriers or gates—their Arab masters never exposing themselves to such danger.

Under Sebastián's direction, the king's gates saw reinforcement by addition of double staves across each portal and angled braces jammed against the wood from the inside.

"Most excellent," Sebastián told the guards after viewing the preparations and doubled back from whence he came.

Reaching the palisade, Sebastián climbed onto a platform a step higher then the walkway. The extra height afforded sight toward the forest in an 180° degree arc.

"I must be able to see the battlefield," he had explained to the king when the sovereign demurred over the Sebastián's exposure to enemy fire. Also, under Sebastián's direction, notched embrasures for the archers had been cut into the wall of stakes forming the palisade. Platforms, two paces wide at staggered intervals, ran the entire length of the wall. Two archers manned each platform—overlapping the other man's field of fire.

Sebastián marched down first one side of the palisade, then the other, reviewing the hand signals he would use with the men. Through years of battlefield experience, he knew the clamor of hundreds of men—whether friend or foe—drowned shouted commands.

"After each volley, watch for my signals," he advised each archer. "A triangle over my head means aim for the African chiefs; I will point them out. Both arms over my head means aim for the Arabs, the sun strikes their armor, reveals their position."

A lookout pointed toward the forest. "The enemy approaches!"

At a run, Sebastián took his place midway on the palisade.

First a low hum, the crash of underbrush followed by a roar, then like an angry swarm of ants, the enemy debouched from the edge of the jungle and flooded the clearing in a tide of men.

The tribesmen appeared first. With hoarse war cries and brandishing of spears, sweaty bare chests shimmering in the afternoon sun, cowhide shields held to the side, the Africans surged forward.

A single line of warriors covered both flanks in a half circle while middle ranks reached four warriors deep. The first rank of twenty or thirty men narrowed to a "V," and at a single command from the Arabs, swung shields to the front and aimed at the gate.

Sebastián nodded his admiration. These tribesmen showed some discipline and training. Most likely achieved, he assumed, from the Arabs. Now the enemy would throw itself in a group against the structure—the tactic deduced from countless reports by traders and captured slavers.

Behind the screaming tribesmen skulked the caboceer, the village chief with his coronet of feathers, along with the witch doctor, identified by a cap of steer horns. Close by, the Arab slavers, dressed in white, watched and shrilled commands.

Sunlight glinted off armor on seven Arab chests.

"The Muslims wear chest armor over the white djellabah," Sebastián told the nearest archer. Along with hackbuts, he imagined—not able to see behind the mass of warriors—each Arab stood armed with a scimitar tucked into his waist and a coiled whip draped over one shoulder—the latter a standard piece of equipment for whipping captured slaves to obey.

Sebastián raised his hand. "Crossbowmen. Steady! Pick your targets!"

The king's men nocked their crossbows.

The body of tribesmen reached the blue-painted sapling—the tree closest to the gate.

A stride beyond the mark, they stopped, reached back and, as one, hurled their spears. Dozens of spears slammed the gates with force—the wood trembled, several staves splintered.

Other spears flew over the palisade and into the compound. A few struck down inhabitants. Cries rose from felled men or boys.

Three ranks of the enemy rushed forward. First rank, stone and metal axes aloft, second rank with war clubs raised, third rank shoulders pushed back, spears aimed for release.

Sebastián snapped his arm down. "Loose!"

A dozen bolts shot toward the enemy.

The front row of attackers fell as wheat before a scythe. Behind the fallen men, the second rank faltered, then a guttural shout from their chief sent them charging again. The warriors leapt over their fallen comrades, launched their spears, war cries less strident. Off to the side, half a dozen men attacked the gate with the axes—hacking at the staves. They fell, one by one—impaled by spears from the king's men on the ramparts above, or crushed by heavy stones thrown by the defenders.

Sebastián raised, lowered his hand again. Another fusillade of bolts flew straight for the enemy. The second rank collapsed in a heap. A spear whizzed by Sebastián's head.

Crossbowmen bent over to reload then raised their heads.

Impatient, Sebastián slammed one fist against the other.

"Loose!" Holes opened in the third rank of warriors.

"Longbows now! Sebastián twirled his arm over his head.

Crossbowmen stepped aside. Archers took their place, arrows nocked "Loose!"

Longbow arrows pierced cowhide shields; men behind them clutched their chests, screamed and tottered to the ground face first—bloodied arrow points pushing through their backs. Rear ranks spun on their heels and ran toward the edge of the forest.

Sebastián viewed to his left then right. Three of the king's soldiers lay dead—spears through chests or necks.

He cupped his hands around his mouth. "The enemy is collecting fresh spears and regrouping for another attack. Watch for my signals."

In the center of the milling bodies, he spotted the feathered headdress of the chief and the witch doctor's cap of steer horns bobbing among the men— both leaders exhorting their warriors to attack.

Sebastián formed a triangle over his head and pointed toward the two headmen.

Archers on both sides of him, nodded, aimed and loosed their arrows.

Whistles cut the still air. Both chief and witch doctor fell with a flailing of arms and jerking of bodies.

Immediately, the Arabs took command. Two uncoiled whips and lashed out at the Africans, forced them back into attack formation. Four slavers in chest armor ran toward the gate, hackbuts held at the waist. They knelt and fired. Splinters and chunks of wood flew off the gate. Behind them, the line of warriors, their ranks now broken, rushed in fits and starts for the palisade.

This time, Sebastián held both arms above his head.

In swirls of white and spurts of red, the four slavers fell with twitch of limbs and screams—while reloading for a second volley. The remaining natives ran for the safety of the forest—and into the last three Arabs.

Sebastián smiled. "They have reached the yellow mark and think they are at a safe distance, eh? Loose!"

The enemy's entire rear rank collapsed. Tribesmen, backs cut and bleeding from whiplashes from the Arabs ran into each other. Several tripped over dead bodies now two deep while dozens of others circled away from the merciless whipping and retreated into the forest.

Others, as though dazed, confused, discipline broken, dashed back toward the palisade. Arrows felled them.

Sebastián leaped from the platform, sword held aloft.

"By Saint James, at them!" He bounded for the entrance of the compound, followed by the archers and a dozen soldiers.

"Open the gates!" he called to the sentries.

Cries of victory rose from the throats of the king's men. "For our Lord Sovereign!" They raced through the open gates and across the open ground in pursuit of surviving slave merchants and their African allies.

At the edge of the forest, a swarthy Arab whipping a cowering native spun around, djellabah billowing under a short cloak, to face Sebastián. The native scrambled to his feet and stumbled off.

As tall as Sebastián, the Saracen boasted a red turban. Dusty red boots shod his feet. Sunlight, almost blinding, glinted off the man's scimitar as he drew the weapon from an exquisite ivory and gold scabbard. The Muslim peered at Sebastián with contemptuous curiosity. Perhaps he wondered why a man in European armor challenged him.

The Muslim circled slowly, each step skillful, his dark eyes above a black, snarled beard narrowed into slits. Sebastián followed his opponent's every move.

"Die, Christian dog," the Arab screamed in Portuguese, then, scimitar held to his side, charged and slashed at an angle, aimed for Sebastián's sword arm.

Sebastián parried; the scimitar slid along his own sword's edge and missed, but Sebastián slipped on wet leaves and fell onto his back.

"*Allah uh akbar!*" Mouth open, spittle running down his mouth, the slaver raised his scimitar to deal the fatal blow.

Sebastián rolled as the Arab's blade cut through the leather strap of armor and into his shoulder. In the same instant, he swung wide with his own sword. It bit at the man's knees.

Blood sluiced through the white cloth. The Arab gazed at the wound, sneered and spit toward Sebastián. The slaver stepped back and uncoiled his whip with his free hand.

Once on his feet, Sebastián circled out of range of the lash. *Watch your opponent's eyes when a cloak hides his movements.* He watched for a telltale blink, a widening of the eyes, a flicker.

The slaver's eyes above the crescent of kohl widened, and he raised the whip.

Sebastián leaped forward. In a blur, his blade struck, cut an arc under and across the man's elbow and sliced into the exposed neck.

Blood spurted, the white djellabah mantled red. Whip and scimitar fell to the ground; the slaver clutched his neck and crumpled onto the ground, dead eyes defiant.

Sebastián raised his sword, saluted the dead Arab, wiped his blade clean on the hem of the djellabah, then ran to join the king's soldiers in pursuit of the enemy remnants. He passed by the last two Arabs.

They lay by a dirt path, arrows sticking out of their chest armor.

Alongside the Arabs, sieved by many wounds from spears, he saw the body of Sinhue—the former suitor for the hand of the princess.

"*That* is how the slavers received their information and gathered a large force. A traitor!"

If the slavers were victorious over the city, Sinhue would have received his reward: Cebellina. Sebastián harbored doubt. The Arabs held the promise of riches over any empty promise given to Sinhue. They would have killed Sinhue and sold her to a sheikh for a king's ransom.

"Sinhue, either way, your life was forfeit."

Sebastián pressed forward. Reaching the temporary enemy encampment, where scattered clothing, uneaten food and broken weapons bore witness to the slavers' haste to attack the city.

Epicydes, joined him, the king's field commander, face sweaty, his breathing rough, gazed nervously at the surrounding dark forest.

A quick look at the commander's demeanor exposed the inexperience. Sebastián lowered his voice and spoke in a calm, reassuring manner. "Only a few escaped. They are physically tired, winded and face a long distance before reaching the mountains. They will be easy to pursue."

Epicydes offered an appreciative tilt of the head and cried out, "Trackers. Hunt the retreating enemy down!"

Three men detached themselves from the group and disappeared into the brush.

The commander turned and gazed at the bloodied sleeve. "Captain, you are wounded. Permit me." He ripped off a portion of Sebastián's sleeve and tied the cloth above the wound.

"Thank you."

"I must leave and report to the king," Epicydes said.

"Yes, sir. Let the deaths of these men remain a mystery to their kinsmen. How many of the His Majesty's soldiers were lost, Commander?"

"Twelve."

"In spite of the losses, it is a magnificent victory. Congratulations to you and your men. Shall we gather the enemy's weapons for the king to view?"

"Yes. Thank you. His Majesty will be pleased," the commander said. "Captain, a question, if I may."

"Of course."

"How did you know exactly in which direction the slavers and their African allies would use for retreat?"

"I did not. The rabble we routed was a body without a head. With their Arab masters dead, the only thought the tribesmen held was to reach this camp and then home over the mountains. Their desperateness made their path easier to follow."

Epicydes nodded. "I will leave three men as a rear guard, take some of the weapons back with me. The king awaits my report."

"I will remain here and erase all traces of this camp," Sebastián said. "But first, I would like to address the men who came with me. With your permission, Commander?"

"Yes, of course."

Ignoring the building fiery pain in his shoulder, Sebastián addressed the archers assigned to him by Telemesus.

"This great victory would not have been possible without the dedication and skill demonstrated today. I wish to congratulate you all. For that, I humbly thank you."

The men responded by tapping their bows on the nearest shield.

Epicydes signaled to the soldiers and they marched off.

Making a mental note of dead tribesmen, slavers and the death of Sinhue, Sebastián and the rear guard cut off leafy branches and set to work throwing into the brush broken spears, uneaten food and sweeping away the many footprints, he, grimacing from shoulder pain with each stroke.

How Sebastián wished he could share today's magnificent victory with his father!

THIRTY-FIVE

Early twilight beamed across the river when the sentries closed the gates behind the last of the king's men. Arab slavers and their African allies vanquished. Those of the enemy who survived were now being hunted down by skilled trackers and killed. No one would live to tell what happened or reveal the location of the kingdom.

A dirty, exhausted Sebastián entered last through the gates. He had waited with the rear guard until the last of the soldiers left the forest, then threaded his way through the battlefield. Flies buzzed among the dead. The bodies needed burial as soon as possible.

The gates shut behind him and he veered off to his quarters, intent on bandaging his wounded shoulder—the throb insistent. He glanced around him. Why was the square empty? The emptiness gave him the feel of the somberness of an empty cathedral in Spain. The battle had ended much earlier. A breathless Abydos ran up to him.

"Captain, make haste! The king summons you."

For an instant, Sebastián thought the summons meant punishment awaited him. His heart lurched, his tongue scraped over dry lips. Voice raspy, he asked, "You are shaking, Abydos. "What is the matter?"

"Our lord king is wounded."

Both men bolted toward the Royal Chamber. Boots kicked up dust, Sebastián puffed his breaths, grimaced from the slash on his shoulder.

"How did it happen?" Sebastián asked.

"A slaver we thought dead leaped from the ground and speared his majesty. The Arab's body rots on the field, carrion for vultures."

197

Victory now tasted bitter. What did this turn of events mean for him? He centered his thoughts on the message. The urgent summons meant a serious wound. What if the king died? Sebastián felt remorse. He had betrayed the trust awarded him by Telemesus and the people. Unworthy of a guest. Never again.

He and Abydos rounded a bend, passed the candle maker's and carpentry shops, both closed.

Close to the Royal Chamber, they stopped. A jostling crowd blocked their path on this late afternoon. Women wailed, some men wept openly. A somberness filled the air.

"Stand aside, please," Abydos said, pushing his way through. "His Majesty commands the captain to appear at once."

Half a dozen soldiers appeared, spears held lengthwise, they walked alongside Abydos and Sebastián to clear a path.

Inside the chamber, Cebellina, in a purple robe, knelt beside her father, wiped away the perspiration on his temple. In a corner, the sorceress squatted on the ground, rocked and keened. Her once demonic eyes now dull and lifeless.

"The witch was already here when the soldiers carried the king inside," Abydos whispered to Sebastián, who noticed the king's bed had been moved to the center of the chamber.

Near the throne, in a cluster and on their knees, Cebellina's menina sobbed. In their middle, Amanuet wiped away tears. On the sovereign's left knelt Aton. At the head of the bed stood Epicydes and two officers, ceremonial spears in hand, heads bowed. Off to the side, the priest murmured prayers. Other soldiers and townspeople filled the chamber.

Aton pressed a hand over a bloodied coverlet covering the wound. The king's features were sallow, the strong jaw quivering, the pain obvious. Overhead, the flames in the hanging oil lamps shivered.

"He is here, Majesty," Aton said.

"Captain, come closer," the king said.

Sebastián fell to his knees next to Cebellina. She turned at his gentle touch. Tears welled in her eyes, jaw clenched, fist balled. *She is struggling to control her emotions.* "Sire?"

"My daughter will now be queen. Aton will guide her." The king's eyes turned toward the scribe.

Aton bowed. "I will obey her as I have Your Majesty."

"Captain de Aviles?"

"My lord?" Sebastián swallowed hard and moved closer.

Telemesus grasped Sebastián's forearm in a vise grip, the wine-dark eyes bored into his. "You will obey her commands? You will protect her?"

Sebastián drew his dagger and held it by the blade. "I will obey her commands as queen. I will protect her until my last breath." He kissed the handle of his weapon. "I swear this before my God and your gods, upon my honor."

"Then before these witnesses," the king rasped, "I unite my daughter and you. Now I will rest. I am tired." The king closed his eyes as his head lolled to the side.

"Our lord sovereign, our protector is with the gods," Aton said. The sorceress had disappeared.

Aton rose to his feet and bowed to Cebellina. "You are now queen. Shall we follow the custom of your people?"

"Yes. Our king shall be buried without a headstone or markings of any kind. His burial place shall be known only to us, not to our enemies."

"So shall it be," Aton said.

Cebellina leaned forward, kissed her father on the temple and addressed those in the chamber, chin raised, voice strained but firm. "His Majesty, The King Who Lives On The Red Mountain is dead. He will surely live forever in our memory. I will now be queen. It was our lord king's command that Captain Sebastián Alejandro de Aviles be my consort. The ceremony will occur a month from today. I will return in a moment. Captain, please follow me."

Gaze turned toward the dead king to hide his own pain, Sebastián spied blood on the ground from where he had risen—*his* blood, his fingers now dribbling red drops. Instead of elation at the sovereign's word of approval, Sebastián could only feel despondent.

He would have preferred to offer apologies to the court for his conduct and accepted whatever punishment meted out. Clutching a portion of his blouse against the wound and summoning his remaining strength, he followed Cebellina.

She led Sebastián into an adjoining room.

He turned to face her. "My sincerest condolences…"

Cebellina collapsed in his arms and broke into loud sobs.

THIRTY-SIX

Over the thirty days, Sebastián saw Cebellina but rarely and only to offer military advice to her, Aton and Epicydes. The days dribbled by as though each drop weighted. Finally, on the thirty-first day...

The priest, dressed in a black sleeveless outer garment stitched with the symbols Aton called *hieroglyphikos,* over a white linen robe, strode into the center of the clearing—an area circled by acacia trees at the rear of the king's chamber and set aside for special ceremonies. Between two olive trees, Sebastián spied a statue. Though badly chipped and blackened by age, dressed with full armor carved in marble by the sculptor, the female figure still displayed elegance of form. Now draped with garlands of flowers, the statue reminded Sebastián of a drawing he had seen in an old manuscript of the Greek goddess...

"Athena!" He peered closer.

The virgin Greek Goddess of the arts and prudent war, stared out of her intense, stone gray eyes, shield in one hand, spear in the other, ever vigilant, ever ready for battle.

"All these centuries and they still believe in their ancient gods..." he muttered. Neither Islam nor Christianity had influenced the descendents of Alexander The Great and his Macedonian conquerors. Sebastián shrugged and, eyes widened, watched the ceremony unfold.

In one hand, the priest held a long staff and stood still under a full moon while shafts of moonlight glinted off the man's shiny bald dome. Behind him, acolytes swung censers of burning incense. Whiffs of eucalyptus and jasmine filled the still night air.

A murmur of voices rose from the audience as the priest and his assistants intoned prayers in a language Sebastián did not understand.

How similar to the rites of the Church.

Observation of a religious ritual in a language most or all of the congregants did not comprehend. Or did this audience understand? One of the arguments he had had with the Roman Catholic clergy and roundly condemned for his audacity and heretical words. Well, what difference did it matter now?

The priest droned on, chanting and bowing to the carved figures of the Egyptian goddess, Bastet represented by a cat, and the goddess, Wadjet in the form of a flared cobra. A few paces away, Sebastián, resplendent in polished breastplate and sword, cradled his plumed helmet, noticed the weaving of Greek and Egyptian religious beliefs and perhaps other religions. An idea originated and promulgated by Alexander in lands conquered by him.

Did the idea of intermingling religions merit discussion? Sebastián wondered, the thought broken by the whisperings of the wedding guests. The soft voicing grew in volume with audible sighs and many nods of approval. He turned to his left.

As far as Sebastián could see, men, women and children filled every square yard of space in the clearing, doorways and paths. A gentle breeze fluttered by, lifted hems of fine gowns worn by the bejeweled women.

Except for the advisors and a few others, the men wore simple tunics, several boasted circlets of gold around their necks. Minutes passed and the audience turned restive and jostled each other for a better look.

After what he thought an eternity, he saw Cebellina emerge from the royal chamber and walk under a pergola festooned with purple, pink and red orchids. Along the path, rows of young women held lit candles in their hands. Petals generously strewn by the youngest of the menina, The Rose That Blooms Early, added to the aroma of the night.

A breath caught in his throat at the sight of his chosen bride.

A snow-white pleated gown, its hem edged in gold thread, flowed from neck to ankle. A red sash, the symbol of royalty, cinched her waist. Her collar of precious stones shone even more lustrous in the moonbows. Embroidery sewn on each of the billowing sleeves featured a snake—a cobra with flared hood. A wide band of gold encircled Cebellina's temple, a single turquoise in the shape of a falcon adorned the center.

"She's more breathtaking than ever," he said aloud. How he wished he could lean over and kiss that bow-shaped mouth! Even after being chosen as consort, Sebastián had not been able to step closer than three arm lengths.

"Princess, please step forward," the priest said. He motioned to Sebastián. "You also, Captain."

Sebastián clasped Cebellina's hands, her fingers felt cool and trembled; equaled the tremors in his legs at this most auspicious time of his life. They both knelt on crimson cushions.

Breathing deeply of her exotic fragrance of unknown origin, he closed his eyes for an instant as the scent embraced him.

To the right of Sebastián, propped on a chair, sat the dead king's jeweled sword and contoured chest armor—his silent presence to the wedding. To Sebastián's right stood Aton, the scribe silent and in a plain white robe, although a wide smile wreathed the scribe's face.

The queen raised her hand for silence.

"You may begin," she told the priest.

The ceremony proceeded, all foreign to Sebastián.

A half hour later, Sebastián thought, passed before Cebellina stood and turned to him. "Do you wish to say something?"

"Yes. If I may have Her Majesty's permission?"

The queen nodded.

Sebastián swallowed the hard ball of nervousness in his throat. "I would like to express my love for The Daughter of The King Who lives on the Red Mountain in your language and then address my God, in my language."

Raising himself on one knee, Sebastián drew his sword—lightly placed the point in the ground, and reached out for her. She squeezed his hand as he took hers and Sebastián placed his fingers over her palm.

"Cebellina, please kneel with me."

For the first time since he left da Gama's ship and its companions of calamity and death, he felt a bottomless peace and satisfaction. Sword pommel grasped, heart pounding in his ears, he gazed at her.

"I swear upon my honor as a soldier and hidalgo, that from this day forward, I will be your champion and protector. I will love you with every fiber of my being and will cherish you to the last breath of my days."

Sebastián stood, sheathed his sword and turned toward the queen. "With Your Majesty's permission, I will now speak in the language of Castile and my ancestors." Fingers steepled, he lifted his chin toward heaven and knelt again.

"Almighty Father, I know I have offended thee. For those sins I will answer to You in the hereafter. I love this woman and wish to marry her in your presence. I have neither Christian priest, kin nor friend by my side as witness to this most glorious day for me.

"I beseech You, God, our Lord, to witness my marriage to Cebellina. She is a pagan, but it does not diminish my love for her. I will hold dear her life as I do my own. I will challenge any man by force of arms, be he Spaniard or foreign, noble or peasant, who seeks to break this unshakable bond between my chosen bride and I, your humble servant. Please bless this union."

Sebastián crossed himself and stood. "I used the words I have heard many times. Cebellina, did your priest say or pronounce…husband and wife?"

She placed her fingers with thistledown grace on his arm. "Yes! You are now twice wed, once under my gods and once under your god. It is too late for you to run."

Cebellina laughed her soft velvet laugh, slipped her arm through his, as clapping broke out. All heads turned toward the chamber's entrance.

A group of young women appeared from inside, musical instruments in their hands. Heads held high, regal in their walk, the women took their places on stools. The thrum of drums began.

The audience raised their hands to the sky and burst into song.

> *"O, Isis, we sing this Evening Song with hands upraised*
> *To give our thanks, give our praise*

The reedy sound of flutes joined in.

> *O Isis, you are the Breath of Dawn*
> *You are Night and a New day born*

Tambourines, entered, added their tinkling.

> *Let us sing our song to thee*
> *Mother of Land and Sea*

Finally, the dignified sounds of the lyres.

> *Let our words echo o'er mountain and stream*
> *Fill our hearts, fill our dreams*

> *Isis, spread your wings and fly*
> *Embrace the Earth and Sky*

Wax cones on their heads emitting fragrances, filmy long dresses swaying as though wedded to the music, the guests swayed back in forth; the movement as that of deep ocean swells. Captivated by the regal movements of singers and music, Sebastián, although the words unfamiliar, hummed along until the end. In Spain, only peasants celebrated weddings with such feeling and joy.

The music ended with enthusiastic clapping and musicians and guests helped themselves to wine, beer, figs and honeyed cakes and pastries set on tables.

After hearty congratulations from Aton, and well-wishers, she and Sebastián strolled down the petal-strewn path and between walls of candles to the Royal Chamber.

Inside, censers set at the corners of the chamber, filtered their vapors through the air, breathed out their provocative scents.

A bed, comfortable for two and similar to the king's—his had been buried with him, occupied the space. A foot-long candle flickered at the headboard and played soft shadows on walls decorated with sprays of orchids and other flowers.

In the soft light of three-wick oil lamps, Sebastián unbuckled his armor, let if fall to the ground and took her hand in his. He sniffed the air. She had perfumed herself with the fragrances of wildflowers. He imagined Cebellina in a field surrounded by yellow jasmine, the red petals of roses, and pale purple lips of lavender, all of them rushing to embrace her with their scents. Essences to feed his spirit, gladden his heart and quicken his pulse.

"Cebellina, that day in the clearing, when I first saw you, my breath faltered, my body refused to move. My heart wished to burst from my chest and pounded in my ears. From that moment, I knew I would love you through eternity."

She touched his cheek with her fingertips. "And when I saw you, at first I was frightened and thought first to kill you, or kill myself to avoid capture— never be a slave in the harem of an Arab. But when you spoke…a calmness settled over me. I was not afraid anymore."

Sebastián leaned over, kissed her temple, moved to her lips…He reached behind her neck and untied the gold cords of her jeweled collar. Placing the collar on a wooden chest, he shrugged off his blouse.

Her hand flew to her throat as she gazed at the spidery network of raised ribbons of cuts from sword and daggers on his deep chest. "I thank the gods for sparing you and may they protect you in the future, my husband." Caressing the strong muscles at the back of his neck, she returned his kisses and pressed her perfumed body against his. Her mouth kissed away his loneliness and his last dark shards of melancholy.

Gently, Sebastián parted the silken cords encircling her narrow waist. Her white gown slid down and gathered in folds at her feet. He lifted her willing body to the bed. Her body writhed beneath him and melted into his.

"Oh, Sebastián, my beloved…"

THIRTY-SEVEN

Twice during the night, Cebellina woke him with caresses and whisperings of love.

Night fled reluctantly—its black and gray streaks in slow retreat before a new dawn.

Days sped by, turned into weeks, then months. One morning she woke him with the message: "I am with child."

This morning, a breathless Abydos, now the queen's messenger, ran up a wooden ladder set against the wall of the royal Chamber. The rungs led to an overlook with a magnificent view of the river and the distant gray blur of the aloof mountain range.

Abydos shouted as he climbed. "Captain!"

Sebastián left his repair work on the crumbling mud-brick belvedere and peeked over the edge. "Take pause," he said. "Then speak."

Two deep breaths later, the man said, "We have received news from one of our outposts. Twenty Portuguese ships are making their way down the coast. At last report, they are three suns away."

Sebastián slapped his thigh. "It must be Vasco da Gama! Have you informed the queen?"

Abydos lowered his head. "I dared not enter her personal quarters."

"I will inform her."

Abydos nodded and hastened back down the ladder.

Two years. That's what Da Gama had said for his return to Western Africa. His former superior, Sebastián surmised, most likely on his way to consolidate Portuguese trading rights and further conquests in Africa, India and Cipangu. If Sebastián moved with utmost haste, he could meet da Gama at the bay. Then he would receive tidings from Spain, and, most important of all, news about his parents—four years had passed since he left Spain.

So much had happened since his being marooned on the beach as punishment with death as his final companion. He would ask da Gama to send a messenger to Spain with a long-ago-written letter to Sebastián's parents about their son's marriage to Cebellina. What would his parents say? His father? Of all the cavaliers Sebastián knew, his father was the most flexible in matters of religion. Over many years, Don Avíles had attended mandatory twice-a-day masses. He had found, Sebastián also knew, some priests dedicated to their calling, others avaricious, even criminal.

Sebastián's mother? She would light innumerable candles and wear out her rosary in prayers at endless masses. She and the Church would never accept his marriage to a pagan—even a queen.

Well, somehow, he would convince his mother. The Church? He did not care. The Church no longer controlled his destiny. God our Lord commanded all destinies.

Cebellina! What would she say? At this moment she nursed their first child—a girl.

Crossing to the anteroom, he filled an earthenware basin from a jug of fresh water and washed his hands and face. On a shelf above him next to a vase with jasmine flowers sat the silver goblet from da Gama. He glanced at the object. Visions of the tortuous return voyage, the hardships on body and soul, battered by angry seas, ugly sickness and…

Cebellina appeared, her exposed nipple still wet from the nursing, their daughter, Caterina, Pleasure of Our life, asleep in her arms.

Taking a cloth from a peg, he dried himself, gazing at his wife. Motherhood had bestowed a luminescence on her features. Sebastián smiled.

Cebellina tucked the baby into a wooden cradle lined with soft cotton sheets, turned and raised the tunic to cover her breast and slipped on the ever-present gorget of precious stones.

She saw him polishing his armor and sharpening his sword as though preparing for battle. She arched an elegant eyebrow.

"Where are you going?"

"Vasco da Gama will arrive soon. I have described my voyage with him to you." He shrugged into a clean blouse.

"I will go with you. I will summon Aton and dismiss today's court session.

207

If you go to meet with this…Vasco da Gama, I will be there also." She pushed errant auburn curls away from the infant's face.

"You cannot go."

She spun to face him. Her dark eyes flashed. "Why do you not wish me to go?" Then her features softened. "If you leave, there will be no rest for me. Our bed will offer no comfort to my body."

Sebastián embraced and kissed his wife on the lips, bent over and kissed their baby's head. "I love you both more than life itself. I do not know what my reception will be. Many things may have changed. I will not place you in jeopardy."

Her painted eyes narrowed. "Are there women on these ships?"

"Perhaps, perhaps not. On their first expeditions of conquest, Spanish or Portuguese conquistadors do not take women. There are many hazards. Scores of conquistadors have already died from disease, starvation and battles with indigenes—the native peoples."

Undeterred, Cebellina went on. "If these voyages and conquests are so dangerous, why do these men persist?"

Sebastián sighed. "The light on the path to unknown lands is lit by Glory, Gold, and God. Neither heat of desert, nor winter's cold, jungle, or wild beasts deters a conquistador—these men conquer or die in the attempt. As for your boarding a ship, sailors have deep superstitions. Women on board these ships, seamen say, portend bad luck."

"Well, then we shall all meet on the beach! I have never seen a beach or a ship."

Why was she always so logical? "The journey is fraught with danger," he said. "The march there and back." He recalled, after the destruction of the slavers and hundreds of their allies, peace had reigned for two years. Little danger existed—as long as vigilance stood high.

"My father always advised me that whenever the opportunity arose, I should meet face to face with possible future enemies. Also, you will be there to protect me. You will prepare a plan. I trust you with my life," she said, as though reading his thoughts. "I will wear my armor and take weapons."

Sebastián drew a deep breath, exhaled slowly to sort out his thoughts. If he insisted Cebellina not go…

Da Gama would expect his former officer to greet him on board ship and Sebastián hungered, craved for tidings about his parents and Spain. He gazed at the great fortune resting on her collar, the glint of rubies and other precious stones plus those on armlets, bracelets.

"You may go with me. No armor or javelins. But you must wear a robe that covers you from your neck to your ankles and has long sleeves. Use a white sash instead of the red. No earrings, headband of gold or display of great wealth. Also, remove the coloring on your eyelids. You must trust me in this matter."

She frowned. "But the jewelry belonged to my mother, her mother..."

He circled his arm around her small waist. "Dearest wife, without a hint of gold or glint of diamond, you are still the most beautiful woman in the world. You know why I ask. Do not resist my request." He lifted her chin and kissed her again.

She stroked his cheek and whispered, "Yes, my beloved captain, at certain exquisite moments—many, many—of them, I do not resist but surrender, nay, conspire gladly. And..."

Amaunet who had always blocked Sebastián's nearness to Cebellina entered. She arrived each morning to allow Cebellina to attend court, listen to petitioners and others presenting their cases before the queen.

"Good morning, Amaunet," Cebellina said.

Amaunet offered a slight bow. "Good morning, Highness."

Head held high, she nodded to Sebastián. "Captain."

"Good morning, Widow Amaunet," Sebastián said. He offered a broad smile, trying to break through the usual rock hard expression on her face. *Was that a semblance of a smile on her face?*

She peeked into the cradle, immediately lost her haughtiness and cooed at the gurgling infant. "And how is our little princess today?"

An hour later, after assuring the court only a day's delay in its process, she dismissed everyone and asked Aton to accompany her back to the Royal Chamber.

Sebastián repeated his desire to meet with his former superior, da Gama.

Aton clasped his hands behind his back. "How do you know this da Gama will not march to attack the queen and her people?"

"Scribe, the Portuguese are interested only in cities with ports accessible to their ships. Inland cities pose most difficult problems for them—tortuous supply routes, Portugal's lack of a large army with many trained soldiers, sufficient capable commanders, inhospitable terrain and hostile natives."

"I see. How will you assure the queen's safety?"

"I will do the following..."

An hour passed, Sebastián outlining his plan in detail to the queen and the scribe. An attentive Aton listened, offered advice and asked questions. Finally,

Cebellina and Aton approved and Sebastián then asked preparations be made for the following day's travel to the beach and the meeting with da Gama.

Two days later, standing in front of a tent erected by Sebastián and the queen's soldiers on the beach, he and Cebellina watched da Gama's flagship glide into the bay. Out toward the horizon, the remainder of his fleet furled their sails to half-mast and tacked back and forth within sight of the bay. On shore, as per Sebastián's request, the king's soldiers lay hidden behind trees and thick brush.

Orders rang out on the deck, echoed across the bay.

He watched seamen lower a large skiff with a crew of four and row to shore.

"Dearest Cebellina, I will be speaking in Portuguese to da Gama. Later, I will translate what is said. Do not fear anyone. I have come prepared."

Cebellina raised her chin. "Beloved, I never cringe before an enemy. Well, perhaps that one time with you. But I am afraid for you. I will not show weakness. I have my dagger hidden in my robe."

Sebastián rubbed his chin. Once he had been allowed, he watched her and other women practice with the weapon. He saw Cebellina throw the razor-sharp blade and hit the center of a bull's-eye target—several times. Perhaps the crewmen should be afraid.

"Good, then we are ready."

The skiff's bow lifted on a wave, shot forward and crunched down on the beach.

He marched toward the seamen. Surprise rose on the sailors' faces. One drew his sword. Sebastián raised his hand. "*Alto!* Hold! I am Captain Sebastián Alejandro de Avíles. I am here to pay my respects to your commander, Vasco da Gama. He expects me. Hold the boat steady for the lady."

The seamen hesitated.

"Row us to the ship now!"

Before the seamen could react, Sebastián swept Cebellina up in his arms, waded to the side and settled her on the stern seat of the boat.

Even though covered with a cloak from her neck to her ankles, the mouths of the sailors gaped at the sight of the queen, as though transfixed by this vision of beauty.

Expressionless, she looked neither to the right or left, but fixed her gaze over their heads.

The seamen obeyed, lowered and slipped the oars through the oarlocks and pulled away from the beach.

Red and white plumes fluttering in a welcome breeze, his polished cuirass beaming in the sunlight, Sebastián adjusted his helmet and tied the faceplates.

Next to him, her back straight as a wall, Cebellina stared at the ship. Though impassive at what she saw, she gripped Sebastián's arm tightly.

She is controlling her excitement about her first sight of a ship. If she only knew the truth. These ships can be beautiful to look at, but they are a horror to live on.

The skiff bumped against the starboard side of the ship, a seaman grasped the ladder built into the gunwales and, with Cebellina close behind, Sebastián climbed on board.

On deck, da Gama strolled forward and stretched out his hand. "Ah! Captain Sebastián. Welcome aboard." Sebastián saluted, he and da Gama shook hands, then da Gama turned towards Cebellina. "And who, may I ask, is this young lady?"

The ship's crew drew closer.

Sebastián spoke in Portuguese. "Thank you, Sir. I have the honor to present The Daughter Of The King Who Lives On The Red Mountain.

"Her father, the king, sends his respects." Sebastián forwent any mention of his marriage to a pagan woman. Da Gama was not that forgiving. Also, unsure of da Gama's reactions in dealing with a queen instead of a king, he gambled da Gama would not pursue the matter.

"Where is this Red Mountain?" da Gama asked.

"Fifty leagues from here," Sebastián lied. He was willing to risk his life and hers if warranted to save the new queen and her people from conquest or destruction. Who knew when the Portuguese might extend their conquest inland? What if an invasion occurred? Sebastián would fight the Portuguese. If necessary, even against da Gama.

Da Gama nodded. "I see. I assume she does not understand Portuguese. You will translate, Captain."

"Yes, sir."

Da Gama bowed slightly. "Welcome, Princess. My king sends his greetings and salutations to your king and his people."

Sebastián translated, substituting "queen" where necessary. Cebellina responded with a polite nod.

Da Gama turned to Sebastián.

"First, news from Spain. Christopher Columbus and his brothers, Diego and Bartolomeo were brought back to Spain in chains…"

Sebastián cocked an eyebrow.

"…for disobeying the queen's explicit orders. Queen Isabel had ordered the treating of the *indigenes* to be, '…*muy bien y con amorosamente.*' Treated well and with affection, instead, they governed more with the whip and the gibbet than with good administration.

"Spain also now controls, in addition to Sardinia, Sicily and southern Italy, all of the Caribbean from Bermuda, to Cuba." Da Gama paused, then went on.

"Captain de Avíles, It always grieves me to deliver sad tidings of a personal nature. I have distressing news for you."

Sebastián flinched. "Sir?"

"Your parents are dead."

Sebastián felt color drain from his face.

Her attention on her husband, Cebellina's eyes widened and she shoved her hand under the sash of her waist.

Sebastián shook his head almost imperceptibly at her. She withdrew her hand.

"How did they die?" If his parents had died on orders from Lupiana, Sebastián would search for a way to reach Spain, kill that vicious woman and anyone else involved.

"From what was been reported to me, Don Avíles and Doña Avíles were returning from some festivity, the night dark, heavy with rain. At a turn in the road the carriage skidded and plunged over the side of a cliff. Both, the most honorable knight of the Order of St. James and old friend of my family along with Doña Avíles perished, including the footmen and driver."

Da Gama extended his hand. "On behalf of myself and my family, we express our deepest sorrows and may Almighty God and His Beloved son, Our Lord Jesus Christ watch over their souls."

Sebastián lowered his head. His hopes and dreams of one day returning to Castile had ended with the death of his parents. The rest of his family, adult male cousins and uncles, had perished in battles during the long wars with the Moors.

Only aunts, female cousins and two young males were left to manage the leagues of cork farms, orange groves and other properties of the de Avíles estate, a difficult task. Eventually, the crown would take possession of the family holdings. Nothing remained in the land of his birth to pull him back.

"Thank you, sir, for your kind condolences."

"I ordered my fleet to stop here…" da Gama said, "…to see if you were still alive. You are that and…" He glanced at Cebellina. "…much more than that. I will not ask for details. I am in great haste. The other boat I sent ashore is returning with additional fresh water and vegetables. After my last voyage, His Majesty promoted me to Admiral of The Sea. But my respite was of short duration. I have been asked by my lord king to return to India. There is widespread corruption among the Portuguese administrators, and rebellion by the populace. The governor general who mismanaged the colony is an idiot. I will set things right."

Knowing da Gama, Sebastián visualized the outcome. The incorruptible da Gama would shackle the governor-general in chains and send him back to Portugal, perhaps also the governor's staff and anyone else found guilty—if they were fortunate—torture and hanging for those judged responsible for causing difficulties for king and empire.

"Admiral?" asked the ship's chief officer.

Da Gama turned. "Yes, what is it, Captain Romero?"

"Is not this man a fugitive, wanted by Queen Isabel? There is a large reward. We should arrest him…place him in irons." Murmurs of assent rose from nearby crewmen. "And the woman also. She looks like one of those spoken about…"

Da Gama raised a hand.

Romero's mouth snapped shut.

"What do you say to that, Captain de Avíles?"

Sebastián thought he detected the hint of smile on the admiral's face. No, the admiral never smiled.

"Captain Romero," Sebastián said, "if perchance you have not noticed, the entrance to this bay is quite narrow, allows passage for one ship, perhaps two at a time to pass through. I came aboard peacefully to pay my respects to the admiral. If my party and I are not safely back on shore within the hour, this ship and everyone on board will die."

Captain Romero sneered. "Including you and that pagan woman?"

Sebastián locked eyes with Romero. "Yes. Those are my strict orders."

Arms folded, da Gama watched in silence.

Romero rushed to the gunwales and searched the beach. No sign of armed men, Sebastián knew. The king's soldiers lay well hidden. Romero's glance at the crests would reveal only thick groves of trees and brush. The ship's captain fingered his sword. "You have a dozen savages posted there? What will they do with their puny bows and spears? We have hackbuts, pistols and cannon!"

Sebastián casually brushed some grains of sand from his sleeve. "I have many experienced archers on both cliffs. I will repeat myself. If my party and I are not safely ashore within the hour, this ship will be a blazing torch down to the waterline before its bow reaches open sea."

He faced da Gama. "With the admiral's permission? I will offer a single demonstration. Please clear the center deck."

"Clear the deck," da Gama ordered. The crew dispersed.

Sebastián raised both hands over his head.

As the ship's captain and crew watched from the railings, an arrow flew out of the forest on the bluff, arched, then plummeted. The arrowhead thudded dead center on the deck.

Murmurs ran through the audience of seamen, their mouths gaped and looks of shock crossed their faces as they stared at the quivering shaft. Some cupped their hands over their brows, scanned the heights. No sign of archers appeared.

Da Gama nodded. "Captain Romero, did I not tell you Captain de Avíles is an excellent officer? I wager he has already mapped and taken measurements of this area, positioned his men to inflict the greatest injury with minimal loss to themselves. I will not risk loss of His Majesty's ship or crew for a few gold coins. Raise anchor and make ready to leave." He stepped closer and grasped Sebastián's hand in a strong handshake.

"Oh, yes, I almost forgot. Some months ago your father wrote to me. In his letter he said that Doña Lupiana had been arrested by the Inquisition."

"Why?"

"For trying to seduce and corrupt a cardinal close to Queen Isabel."

Sebastián shook his head. Lupiana's consuming thirst for power might now consume her in flames.

"Go with God, Captain. I will retire after this voyage. I wish you were going with me one more time. At this time, Portugal and Spain are in dire need of good officers. But, I do not think we will ever see each other again. 'Tis a great pity."

"Go with God, Admiral." Sebastián saluted and hurried Cebellina to the railing and helped her into the waiting boat.

From the encampment on shore, he and Cebellina sat on the beach and watched the ships sail away until the vessels faded into specks on the horizon. She took his hand in hers.

"Beloved, when we were on the ship, I saw a great sadness shadow your face. What has happened?"

"My parents are dead. Killed in an accident."

She released his hand and threw both arms around him. "Oh, I am so sorry. I lost my dearest mother and father and will always carry the pain of their deaths in my heart. Will you return to your land to pay your respects to them? Our baby and I will go with you."

"No. I cannot, as I explained to you. The Church, I would wager, has excommunicated me. I am no longer welcome in Spain." The Church, he knew, long on memory, short on forgiveness. Previously, Sebastián had revealed the duel and the outcome, but not the affair. "Nothing remains there for me. What I need, what I desire most in the world is being here with you and our daughter. I love you, Cebellina. Your smile brightens my day, your sweet words bathe my heart and your touch gladdens my soul."

She placed her head on his chest. "And I pray to the gods each night for your safety, for your nearness to me each day and night."

"Always, Cebellina. Today, on the morrow, all the days and years after." He kissed her on the lips, his kiss long and thoughtful.

Towards twilight and finished with their meal of venison and vegetables, Sebastián set guards and ordered preparations for the next day's march back to the queen's compound.

Off to the side, sentries paced the perimeter.

"Come," she said, taking him by the hand, "let us sit on the sand and watch this wonderful setting of the sun you always praise."

Submerged in the soft shadow of their tent, she and Sebastián viewed the sunset.

Far out in the horizon, pink-hued shafts of sunlight arrowed between the bluffs and walked across the still waters. Soon, the bay, afloat in a pool of liquid gold shimmered in the twilight.

Cebellina clapped. "It is like a large bowl filled with melted gold!" She clutched his hand. "Will our lives be like this always?"

"Yes." He hid the doubt he felt and drew her closer to him. How long would their happiness last? Slavers would return sooner or later, he vouchsafed the fact. The slave merchants had been destroyed once. But others as greedy would take their place.

When? Only God our Lord knew.

THIRTY-EIGHT

In The Year of Our Lord, Fifteen Hundred and Three, an elderly white man, half-delirious and muttering, his tattered clothing hanging on a skeletal frame, staggered into a Portuguese trading port on the Western coast of Africa. Stray dogs yapped at his heels.

"Help me!" the man cried out in Maltese, stumbled forward, then rasped in Portuguese. "For the love of our Lord Jesus Christ, have mercy."

"Another drunk," a passerby said and moved on.

The derelict shuffled past one of the rough-hewn shacks of logs and mud and collapsed on the dusty, rutted single street in the town. "Water, please!" He stretched out his arms in supplication.

Curious, several town inhabitants gathered closer.

"I work in the tavern," a beefy man said, "I know drunkards. He is not drunk."

"Look," a stout woman said, pointing, "he is bruised, full of cuts, insect bites. I'll get some water." She waddled off.

Water arrived. Half swallowing, half spilling the liquid on his sweaty, grimy chest, the man emptied the tankard. The barkeep and another man took hold of the derelict's bony shoulders and dragged him over to the shade of a tree. One of the men propped a piece of firewood under the straggler's head.

"Listen to me," the beggar said when bystanders started to drift away. "I have a story to tell. I swear by Almighty God every word I say is the truth."

"We have heard that before," an onlooker said. The others nodded.

"Wait! My name is Palen Andrus from the island of Malta. I was formerly

217

a professor of history and literature at the university. But one day, I wished to make and live my own history. I longed for adventure, to visit faraway places, exotic ports of call; hear the siren's song. I abandoned the mustiness of the library for the brine of ocean. I signed on as a sailor on *The Star of the Sea*. The ship stopped at this very port for fresh supplies before setting sail to Italy. While in the tavern, some shipmates and myself heard about a slave-gathering expedition getting under way. Men rushed to join because of a certain rumor running through the taverns."

The stout woman pushed through the growing crowd. "You must be one of those that left weeks ago. What befell all of—?"

A bystander shook his finger at her. "Let him finish."

The woman crossed her arms. "Very well."

Palen Andrus continued. "The rumor spoke about a village or town in the south, filled with beautiful women, much gold, silver, and precious stones—a part of the kingdom of Prestor John.

"These women, the tale went, possessed such beauty they brought princely sums in the slave markets. When someone asked for details, none could actually say they had seen one of these wondrous creatures in the flesh."

Palen coughed. Yellow phlegm splattered into the dirt. "I curse the day I heard about those women." He hacked again. "Please, more water…or wine."

A flacon appeared. He coughed back a mouthful onto himself and two of the closest listeners.

"Filthy beggar," one said.

"I beg your forgiveness. I am not myself." Palen inhaled a deep breath, wiped his mouth with a torn, dirt-encrusted sleeve and went on.

"Some sailors said they heard the rumors from the crew of a Portuguese ship under the command of the famous Portuguese Admiral of The Sea, Vasco da Gama. They boasted of seeing one of these extraordinary women on board ship.

"With each telling, the tale grew more grand. The village turned into a magnificent city and the number of women rose into the thousands. By the time the expedition set forth, the numbers of men joining had swollen to over five hundred strong. Among the group were sailors deserting their ships, soldiers, escaped criminals, Arab and European slavers. Half a dozen camp whores from different lands fattened the number. Within a fortnight we marched into the surrounding forest. Because of so many men, we traveled slowly. For safety, some men said. Others disagreed, saying it was due to an incident two years before. This is what I heard: A group of Arab slave traders and tribesmen had traveled south in the same direction as ours.

"They disappeared and were never heard from again. Drunkards and others in our expedition group laughed heartily. The Arabs among us, sullen as always, kept silent at the story."

"They were Arabs, what else could you expect?" one of the bystanders said. The crowd roared. Palen glared in annoyance, but spoke on.

"It is getting hotter," the stout woman said. "Let us carry him inside."

A muscular man picked up Palen as though the Maltese a child and laid him on a wide table of planks in the tavern. Two men pushed the table against a wall for Palen to lean on so the lone survivor could continue with his story.

"Thank you, sirs. On the second day, we happened upon a small village. Men rushed in thinking they had found the wondrous city. They searched the huts, but found only a few trinkets of any value and the women not the ones they sought. Angry at their misfortune, they slaughtered all of the men and children in the village, the women raped before having their throats cut. Finally, the village put to the torch."

Palen raised his hand. "I swear to you before Our Lord Jesus Christ, I did not take part in those atrocious acts." He crossed himself.

"The expedition cautiously made its way south. From the beginning, the nightly encampments consisted of heavy drunkenness. Men gambled, argued, drew knives, pistols, stabbed and shot each other. By the fourth day of our march, three of the camp followers had been killed over who had rights over them. That very night, the remaining three slatterns fled the camp.

"Only God knows what happened to those unfortunate creatures. We decamped the next morning at break of day and waded through mist-covered, poisonous swamps and their most odious stench until sunset. Several drunkards fell into the slime-covered water and drowned. Others, seized by crocodiles, were dragged under the black waters. Footsore, weary by the rigors of the march, beset by hordes of bloodthirsty mosquitoes and other insect societies, plus twilight upon us, several self-appointed guides told us we stood only a day's march from the fabled city. After much argument, we decided to make camp.

"Good fortune had smiled on us. A cool stream and fresh grass in an open clearing two hundred yards from the jungle on either side, looked ideal. Truly, a vision of restfulness and beauty to my exhausted body and mind. Along the muddy curved bank and out about two paces into the water, reeds, a yard high, grew in scattered, thick clumps. A few acacia, eucalyptus trees and scrub grass carpeted the rest of the clearing.

"To a man, all approved of the chosen ground. Some of our more boorish men boasted, 'Any savages foolish enough to attack us across open ground would be easy targets. Heathens have never bested us! Their arrows no match for our hackbuts and pistols.' Armed with these weapons plus two small cannon pulled along on sleds, and our host of men, we all felt safe. Everyone shouted, excited, bragged about the next day's riches and capture of the legendary women, and the princely fortunes they would bring at the slave market.

"We pitched tents—those fortunate enough to have them. Some of the men gathered reeds, tying the bundles into tight fascicles, then lit them to use as torches.

"I, fatigued beyond measure from the endless walk through inhospitable forest and my stomach ill tempered, I borrowed a pot and boiled an infusion of anise seed purchased in Malta before retiring for the night. I draped my tattered cloak over a low branch, a clod of dirt for my bed. Fires and torches lit, the camp quickly turned into an expedition of drunks."

Palen spit up blood, swallowed another mouthful of wine and spun his tale.

"The next day, I rose early, a moment before dawn, to relieve myself. A bluish mist, waist high, was slowly lifting, rendering a poverty of vision. A strange quiet for the middle of a forest, I thought, not a single birdsong.

"After some stumbling in the fog, I found a spot between a tree and a clump of reeds and out of sight of the nearest tent. I squatted down, did the necessary, stood and bent over to pull up my pantaloons.

"Suddenly, a whistling sound rent the morning's stillness. Half a dozen arrows buzzed over my head. One embedded itself in the tree behind me— right where I had stood a moment before! Mother of God. I crossed myself several times at my good fortune. The other arrows struck camp tents, makeshift coverings and men stirring about. Without lifting my pantaloons, I dropped to all fours, crawled into the reeds and struggled to remove my pantaloons. Cursing my fruitless efforts, I surrendered to the impossibility, knelt on the river bottom, smeared my face with mud, and kept only my nose above water. From my concealment I could see most of the camp and the opposite bank. I parted two reeds and watched.

"Inside the camp, amid shouts of alarm, screams of those hit, and others laboring to shake off their drunkenness, another volley flew over. This time the arrowheads held fire.

"I cursed those heathens with every oath I knew." Spittle ran down both sides of Palen's angry, wine-stained mouth. "We had been taken by surprise— our entire army. I would swear the flames of hell would consume us.

"Fires crackled everywhere—devouring all in their path, columns of smoke like sea snakes rose from pyres of cloth, wood and our supplies. Men fell with burning arrows sticking out of arms, legs and chests. Even those with chest armor."

A listener interrupted. "Savages using arrows that go through armor and at the distance you say? That is impossible!" The crowd nodded in unison.

"Please, let me finish," Palen said. The crowd murmured then grew silent.

"That's what I thought at the time. Scores of our Europeans along with the Arabs recovered from the surprise, loaded and fired their hackbuts across the stream into the jungle. All of their shots fell harmlessly to the ground, many yards short. With angry shouts of revenge and oaths, the men drew swords and pistols, splashed and swarmed across the water to shorten the range and close with the enemy.

"Half a dozen men rushed to the sleds and the cannon, pushed the artillery to the edge of the embankment. They loaded powder and shot. About to light the fuse, a flock of arrows felled them. The cannon stayed silent.

"Another storm of arrows struck, quickly followed by another. Dozens of men fell with dreadful screeches, clutched at the arrows, the feathers at the ends growing like flowers in their chests.

"One of the men, an Englishman I had seen in camp, as huge as a bear, still standing unhurt after the fusillade, stopped in mid-stream next to a dying Arab, an arrow in the slaver's chest—blood fountaining a deep red across the Saracen's white djellabah As I watched, this Briton placed a cavalry boot on the dying slaver's chest, grasped the arrow, and while the Arab screamed with a final piercing cry of anguish, the Englishman yanked the arrow out of the man's chest. The Briton then placed the bloody shaft between his fingers to measure the length and examined the arrowhead.

"'The bloody bastards are using longbows!' he shouted over his shoulder. 'With bodkin points that go through armor!'"

"The next instant, a fiery arrow rammed itself through the Englishman's throat, the shaft emerging the length of two hand spans, another pierced his breastplate. From his throat, a hideous gurgling issued when he fell face forward into the already crimson river. When his huge body hit the stream, a hiss arose from his burning clothing and hair as they touched the water—his fingers still tightly gripping the arrow by the ends.

"I can still smell the burning flesh of hundreds of bodies. I thought about what the Englishman had said about the longbows. How did this favorite weapon of the English come to be in Africa? What fiend used them with such ruthlessness?" Palen stared blankly ahead.

His audience looked at one another, some shrugged uncaringly.

"I swore at my ill-timed decision to seek adventure, fame and fortune. As for those accursed women of beauty, a plague on them!" He placed finger on his blistered lips and whispered the next part. The crowd shuffled closer.

"All this time," he rasped, "not a sound from our attackers, no bloodthirsty yells, no onrush of savages brandishing spears—only the endless whistling of the infernal arrows, enough to drive anyone mad. Volley after volley, rained down on the camp.

"Surely, I thought, this is the scourge of Almighty God, descending on us for our sins."

Whimpering, Palen held his palms up towards the heavens, then dropped his chin to his chest. Slowly, he raised it again and resumed his tale.

"The fusillade suddenly stopped—the only sounds rising with the mist and tearing the morning air were the cries of the wounded.

"'Holy Mother, save me'," from the Christians, praying, asking God for forgiveness of their sins. "'*Allah uh akbar!*'" from the Muslims.

"Morning sun rose, burned away the last wisps of fog along with a friendly breeze that rid the stench of burning bodies." Palen stopped and his eyes almost bulged from his sockets. Leaning forward, he raised his voice, swore and croaked his words. "It was then I saw *him*!"

"Who?" the anxious crowd asked in unison.

"The demon of our destruction. A white man! He stood on the opposite bank a moment then waded across, careful to avoid the bodies choking the stream.

"A polished helmet cradled his head—a panache of plumes in the crest, one red one white waved in the morning breeze. Strapped to his chest was an embossed breastplate—his coat of arms out of my vision. But I would swear this man to be a brutal Portuguese or an arrogant Spaniard. In one hand, glinting in the rays of sunlight—a slim, naked blade.

"He marched to within two paces of where I knelt in the mud, and paused. I observed him closely. What I saw of his hair was color of deepest night, his eyes the color of emeralds. How those eyes sparkled in the morning sunlight. Mother of Heaven, the man was Lucifer at his handsomest!

"This devil incarnate glanced over the remains of the razed camp and I sensed cool contempt in his look. This demon then raised his sword. The next moment I heard a rustling and the savages bounded out of their hiding place. To my utter amazement, they were not half-naked savages I had seen in my travels. No animal skins covered their bodies, but short, white cotton tunics.

"Some held spears and shields, but most had that most foul weapon—the

222

long bow, an arrow at the ready. They splashed across the crimsoned stream. Those with spears quickly dispatched those still alive with a quick thrust to the throat. I thought I, alas, would also meet my doom." Palen fell back, breathing with difficulty. Then he bolted upright as though infused with new strength, his face white as bleached bones and twisted with anger and hate.

"Then I saw *her*!"

"Who?" the chorus of voices asked again.

"A woman, possessed of such beauty it struck terror in my soul. Only The Prince of Darkness could have produced such a woman. Surely the spawn of the devil!" A convulsive seizure clutched Palen. He sobbed and mumbled while his head bobbed.

The crowd cast glances at each other, shook their heads. "We all know about sailors," someone whispered. "Drunkards and braggarts. These women exist only in their sodden madness."

Palen caught disbelief in their eyes. He feebly made the sign of the cross and muttered, "I swear by all the saints. You have to believe me! You must believe me!"

"Let him continue," a woman said. "Though it be a lie, his fanciful tale is a most wonderful story."

"She appeared from nowhere," Palen said. "Two of the savages took her by the elbows and carried her across the stream. She strolled gracefully up to this man and he offered her his arm. She rested her arm on his, raised her eyes to look adoringly at him. He lifted her chin and kissed her. Try as I might, I could not release my eyes from her.

"Along with her incredible beauty, there on her person, rested the riches all those dead men had sought. From the diamonds, rubies and other precious stones of her collar to the ornaments on arms and wrists—she wore a king's ransom! In daylight their brilliance almost blinded me.

"Then the heathen army trotted by; I could not believe my eyes. Barely a hundred of them. This small number had annihilated a body of men over five hundred in number and with superior weapons.

"This foe had to be in league with Satan, I told myself, that was the only answer. Well, as these denizens of hell drew abreast of the devil's daughter and her consort, they raised their spears and issued a hideous yell in salute.

"I tell you, my brethren, the sound rose from the deepest bowels of hell."

Palen slumped back, stabbed the air with his finger, and an instant before his death rattle, Palen, professor of history and literature and erstwhile sailor, screamed his last words, "This woman possessed an hour-glass figure and painted eyes!"

EPILOGUE

In 1642, 100 years after the death from exhaustion of Vasco da Gama in Cochin, India, a fleet of Portuguese ships with several hundred troops on aboard, landed along the Gold Coast of present day Ghana. The troops marched inland, intent on conquest and capture of a reputed fabulous city and its extraordinary women—the city long rumored to be a deathtrap to slave merchants and their allies.

About ten leagues or so from the beach and close to a meandering river, the Portuguese found walls and a roof formed into what might have been a belvedere—the structure built as an overlook for a pleasing view of the river. Weeds and thick brush choked smoothly dressed stones in the surrounding area.

When asked about the former inhabitants of this building or buildings, the few frightened natives the troops could drag out of hiding answered:

"Many, many years ago, our grandfathers told us, all the people from that cursed City of No Return…"

"Why City of No Return?" the Portuguese commander asked.

"Anyone who approached or attacked the town died and never returned home. Demons protected the people inside. The land is now haunted by their ghosts."

"Where did these people go?"

"We do not know."

After a long fruitless search for the town or city, the Portuguese packed up and returned to their ships. To this day, the city, its fabulous treasures and beguiling women, and what happened to them remains a mystery.